Moose House Stories
Volume 1

24 tales by

Eloise Comeau Murray
Bob Bent
Gordon Wetmore
Kerri Leier
P. E. R. Sprague
Gary Lovett
Angel Flanagan
Grace Keating
Debra Whittall
Connie Jodrey
Vernon Oickle
David Wiseman
Kathy Brooks
James Whidden
K. R. Byggdin
Daniel R. Lillford
Rhoda C. Hill
Thibault Jacquot-Paratte

Edited and with an introduction
by
Andrew Wetmore

Editor: Andrew Wetmore

ISBN: 978-1-9992687-0-1
First edition November, 2019
Second edition October, 2022

2475 Perotte Road, Perotte,
Annapolis County NS B0S 1A0

moosehousepress.com
info@moosehousepress.com

We live and work in Mi'kma'ki, the ancestral and unceded territory of the Mi'kmaw People. This territory is covered by the "Treaties of Peace and Friendship" which Mi'kmaw and Wolastoqiyik (Maliseet) People first signed with the British Crown in 1725. The treaties did not deal with surrender of lands and resources but in fact recognized Mi'kmaq and Wolastoqiyik (Maliseet) title and established the rules for what was to be an ongoing relationship between nations. We are all Treaty people.

Introduction

When we announced that Moose House wanted to see short stories for possible inclusion in an anthology, we did not know what to expect. Was anybody listening? Would anybody take the project seriously? 2019 was, after all, our first year as a publishing house, and this anthology would be among our very first books.

In the event, we did not have to worry. Manuscripts started appearing almost before the pixels were dry on the call for submissions. Some stories came in from well-established authors taking a break between books; others arrived from writers who had never yet sold a story. Not all submissions found a place in the collection (if they had, this book would be twice as thick as it is), but all rewarded attentive reading.

I knew some of your writers before we started the project (I even competed against David Wiseman in the Inland Nova Scotia Croquet Tournament one summer). Others were strangers to me, and as I write this there are still several whom I have not met face-to-face. But as I have worked with them to get their stories into shape for publication, I have come to admire them all. They share a delight in stories and an urgency to tell them, good observational skills, and the ability to speculate about what might happen next.

No matter what their experience level, I did note a universal constant: all the writers seem to have found writing one hundred words about themselves for the "about the authors" section the hardest part of the project.

I see some themes that quite different stories share. Often, times are hard and options are limited. Straitened circumstances are at the heart of the rural Nova Scotia experience. But there is also a thread of wonder, of the expectation of miracles.

Finally, good times or bad, the stories are about people connecting (or failing to connect) with the people around them, and how that changes their lives. In these tales, people matter far more than possessions, political stances, or the team you root for in these tales.

Welcome, then, to an anthology that may take you to unexpected places and bring you back with your eyes wide and your senses tingling.

Andrew Wetmore
Editor

These are works of fiction. Some, like "The Little Red Sled", follow historical events fairly closely; and one public person, curler Brad Gushue, makes a cameo appearance. However, any other resemblance between the characters in these stories and any real persons, living or dead, is entirely coincidental.

Contents

Moose House Stories

Back in the Day

The way things were helps make us the way we are. Even if you arrived in the Annapolis Valley too late to ride the Dominion Atlantic Railway, your drive along Route 1 is guided, in part, by dodges and swoops the road takes across and around the old railway right-of-way. The gracious open space that holds the farmers' market in Annapolis Royal was once jammed with the buildings, machines, noise, and products of the Annapolis Hardwood Company, in its day the town's largest employer.

Relationships between people living now may be tinted, even tainted, by events that took place involving their families decades or generations ago. One of the high costs of the mild peace of rural Nova Scotia has memorial markers in village after village, listing those who fought and often died in distant wars on behalf of this place.

If we dismiss or neglect our history, we dismiss and neglect a part of ourselves.

The Little Red Sled

Kerri Leier

A way back, not long after the first World War but before anyone had heard of rock and roll, rocket ships or Hitler, when movies were not yet made in glorious Technicolor, there lived a family on the quiet Canaan Mountain that rolled alongside the Annapolis Valley. This family didn't have much, except quite a few children and a lot of grit. There were times when there wasn't enough to eat and being cold didn't seem like anything out of the ordinary. However, they had each other and the will to work hard.

Back in this time there weren't computers or television to keep a boy busy when his toil was done in the deep of winter. The greatest thrill one could have was barrelling down a hill on a sled. If you were particularly lucky, or had a little money, your sled might even have a rope to help you pull it back up the hill, making it easier to beat the crowd for a second run.

Phil, the middle son of this family, was a tenacious boy with a strong back and a keen sense of adventure. He had longed for a sled for quite some time, and he knew he had to work for it. So he spent all his extra time doing jobs for friends and family, squirrel-ling away what little money he could.

Phil dreamed of the day when he would have enough to take the lengthy journey down the mountain into Kentville—a full day's walk—to purchase a sled from Rockwell's Hardware Store. Not just any sled, mind, but a little crimson beauty that was sure to whisk him down the hill in the fastest and most glorious fashion. Whenever he was tired, he would imagine himself flying across the snow, wind screaming past his ears, and he would find the energy he needed to go onward.

Finally the day arrived for Phil to make his journey. He carefully counted his coins and put them in the pocket of his pants. He packed himself a lunch to munch along the way and headed out for his long trudge down the mountain. The trek was imposing, but the lure of the sled at the end—the picture of himself zooming down those slopes—kept a bounce in his step until he reached his destination.

Sure enough, she was there: resplendent in red and looking better than Christmas morning. He had done it. He had won the right to take her home through sweat, and savings and determination. He proudly marched her to the counter and took out his money.

Mr. Rockwell couldn't help but smile as the earnest young boy laid down his loose change with care. He watched as Phil counted out his money ever so meticulously. Then, to his dismay, he watched as panic swam in the boys bright eyes. He was short!

Phil knew he had the right amount when he left home. Where had that last nickel gone? He searched his pockets, checked the cuffs of his pants and in his boots. He could feel the overwhelming disappointment swell in his throat, a thick ball, heavy as a boulder, making it hard to swallow. He took a shaky breath, so the tears welling in his eyes would fade.

Mr. Rockwell watched him carefully. "Do you know what we do with boys who are a nickel short?" he demanded, sternly.

Phil shook his head, too overcome to speak.

"Come with me."

Phil followed the man to the back of the shop, too frightened and embarrassed to ask why. His dream, all he had struggled for, was slipping away.

Mr. Rockwell had Phil stand where he could watch, and measured off a length of rope from a spool. Then he cut it and handed it to Phil.

"To pull it up the hill." He said, and his stern look changed to a smile.

Phil shook his head in disbelief. It was too much. The man had given him back the world.

Reverently, Phil took the rope and followed Mr. Rockwell back to the front of the store, where he watched carefully as the man demonstrated the perfect knot to use to tie the rope to the sled.

"Thank you, sir. I will never forget this." Phil exclaimed. He clutched the sled to his chest as he beamed at the man.

Mr. Rockwell smiled and nodded, not fully understanding how much his small kindness impacted the boy.

As Phil turned his feet for home and headed back up the mountain, his heart was warm and full. He was well into his journey but still had miles to go when he felt a tugging urge to check his pocket one last time.

He set down his hard-earned sled and slid his hands into his pockets. He felt around to satisfy that they were empty, and his finger hit against something cold and metal. Grasping it tightly, he lifted the offending nickel out of the depths of his pocket.

He stared at it for a moment in disbelief. Then, sled held tightly to him, he took off at a run for Rockwell's.

Out of breath, but proud, he marched up the steps and headed to the counter.

Mr. Rockwell regarded the boy quizzically, then broke into a wide grin when Phil placed the nickel on the counter.

"Here's the nickel I owe, sir. I guess it got caught in the corner of my pocket."

Mr. Rockwell watched the boy leave, walking tall, with deep approval.

Phil's trek home was long, uphill, and it was getting late. However, he paid that no heed. The sled had taken much effort to buy, but with all he had gained that day in the purchase, he didn't feel the burden of carrying her home. Instead he felt filled with pride, touched with kindness, and satisfied in the knowledge that sometimes hard work is rewarded in the most unlikely ways.

The Hall

K.R. Byggdin

There's not a lot left of Robertsport these days. The fish-gutting factory is long gone, as are the church, the school, and the post office. All that's left off the exit from the new highway is a smattering of houses strewn along Shipwreck Road, a crumbling cemetery which fills up with lupines in the late spring, and, of course, the old hall.

The hall has been the heart of the village since it was built in the mid-1930s. Countless dances, birthday parties, and family reunions took place under its slightly sagging roof over the ensuing decades. A low fence built of moss-covered stone and the occasional whale vertebra surrounds the squat, white building on three sides, separating the hall grounds from the woods which have slowly but surely reclaimed most of Robertsport.

It's easy to miss the place today even if you know where it is. A towering chestnut tree at the front of the property obscures the view from the road. Many a motorist coming for a bingo night or the village's annual lobster boil has missed the turnoff completely, stopping up the hill at Old Man Nickerson's place to obtain his assurances that the grassy gravel parking lot is still there beyond the chestnut's leafy branches.

Inside the hall, a dusty portrait of King George V presides over the festivities from his place of pride on the north wall. Dozens of sturdy spindle chairs built by local shipwrights are stacked up in one corner, ready to be arranged around the room for card games or luncheons. The chairs have stood the test of time since the hall held its first function, outlasting most of the fancy plastic folding tables purchased more recently by the hall committee with a provincial grant.

The oldest residents of Robertsport are quick to remind the committee of this fact. They resent any attempt to modernize the space, though they don't protest certain additions such as indoor plumbing or the fully furnished kitchen too vigorously. But they constantly remind the committee that its mandate is to preserve, not improve, the space. It's what the people want. In Robertsport, the hall is the last relic of the Good Old Days left in town, and everyone treats it with great reverence.

~

"Who are you?"

The little girl with the bright red curls and large hazel eyes stares up at the boy in front of her. He is standing in the hall among her family, but she can't remember ever seeing him before. That in itself is quite something. Strangers are a rare commodity in Robertsport.

"Hello, my name is Charlie Nickerson the third. I was named after my grandfather, like my father before me."

The boy stretches out a hand to her. He has a curious face which makes her want to study him in great detail. In particular, she can't help but stare at his pronounced lower lip and small, squinty eyes which make him look as though he is perpetually on the verge of sneezing.

After a moment the girl remembered her manners, shakes his hand, and then curtsies to him in her yellow party dress for good measure. "I'm Dorothy but everyone calls me Dotty and you can too, and I am six years old and aren't the party decorations just wonderful, I helped mother make the crepe paper rosettes which she says is just a fancy way to say 'flower' I think the hall is just the very best place for a party, don't you agree?"

Charlie Nickerson blinks back at her, baffled. "I am ten," he finally offers by way of a response.

Dotty reaches for his hand again and this time she doesn't let go. She pulls her new playmate through the milling crowd of adults towards the door.

"Come on, let me show you the woods behind the hall, I call it the land of the fairies 'cause I have a fairy castle all to myself but I can share it with you 'cause mother says it's awfully important to share things so the baby Jesus will know you have a good heart when you die and go to heaven."

Outside, Dotty finds the spot in the stone wall where a jagged hunk of rock juts out, and uses it to step up and over. She looks back, expecting Charlie to follow her, but he is still standing on the other side of the wall with his arms most decidedly crossed.

"Come on, the fairy kingdom is this way, you can't see it from here you have to come into the woods with me if you want to see it, Charlie Nickerson."

The boy shakes his head. "I can't, Dotty. I'll scuff my new boots and then mother will be awfully cross with me. Besides, the party will be starting soon. We should go back."

"We'll be back before you know it, and besides you can take your boots off and leave them here and roll up your trousers and we'll walk on the deer paths my grampie showed me and then you don't have to worry about your mother getting cross, there's a brook and a big tree split down the middle by actual lightening and the fairy castle is there you'll love it, you'll see."

Dotty reaches down, unbuckles her patent leather shoes, and throws them back over the stone wall. They land with a soft thud on the grass beside Charlie.

He considers the shoes for a moment, sighs, and bends down to unlace his own brown boots in a slow, deliberate manner. He steps out of the left one first and then the right, takes off each of his socks, and folds them with a military precision before tucking them carefully inside his boots. Finally, Charlie rolls up his pant legs until they are almost at his knees and climbs over the wall after Dotty, who is already skipping down the path into the woods.

"What do you want to play when we get to the castle Charlie, I play all sorts of games by myself except when my brothers come, they only want to play war and I'm sick to death of being a damsel in distress that has to just sit in a tree until they save me from the

Germans, so we can play anything you like except maybe not war for now okay?"

"War is not a game, Dotty," Charlie intones with a sternness far beyond his years. "Many men are dying every day in Europe to keep us safe at home."

"Oh, I know that," Dotty replies. She hops across the brook on several large stones and indicates that Charlie should do the same. "But it's okay, mother says the war will be over by Christmas and then all the soldiers can come back from away and we'll have fruit cake and oranges and sing carols together."

Charlie stops suddenly on a big, flat rock in the middle of the brook and scowls. "Your mother is a fool."

"Don't you say that about mother you, you, you lard licker!" Dotty shouts, summoning the nastiest insult her young mind can compose on such short notice.

Charlie stares back sullenly. "My father's in the navy. He wrote my mother a letter and I read it even though she hid it in the top drawer of the big dresser beneath her underthings where she thought I wouldn't look. Father said the Germans are tough sons of bitches and the war could drag on for years and years and now he's got insomnia because he's worried a torpedo will hit his boat and he'll drown in his sleep."

Charlie's face stretches into a thin, tight-lipped smile. He is pleased with himself for remembering such a big word as insomnia.

Dotty, mistaking this expression and thinking the boy despondent, rushes back out onto the brook to take his hand and guide him to the other side. "Oh, Charlie, don't cry your mother must be worried sick, your father is very brave, I'm sorry I called you a lard licker I didn't mean it, my papa can't fight on account of he's got weak eyes according to the army doctors and he's very sad about it but he says our side is fighting for freedom so we can't lose and we're almost at the fairy castle, I'll let you use the rope ladder first if you like and you can sit in the really tall part where you can feel the wind in your hair, it's simply marvellous!"

The fairy castle is indeed a sight to behold. Someone has built an impressive wooden fort in the cleft of a large split oak tree, complete with a small round lookout turret and an intricately knotted rope ladder to climb up. A solid roof of thick wooden shingles shelters the space from the elements.

Charlie thinks the fort looks strong enough to weather a hurricane. He notices that someone has carved two large letters into the base of the tree: C.N. Realization clicks into place for him then.

"Grandfather is a wonderful craftsman, isn't he Dotty? He carves me something every year for Christmas."

"Hey my grampie does that for me too, except last year he built me this instead and he called it an early Christmas present and he said an artist always signs his canvas even if the canvas is a fairy castle in a tree isn't it wonderful I told you it was it's my favourite place in all the world!"

She doesn't understand. He hasn't lived here since before she was born, so of course she would have no memory of him.

"Dotty, what's your grandfather's name?"

For once, Dotty is at a loss for words. The thought had never occurred to her that the man she calls grampie might have another name. She stares at the boy with wide eyes, uncertain.

"Okay, what's your last name, then?"

Dotty grins. She knows this one. "Dorothy Elvira Nickerson," she says with another curtsy.

"And who's birthday is it today, Dorothy Elvira Nickerson?"

"My grampie's!"

"Yes, that's right. It's our grandfather's birthday. Yours and mine." Charlie smiles again, but this time he shows his teeth. He can see the gears turning furiously in the little girl's head.

"But if your grampie is my grampie then that must mean we're family!"

Charlie nods. "That's right. We're first cousins. My father and your father are brothers. You see?"

"But how come I've never seen you at none of his birthdays before or church or Sunday dinners or nothing?" Dotty asks, suddenly suspicious. Her family is the most constant presence in her life. How could this boy be related to her if he wasn't always going to the same places and doing the same things with the same people as her?

"Father's in the navy, remember?" Charlie explains. "He joined up a long time ago, just after I was born. We had to move to Halifax and my mother and I don't often get down this way to visit. But with the war on she said it was important to make the effort for grandfather's birthday because it's times like these we need our loved ones the most."

Dotty has a thousand questions for her newfound cousin, but they will have to wait. Her mother is calling for her from the hall.

"Oh that must mean they're about to sing happy birthday and that's my favourite part, my grampie says I have a lovely voice, just like a songbird or an angel, come, Charlie, we mustn't be late you can stand next to me and we can sing together!"

~

It's been years, but all the same Dorothy recognizes him right away, even from across the room. His expression is instantly familiar, as though he's very recently sucked on a lemon. She smooths her black dress with a lace gloved hand, clutches her mug of tea tightly to her chest, and walks over to him.

"Hello, Charlie. It's been a while, hasn't it?"

When he turns towards her, his eyes are questioning, confused. Does he not remember their last play date? Her feet have been burning since the second she saw him. Phantom tendrils of poison-ivy-induced pain wrap around her soles again, just as they had after that ill-considered barefoot romp through the woods a decade ago.

"Sorry, have we met?"

"Cousin Dotty. Dorothy. I showed you my fairy castle out behind the hall once, remember?"

"No, I'm afraid I don't."

An awkward silence passes between them. His eyes scan the room for someone else to talk to. It is obvious he has written her off as childish and uninteresting. She feels her cheeks redden.

"Fine service," she offers, trying to salvage the conversation.

He grunts and sets down his plate of baked goods, wiping crumbs from his hands onto the over-sized suit jacket which makes him look like a boy playing dress-up in his father's clothes. "I thought the minister might have selected a more suitable scripture for his homily. Something nautical perhaps. Grandfather was renowned for his skills as a shipbuilder, after all."

Dotty suddenly finds herself blinking back tears. Since her grampie passed away, she can't help but cry every time someone mentions him. She bites her lip. She doesn't want her long-lost cousin to think he is the cause of her emotion, and tries to steer the conversation in a different direction.

"It's been a long time since I've seen you in Robertsport, Charlie."

"I suppose. And it's Charles now, if you don't mind."

She takes a breath to steady herself and pushes through, determined to engage him. After all, they are family. "So what kept you away, Charles?"

"Wasn't a reason to come here after my father died."

"Oh! I didn't realize. What happened?"

Her uncle is dead. She can't recall her parents ever telling her this. How could this happen? This distance. She's not used to not knowing things, at least as far as her family is concerned. Robertsport has always been an open book. So why does she feel like someone's torn out a page?

"It was back in the war. A U-boat sank his ship off the coast of Ireland."

Charles says this matter-of-factly, without emotion, as though he were reciting his times tables.

"That's awful," Dotty murmurs.

He shrugs. "Well, I was only a child when it happened. Life goes on. But mother was never the same afterwards. She stopped writing letters to the people here or even mentioning them really. The village reminded her too much of him, so we stayed away from everybody. Until she heard about grandfather, of course. Thought it was probably best for us to put in an appearance today, considering the circumstances."

This frankness, this cold, dispassionate tone shocks her. She can't think of a suitable response.

"Guess I haven't missed much though, have I?" he continues. "You're still holding every wake and wedding in this musty old hall. My goodness, place could certainly do with a fresh coat of paint, couldn't it? Come to think of it, probably best if they just tore the whole thing down and started over again."

"What?"

"But I suppose that's not the way they do things here in the boonies, is it? Nobody's willing to change. It's no wonder people our age are leaving places like these in droves for the city. I imagine it must be awfully boring on the weekends, with nothing to do but sit and stare at the water or hole up in this grubby dump and play cards with the old folks."

Dotty blushes a deeper shade of crimson, her face becoming indistinguishable from her hair. This building had always held a special place in her heart. It is the source of all her happiest memories. She resents her cousin's flippant disregard for her hometown and the time-honoured traditions of his own flesh and blood.

"Well, I'm sure I could go see a movie up in Halifax, but what would be the point?" she asks. "I'd probably have to go with some lousy, insufferable oaf like you, Charlie, and that would ruin the whole experience."

She turns on her heel then and leaves him standing there alone with his mouth hanging open, a few missed crumbs still clinging to his too-short tie.

~

She feels a tug on her sleeve and bends down to wipe her youngest daughter's runny nose.

"Go on and play with the others now, dear. Mommy's still got work to do to get dinner ready."

Dot stands over one of the hall's two new electric stoves, stirring a pot of fish chowder and talking with the other women in the kitchen. Their chatting and the noise from the men playing cards masks the sound of a fresh set of tires crunching onto the gravel lot outside. In all the hubbub of laying out the food, it's not until she ladles some chowder into his bowl and looks up into his eyes that she notices the stranger in their midst.

"Oh."

It's all she can think of to say. Nickerson reunions are tightly choreographed affairs, a ritual repeated exactly the same way year after year, with RSVPs coming in months ahead of time. Who does this man think he is, showing up uninvited like this? This is strictly a family affair.

"Hello, Dotty. I recognized those red curls of yours a mile away, but then time's been a lot kinder to you. I suppose you'll need some help to place my craggy old mug, eh?"

He chuckles and sidles around to her side of the table so as to not hold up the food line. "It's me, Dotty. Cousin Charlie. God, it's been, what, twenty years now?"

"Almost thirty since grampie's funeral," she breathes, amazed.

"Time sure flies doesn't it?"

Dot shakes her head slowly. "Sure does."

They sit together for dinner and catch up on each other's lives. She is a nurse at the local hospital now. Married with three children. He is quite well off, a Vice President of something or other up at the big shipyards in Halifax. Divorced, twice. No kids.

"I've gotten the reunion invitations," Charlie says, "but I just kept making up excuses. I don't know how your mother kept up with all my address changes over the years."

She chuckles. "I guess you just can't shake the Nickerson family."

His smile fades. "No, I guess not. I tried, though, for a good long time there. I was bitter about the way things went down after my dad passed."

"What do you mean?"

"Well, there was always a bit of a rift between us and the rest of the family. I guess our grandfather wanted dad to take over the family business, and he wasn't happy when dad chose the navy instead. People seemed to blame mom as well for taking him away, because she was from the city and all. Then when dad was killed, well, it was hard to be a single parent back in those days. But mom was too proud to ask for help, and no one from the family ever offered any, or at least that's what she told me. So over time we just drifted further and further apart."

"Charlie, I had no idea! I'm so sorry."

"Well. It's in the past. I've been meaning to reconnect for a while now. I realized it was silly to hold a grudge when you don't know all the facts. I mean, I was just a kid, who knows what really happened? Mom didn't like to talk about it. But that's what got us into this mess in the first place, you know? Not talking."

He shifts uncomfortably in his seat. "I never did it though. Reached out. Until now. You just lose track of time in the city. All those deadlines, meetings, fundraising galas. Before you know it you're an old man."

"Well, I think grampie would have been proud of you," Dot says. "You did take up the family business! In a way. Shipbuilding just looks a little different now then it did back in his day, that's all."

"I never thought of it like that, but I guess you're right." He grins, revealing a gold tooth. "Though, to be honest, I'm about ready to retire. The long days don't excite me like they used to. And neither does the traffic. No, I envy you, Dotty. It's so peaceful down here. And I'd forgotten about the air. It's different from Halifax. Saltier somehow. More pure."

"Well you've certainly changed your tune since we last met. Guess Robertsport isn't such a dull place after all."

He sighs. "I did have my head up my ass last time we met, didn't I? What can I say? Blame it on the ignorance of youth. I guess it takes time to figure out what really matters in life."

"You know," Dot says, her tone warm and forgiving, "Robertsport has lost a lot in the past few decades. But if there's one thing we've still got in spades, it's real estate."

"Really?" He leans closer towards her in his chair.

"Oh yes," she replies. "It's a buyer's market for sure. The d'Eon's house back near the highway took nearly six years to sell. There was a young family renting grampie's place up the hill for awhile, but they moved away to Ontario and it's been vacant ever since. The realtor in Yarmouth says there's not much else he can do at this point. People want to live where the jobs are, and there just aren't any around here. But if you're a retiree, well, I suppose that doesn't matter. Does it?"

"You mean the old Nickerson homestead is actually for sale? Can we see it?" Charlie is half out of his chair already. He sounds giddy, like a child.

Dot gives a casual shrug, but her hazel eyes are sparkling. "I don't see why not. It's a short walk and the key's under the mat, same as always. You thinking of buying yourself a summer home, Charlie Nickerson?"

"Actually, I might just stay year round! If you all will have me."

"You're joking."

"No. It's like I told you, Dotty. I really am tired of the city. Robertsport was my home once; maybe it can be again. Besides, with those double alimony payments I'm always on the lookout for a way to reduce my expenses."

She arches an eyebrow and he flinches involuntarily.

"What?" Dot asks.

"Oh, nothing," Charlie answers with a laugh. "It's just, the last time you looked at me like that, I thought you were going to throw your tea in my face!"

~

If you live in Robertsport these days, it's because you've chosen to. You've chosen the woods and the hall over high-speed internet and a short commute to some fast-paced job. It takes a long time to get anywhere from here, and that's just the way the locals like it.

Take Old Man Nickerson, for example. He used to be quite the big shot up in Halifax, they say, but even he came back home in the end. Chose to live in a quiet house on a quiet road in the middle of nowhere. It's not like he's a hermit. He was just looking for a change of pace. And he certainly found it here.

If you ever need something, if you're ever looking for the hall and get lost on Shipwreck Road, just knock on his door. He's sure to be there, likely chatting with his cousin Dot over a cup of tea. Take a few minutes to visit with them both if you can. They'll be happy to brew a fresh pot to share, ask what brings you down this way, and talk your ear off with stories of the way things used to be here back in the good old days.

Old Man Nickerson will get round to giving you directions, eventually. In his own time. "Sure the hall's still here. You've just passed right by it in point of fact. I suppose we ought to trim back that old chestnut a bit," he'll say, his eyes twinkling, "but it seems a shame to touch it, really.

"Tell you what, why don't I hop in with you? Show you the way. No, it's no bother. I've got nothing better to do. Dotty, you just let yourself out whenever you please now. You know where to leave the key.

"What's that? Oh yes, it's a beautiful spot this time of year. Well, any time of year, really. Isn't that so, Dot?"

We Smoked Salvia

Thibault Jacquot-Paratte

It was some months before finishing high school, that time when you are bored beyond belief out of your young mind, because not only have you been learning so little from school that you cannot but feel you are wasting your time (time out of your precious, young, yet already too-fast-fading life) sitting around, smiling pretend smiles to people who disrespect you due to your age and legal status, in an institution so caring that it censors what you read to ensure that you do not get traumatized by horrible curse words, and that you don't read what they do not wish to approve.

My friend and I drove to Wolfville because I knew a guy there from whom we could buy weed and salvia. Of course weed wasn't legal then, but that didn't stop anyone from smoking it. But this isn't a story about smoking pot, since when we got to the place, the guy I knew didn't have any (all sold out, as does happen in a university town where students spend their money on beer and ganja).

We were used to that dope, and not to the other herb which we came to purchase in order to try it. During the transaction he inquired if we had tried salvia before, to which we answered "no".

"How are you going to smoke this?" the guy asked.

We shrugged. "We were just going to roll a doobie with it," I answered.

An expression dawned on his face suggesting a certain amount of pity and déjà-vu. "You can't do that. You need something that will get some real heat in it. Also, it doesn't get you high like weed. It will give you a heavy trip that'll last about 15 minutes. It will be something closer to 'shrooms or acid, if you ever tried those."

We hadn't.

"How this works is usually one of you lies down on a couch after taking a dose, and the other sits next to him until the trip is over, to make sure that everything goes well."

He scratched his head, "Now, you'll need a pipe. You guys go to The Market—they sell them there. Just tell them you need a pipe for smoking salvia, they'll know what it is. It should cost 15 or 20 bucks."

As inexperienced as we were, we did what he said, though we weren't thrilled about the 15 bucks, perceiving it, as we did then, as a substantial sum of money.

We took the cash we had earned picking apples on the weekend and bought one small, golden metal pipe, to share. With all this we headed back to my place, a 20-minute drive towards the North Mountain. We were psyched. Virgins as we were, with so little contact with girls in our age group, and bored out of our minds because we had nothing to do, nothing to learn, little possibility to work especially under the constraint of our school-day schedules, and little space to be creative, getting high was the only thing which seemed within our means which could give us any feeling. We went to my home as I was alone at that moment. Where were my folks? How should I remember? They were elsewhere, and that's all that mattered.

They weren't there, and my friend and I were able to act according to our mental age, which is to say to enjoy a friendship which wisdom limits to a selected few, to break pleasureful solitude only to appreciate the company of another, and to enjoy that which modifies sensations within an agreeable context. Adults are often not wiser than children, and maturity only exists where maturity is allowed to grow.

Yes, we were going to smoke salvia, not unlike how some elders get so drunk they can barely walk out of their dinner parties. But we had the decency to know that this wasn't something to be particularly proud of. No, we only wanted to feel and exist; we didn't want to get intoxicated to follow social norms and conventions, or without an ounce of reflection on the matter, as is the case with most people who drink.

I felt the comfort of my bed's soft mattress under my backside while I examined the small golden metal pipe in one of my hands, and the small glass vial containing the herbs in the other. My friend was on a chair facing me: he was too nervous to take the first hit.

We stuffed the very small bowl, and he handed me his lighter. The flame flared and I held it to the bowl, burning my thumb on the way down.

On the second try I was holding the lighter on the side, as I figured one should, lit the substance, and promptly inhaled. Throat dry, lungs slightly inflamed, I held the smoke in as long as I could, and placed my head on my pillow.

I was watching my unshaven friend with his already-tanned skin (though it wasn't summer) peering down at me through his glasses. I remember a great sensation of falling, followed by that of being projected back into place in the space of a second—like an immediate zoom-in.

Everything became quite real and tangible—I could feel the tips of my fingers and the tips of my toes unusually well—but most of all, it all came apart.

I saw the walls, the ceiling, the Marilyn Monroe poster I had above my bed disintegrate into small geometric shapes. The shapes were static, but they weren't. They were shimmering, but they weren't. At times, I was wondering if they were really there, and when that happened, the whole world became blurry.

My friend asked me if I was okay at one point. I wasn't sure—I reached out my hand and touched him. I would learn by observing him, and by stories I heard later, that my reaction was rather weak, that I hadn't been affected as much as I could have been. It affected my friend a lot more.

He had his eyes closed the whole time, and at one point he started screaming. Not a scream of fear, or pain; more of a healthy yell. Something just to be heard.

He later told me he had been in a hallway which was grey and very large, made of shiny stone, and he wanted to hear the echo. That's what he said to me when he came to: "I wanted to hear the echo, I wanted to hear it resonate!"

He had decided to study psychology at Acadia, and he almost convinced me to do so as well, though I opted for economics instead. I figured I would prefer working with figures and papers than with people, especially problematic people. Not that everyone who sees a psychologist is problematic. People don't necessarily attract problems or seek them out, but when their problems start to take control of their lives, they seek help. Their nature isn't problematic, but circumstances have rendered them so, if you see what I mean.

Now, with time that's gone by, I've also heard the stories of people who are problematic by nature, or, as we could say in simple terms, fucked. One girl with whom I flirted at one point wanted to show me something she had in her large red purse. She started pulling out everything in her purse in order to find it.

Seeing an object which looked like two miniature gongs linked by a piece of string, I asked what it was.

"I'll show you!" she happily said. She took the object by the string and manipulated it so that the gongs hit each other, producing a loud ringing, similar to a bell, the kind of meditative sound you would hear in a Buddhist temple.

"Why do you carry this around?" I asked.

She said she rang it before every session with her therapist to set a good aura in the room, to create a good ambience so she could clear her mind.

I nodded and said, "Interesting," before excusing myself and getting out of there.

You don't want to be with someone who's problematic, and who needs to ring a miniature gong in order to confide in her therapist. Lucky therapist, seeing a client they'll be able to keep for a long time, at some amazing price per hour.

I mention my friend's desire to study psychology because, in our zeal to advance in life, we had purchased an introduction to Freud, which we both read and debated in the school bus, when we weren't playing harmonica and singing gospel songs.

Once someone complained about it and I told them to shove it.

My friend commented, "With that attitude and a harmonica, if I'm ever sent to jail, I want you as a cell mate."

A true compliment. You would not want to be locked into an uncomfortable, dirty cell, where you would have to go to the john one in front of the other, and satisfy whatever other urges one would have (pace, talk to oneself while going mad, sing, masturbate) with just anyone.

Wanting to understand and interpret the mind, I figured then that the image of a long, dark hallway in which one would wish to yell in order to hear an echo was like being in a large yet locked area—society perhaps: dull, not colourful, and cold. One would want to try any desperate (if not also incoherent) action in order to feel like one could make any difference at all; to get feedback, receive in return. When you hear the echo of your own voice, you know your voice has travelled, however it may sound, whatever it might have said.

I told my friend all this, and he agreed it was a possibility. We didn't know anything back then in comparison to now, but he would probably still agree it's a possibility.

We both took another hit. Slightly stronger for me, and about the same for him. Afterwards we stepped out, where nature was becoming nice after what we call "mud season", that period after the frost where everything is mushy, and which always felt worst in the Valley.

We walked around and talked about anything and everything. School was coming to an end, a good thing given that the small nucleus of friends which we had managed to form had decided to explode H-bomb style just at that time. That semester, there was no staff member available to manage a drama or AV club. Losing these options only increased our desire to emancipate ourselves from it all and go out into the world.

I questioned my friend again. "Why did you choose Acadia?"

"Why?" He pondered. "Honestly? My parents work there."

"It's a mediocre university, and it's their own damn fault, too."

"I looked into it, and I like it."

"And it's ridiculously expensive! Isn't it even more expensive than Dal?"

"Yeah, it is. But not if your folks work there."

I stopped asking questions. Looking back, I think that he was afraid to move too far away. Not I, no sir. I wanted to go far away. I had applications going out all over the country, and though I wouldn't be thrilled to go to a big city, it would be what it had to be.

I did hate the idea of living in a place with more cement than trees. Why is it, I anguished, that the country should stay backwards and uninterested—why does it stay conservative, with all that entails (for we should include everything pertaining to a lack of intellectual curiosity)—and that if one wanted anything progressive, any culture, one had to go to a city. I hated that universities that could have been hubs for out-of-the-way places, like Acadia, were dragging, held back by petty rivalries between professors who each tried to do less than each other while looking good doing it.

We came back to my place, and I started making us some eggs and toast, with fried zucchini on the side.

My friend said, "I was thinking about what you saw."

"Yes?" I replied, flipping my egg to have it over-easy (and aiming to have a nice firm yolk which I could eat with some hot sauce).

"Yeah. I was thinking about it, and it's like this, I think. You saw all your surroundings breaking up into small parts and shapes, because it's like you want to understand it all, in detail."

"Hmm, that could be."

"Yeah, it could be. Like, you want to see what everything is made of, and see how it moves and works together."

"Well, I can't say I don't," I coolly replied. It made sense.

I pulled out two plates and was serving the food when we heard a car door shut. My folks were home.

They came in and found us eating. We chatted of everything and anything. They didn't know we had smoked salvia.

We had yelled in an empty hallway, and we heard an echo.

Boat Harbour

James Whidden

Strawberries don't last forever. After their harvest the days of summer grow long and hot, and weeding becomes a tedious chore. In the brilliant sunlight of the afternoons the adults set the sprinkler running. I put on a bathing suit with blue piping and a fringe. Water guns were filled. Cardboard boxes could be turned into automobiles or sailing ships that slid across the lawns.

Because my father had returned to the base, there was no one to drive us to the beach. My grandfather's car was parked in the barn and only taken out for exceptional occasions, like emergency deliveries of strawberries to Carmichael's. My brother Daniel said there was a little pebble beach down on the harbour, but the path was overgrown and the shoreline rocky and full of seaweed. To access it, we needed to cross the Milton farm. Our friend Donnie lived there. He and my brother Daniel worked to open the path. When it was ready, my mother came along and made the journey with us.

We crossed the road where the Lower Road forked away. The Milton farm was the mirror image of ours, two gables, two verandas, except painted yellow instead of white, red trim instead of green. We waved to Mrs. Milton. On the other side of the pasture was the path, cut through the brush, not woods, because this area had once all been pasture and hay fields. The path opening was like a black door.

Once we were in, the bush crushed in on us and the mosquitoes bit. We came to the old rail line, disused now, we followed it a piece, until the path found its way again and wound down to the harbour side, directly across from where the new factory was rising. We could just see Eastvale, and the greasy estuary of the river. The water was slightly oily, with a skim like that from out-board motors, and there were odd bits of flotsam, parts of boats, waste timber, and plastic tubs washed up on the beach here and there. From sea level and up close, the new factory's chimneys rose like towers across the water, with as silvery a sheen as a space ship, the factory walls were low-lying and sleek, not like the great high sheds of the old Steelyard and Car Works.

But we had the beach to ourselves. Mother even shed her modesty and went into the water, something never done on the beach by the open sea. Eyes might be watching. But here we were alone, only ourselves and the factory rising. She even sunbathed.

Daniel and I had recently been debating the difference between living on the farm and in town. My father's family was from town and sometimes we visited his mother, whom we called Nana. She lived with Pops in a house on the back side of the main street. We called my other grandmother Granma, and that's where we spent most of our time when not on the base. We enjoyed the freedom of the farm.

I asked the question that had been troubling us. "Why is Nana so severe? She makes us sit still and won't let us play."

"She had to bring up a big family all alone, without a husband. It is not easy being a widow."

Death was a reminder of all we did not know.

She continued, "As a single woman she had to guard her reputation."

"What's that mean?"

"Oh, nothing at all. But people talk."

"When did she marry Pops?"

"Not until much later, after your father was grown up."

"Did she know him before?"

"Oh yes, she knew him."

"Was Pops married?"

"Yes."

"What happened to his wife?"

She pursed her lips.

"Where did you meet Dad?"

"At Macpherson's. Your father worked there. He had been there a long time. He had to help his mother pay the bills."

"Even as a kid."

"He didn't have a father. Pops is his step-father."

A strange concept, but Daniel seemed to understand. "When did you marry Dad?"

"Only after he went up to the base. That's when we moved away."

"And Sandy?" That was her brother.

"He had already left."

"Why didn't Granddad want him to leave?"

"He thought he should stay on the farm and marry a local girl. But Sandy had other ideas. He wanted to join the army."

"Didn't Granddad want him to?"

"No."

"Why not? Granddad was in the first war. He has all those guns and shells and medals."

"That's why he didn't want him to go to the second war. Anyway, Sandy went to war."

"Dad says he got as far away as he possibly could."

"It's true," she said sadly. "He didn't get along with your grandfather."

"Why?"

But she just declined her head.

~

Granddad had a bottle hidden in the front porch, where the cellar door kept things cool. He took it out and sat in his chair.

Daniel was reading a book. I was peering through the crack of the door that led into the hall. I was a Spy. Agatha Christie.

Granddad said, speaking to no one in particular, that he went West as a young man to work in the harvests. On the train rides West, he and his friends clutched together over cards and drinks, but the greatest joy was out in the fields when the young women mixed freely with the men.

Daniel looked up from his book. His jaw dropped. It was the only time we saw him with a beer or heard him speak of women in that way.

And then I thought of those boxes of stereoscope photographs upstairs in the attic with all their forlorn images of lovers, lingering along the paths of gardens, waving farewell at a train station, or searching the horizon for a ship. Was that Granddad's story?

Granddad was kind and I often tagged along while he was doing his chores, but he could just as easily walk away with a kind of spitting movement of his lips. He was disapproving. He had disapproved of his brother's life. Although it was not clear why (he never married?). He disapproved of his son's choice to go to war and never return. And he disapproved of my father for never being good on a farm, for taking his daughter away, and for filling her head with the idea of foreign fashions and films, and the children were good only for playing games and pursuing dream worlds in comic books and films.

Maybe Sandy was the same as us. In the attic there were old pulp fiction books, fat comic books with corner clips that turned into moving pictures if you flipped through the pages fast enough. Big city detectives and action heroes.

~

Mid-summer involved a trip to the woods, the high woods, way beyond the strawberries, sugarberries, and blueberries, where Granddad collected firewood to provide kindling for the coal stove throughout the winter. He hooked the wagon to the tractor. A chainsaw and gas tin with the long spout.

Because I followed him around like a dog he let me come along. I stood in the wagon. He showed me how to hold on by gripping the rail firmly himself, without words. Every action of his was his way of teaching me, his way of passing on all that he knew, all he had learned down the ages. It was a gift he had to give. It must have hurt when his only son refused that gift.

We putted slowly up the wagon track between raspberries,

strawberries, and hay fields, through the pasture back toward the far line of trees. In the woods the trees soared overhead, leafy and green at first, then the pillars of pine and spruce.

We came to an opening where there were fallen trees. The sky unfolded and around us grass and flowers had turned the opening into a little field. This was his camp.

He would make us a lunch by lighting a small fire and smoking hot dogs. Then he went to work with the chainsaw and arranging the tractor and wagon to collect the logs. I sat on a log and watched while he carved up a tree with expert strokes of the chainsaw. It buzzed, and then all was peaceful while he tinkered with chains and hitches.

I felt I had penetrated the real woods at last, a place eternal in its stillness – these trees had been here before the British and the French, before the US Cavalry. They marked the unchanging, the forever, but even more, offered a chance to plant a seed and let it grow. The woods spoke of time changing, as well as time eternal, saying that we could take up the saw, keep the road open, and every year let a few trees fall so that more might grow.

The birds sang and the insects contributed their strange hum. Everything was alive from the roots to the heavens above. The sun aroused the deep perfume of leaf, fern, needle, and earth.

The song of life gave voice in birds and the splash of water from the marsh; of muskrat, of beaver, and the plop and burp of frogs. A loon called from the far fens where ducks turned tail in defiance of us.

I saw Davy Crockett with gun cocked taking down bird or stag. And just beyond the fringe of trees the Cherokee were watching us.

~

My brother said that sometimes in the evening, after hanging around the Lobster Bar, they went to the beach and lit bonfires. He said that kids from the Reservation came down too.

The Lobster Bar was a canteen up the road from the Ferry Wharf. Young kids hung around after work. I envied Daniel when he left after dinner or later, after supper, after combing his hair and putting on a clean shirt. He seemed all grown up to me, though he was hardly a teenager yet.

He had a scar on his face. That was from when Mitzie bit him. Mitzie was a wild dog, part collie and part something else. She barked madly at everyone; only my mother knew how to ignore her and turn her nose down to the ground.

Except, once a young man from the Reservation came up the drive. She barked, but he went down on one knee and held out his hand and she submitted as if she knew him, as if she were one of his.

He was looking for work on the farm. There was nothing to offer, although my grandparents would offer odd jobs to the Nielson boys at harvest.

Wendy Nielson often came and sat in the kitchen and talked on and on. I had to sit and try to be friends with her. She usually left with something from the garden or the oven. That was Christian charity.

Mitzie bit Daniel while we were playing 'Cowboys and Indians'. Daniel was doing the war dance, chanting and circling wildly. It was too much for Mitzie. She jumped in rhythm and nicked him on the cheek. There was blood.

My grandmother insisted on 'putting the dog down'. That meant killing it. Daniel cried. He begged her not to. If we hadn't been jumping and playing about, she would not have got excited and jumped at him. But it was no use, the dog had to go. Mitzie never really liked us, never accepted our presence; but we loved her nonetheless.

It was the way they did it that seemed to scar. Mother protested, but she would not or could not defy her parents. We found out later that they had paid the Nielson boys to take her away. Daniel said he found her riddled with shot in a box on the back road.

That deep-seated cruelty. Is that what made the dogs howl? Is that why the older men and women on the Reservation were cowed?

~

I thought my brother a crusader for discovering the truth about Mitzie and asking these questions. He was the future. A kinder world. But what sort of change would the future bring? Even the government couldn't agree what it would look like.

That summer the government invested money in the Reservation. The houses on the dune, so impermanent, had some new paint and siding. The new canteen on the beach brought more people from town.

Mother and Granma talked about it in the kitchen, repeating after-church conversations, party line gossip. Grandmother's was the voice of authority. What the churchgoers agreed on was pretty much doctrine. The government was investing in the factory. It would bring jobs to the community.

The issue was that some complained of the idea that there would be standing pools dug for the effluent, next to the factory. It was said that the chemicals released were not so harmful.

From our pebble beach the little steeple of the Baptist Church marked the spot where the pools stood. We could see barefoot children running along the horizon like stickmen from a brush fire.

But the effluent had to be piped out after it stood a while. 'Where were they going to pipe it to?'

But these concerned voices were drowned out by others. The Nielson boys were already employed, trucking. The factory would bring jobs. After sitting in pools, the harmless fluids would disappear into the Strait, through the Gulf. The Atlantic could easily absorb all that.

~

It was difficult getting to the beach. Daniel was busy. Mum wouldn't take us on the path through the bush alone. She spent too much time in the high front room where there was the portrait of the French Lady in an elaborate hat. She would never mess up her hair for a child's whim. She had a kerchief to keep it in place.

Granma took us once. She cried out each time we put our heads under water. We laughed and teased her, 'We're drowning!' But that was just the once.

Daniel had the idea to go to the beach at the bottom of the Lower Road, which meant I would have to cross the highway. Daniel told Mum he would watch me. This was exciting because it took me to his happy hunting grounds, the road on the way to the Lobster Bar, where there were soda pops, cigarettes, and girls.

He called Donnie on the party line. 'Hi Donnie. We are going to the beach.'

Pause. Obviously, Donnie was saying no he couldn't go because that was what he always said. He had an oddly screwed up face and peering eyes. He didn't like to talk. He was afraid of the world.

Daniel said, 'Yes, we will be there shortly...That's all right: you will be okay...I'll bring you a bathing suit. You're coming!' Daniel wouldn't take no for an answer.

We crossed the road. It was the trucks you had to watch for. They were fast and seemed to take pleasure from near murder. On the other side of the road Donnie joined us and we plunged down hill.

The first stage of the walk was drear, under dark old trees, along the side of the Milton hay fields. Then there was the Nielson house, low and dark, with its sagging veranda. Some windows were smashed.

At last we reached the sunny shoreline of cottages, anchored pleasure boats dancing in the waves, close-cropped lawns, dipping willows, high pines. The cottages were brightly painted in pinks, reds, yellows and blues; painted buoys and lobster traps were the standard decorative features. Old dories were pulled up onto the shore.

The beach was next to the boat launch at the bottom of the hill, pebbly with a crust of seaweed. But rather than the factory looming across from us, the old port was opposite.

There were some buoys in the water to mark the shoals. They were our playmates. Donnie gave them names, Davy Boy and Captain Boy. The ships across the way were navy or pirate, although mostly merchant marine, coastguard, and fishing boats. Sometimes a grey destroyer entered the harbour, long and low and mean. Grey, like the Atlantic.

The shipyard was building a ferry, quite large, its bow poking out from the sheds. The shipyard hummed. Voices over speakers could be heard. At noon a whistle wailed. That's when we left the beach and headed toward the Lobster Bar.

On the way Daniel turned us into a drive toward a cottage with a long chrome station wagon at its end. I liked the oval conical, red, rear lights of that model, Ford Laurentian.

In the driveway, Donnie paused and said he had to go home, as if he sensed danger ahead. He turned and fled. Daniel shrugged.

We went up the drive. A girl wearing shorts, sandals and an ordinary shirt ran to the screen door when he knocked. She laughed and smiled.

The cottage was hot inside, all wainscotting or plain boards painted white, with high ceilings showing the rafters and planks. A door led to a kitchen, long and narrow, like the galley of a ship. Open shelves held tin containers, Roasters coffee and Red Rose tea, pots and cups, Kraft dinner and Spaghetti-Os. Beyond there was a room with two day-beds, a table with playing cards, cushioned chairs with metal legs, and a beach stone fireplace. The girl's mother smiled over the brim of her paperback novel.

We went out onto the veranda with its Westport chairs. It looked out over the harbour, with a path down to a little dock where a rowboat was tied. There was a round barbecue.

After sitting a bit with his girlfriend, Daniel gave me that look like scram or I'll fix you for good. He said, 'We will see you at the Lobster Bar.'

His girlfriend smiled at me but giggled.

I went off alone, wishing I were with him. The road followed a rise, where on a cleft was a great house with gables, haunted probably by Peg-leg, and then down a dip toward the Ferry Wharf. The ferry was gone, but that's where the lobster boats docked, traps piled high, netting and rope strewn all along the dock side, barrels, and the strong smell of tar and diesel.

There were a few people at the Lobster Bar, which stood up the road from the wharf. I went and asked for an orange pop. Some kids sat at a picnic table. They glanced and pointed.

One said, 'You're Daniel's sister.'

Giggles and laughs, at an insider's joke.

Eternity passed like a prison sentence. Daniel arrived like a saviour. We took a path behind the canteen that led through the bush and met the Landing Road just the other side of the school, not far from my grandparents' farm.

~

She was from the city. She was going to be a doctor. Her plan was to go to Africa after high school because that was what her big sister had done. Her sister had a boyfriend there.

That appealed to Daniel's sense of mission. At the YMCA he showed films about the world to the kids dropped off for the Saturday events, swimming lessons, track meets, judo and gymnastics. Some films showed the frozen polar north. Others the great train ride from coast to coast. There were animations also from the Film Board about war and peace. Odd tales of back woods and railways. Films on events across the globe.

Daniel had just turned sixteen, but was already an educator, like his girlfriend's sister in a school in Africa. That's where there was a political struggle for freedom.

Uncle Richard's last posting had been in Gaza. He brought back a miniature sphinx and postcards of the pyramids.

I asked him if he liked Egypt.

"Yes," he said.

"What was Gaza?"

"A place near the desert."

"Why were you there?"

There had been a war and he was keeping the peace. He laughed and dragged on his cigarette.

He always looked as if he knew something that no one else understood. He knew what things were really about. He learned all about it in the German POW Camp, but the worst things happened before he got there. Murders. Ritual humiliations. It was impossible to explain and, after that, for him this world was all a joke or a sham. At any rate, it didn't add up to what he knew. Richard never stopped smoking.

The kids at the Lobster Bar smoked, Export A or Du Maurier. They drank beer, too, like Richard, from the bottle. My dad always poured it in a glass and then only on Saturdays. It was a sin to drink on the Sabbath, but Richard couldn't have followed that rule.

His kids were experts at torture. They could twist your arm in a hold that you couldn't punch out of. Headlocks were the worst.

They could use magnifying glasses to turn a grasshopper to flame. Their dog, Deuce, could sit forever with a treat balanced on his nose.

When that dog saw Mitzie, it was a fight from start to finish. It seemed to be a fight to the death, so the men pulled them apart and tied Mitzie to the barn wall. Deuce danced a sort of jig afterwards and Mitzie growled. That was before Mitzie was shot.

My Dad says that Richard woke up in the middle of every night to drink a beer. That was because of the war. After Gaza he came home and was turned off the base. It was an honourable discharge. He was a good soldier. He lived with us for a while, all alone, his wife and kids had gone away, and sure enough he had a beer in his hand first thing in the morning.

~

A boat trip from the Ferry Wharf through the harbour mouth, past the lighthouse, red and white, and beyond the point of pines and spruce, and beyond that there was the Strait onto the Gulf and the Atlantic. The sea could be rough, but it gave access to Boat Harbour. This was a more exclusive cottage country, the other side of the Reservation. The cottages dotted the shore, not more than a dozen. Daniel had a friend from Halifax, whose parents owned a cottage there.

Out to sea there was a good sand bar for diving and catching crabs and other shellfish, and through the narrow neck of water one entered the long sinuous harbour, rich in fish and ducks, and even further inland these turned to fresh water marshes. Granddad's old logging road ended here, or at least one of its branches, others forking off to the highland hills in the distance. The marshes were near the meadow at the end of Granddad's land.

What joy, what paradise, to be at Boat Harbour with friends, parents far away at work, catching free days of youth. There was Daniel and Jenny, Don and Dave—oddly, they all seemed to have variations of similar names. They even looked the same.

I went with my parents once or twice and we passed through. Even my father said it surpassed anything in the picturesque. My father took a photograph. When still, its waters like a mirror reflected the pines and spruces and the sombre image of the cottage fronts like devotees staring into the eternal.

And what is eternal? Was it the world or was reality only a picture, only a reflection of the soul that contemplated something deeper, the everlasting soul? Did each and every one of us share it? For Daniel at those evening rallies of friends it seemed they possessed the eternal, the forever, in this place of shimmering reflections.

The Egyptian pyramids pointed to heaven. The African savanna was the origin of human life. I learned this in the YMCA films. But the eternal for us was the wild, lakes and rivers, forests; there was something divine in cottage life as each of us contemplated it in our lakeside resorts. I saw it in my father's eyes when he stared off to the horizon; otherwise, it was all mess hall games, poker, bridge, cribbage, pool and snooker.

And then there was the war.

He went to the edge of the water and without a word I knew that this quiet sound was the quintessence of his meaning, the stillness, the rocky shore, where he tossed a cigarette between stones.

Father didn't have much confidence in communicating with people. He only had that moment of reflection. Not a lot was said. His brother Richard had his mementos. He handed them around:

the wooden camel from Egypt and a parquet smoker's box; wooden shoes from Holland; the polished boots in the closet; a uniform pressed behind plastic.

They talked about the Casbah, the Medina, Gamaliyya, Ezbekiyya, the men in turbans and robes that followed you about, offering services, the brothel where he only sat and drank a beer and watched a slow and modest waltz of a tired-looking peasant girl, probably from Spain.

He recalled his Moroccan servant at the base was called 'Rat'; another was named after a more exotic creature, but he assumed equally a denizen of the gutter. He heard they belonged to some lower caste, probably Berber.

It seemed relations with the natives easily degenerated. Huge arguments ignited over the slightest thing, usually a bad tip.

Most of the photos were of him lying on the rocks of the palace wall in Casablanca or Cairo, a girly magazine covering his face, or of planes at the base. When Richard and his buddies drank beer and told stories, father walked away, because they were abusive and violent, and things normally ended in a fight.

It was that winter that father had the call that Richard was in the car crash. The eternal took him at last.

Daniel turned sixteen.

There was a better world ahead.

Around Here

Rural Nova Scotia contains, and embraces, all the subtle complexities of any human society. We have our doers and dreamers, our nay-sayers and community builders. You don't have to travel far to find a pleasant person with a secret past; a settled life that was once nearly overturned by a rash act or forces beyond human control. We have grudge-bearers; we have passionate lovers; we have scammers and public servants.

We have ghosts.

46

Two Wishes

Bob Bent

The day started out nice enough, but it clouded over soon after Chezzetcook. That was an hour ago. Now it's drizzling, the windshield wipers can't decide whether to start or stop, and I don't have a clue where we are.

"Did you bring a map?" she asks. "Because there's not a soul around here I can ask for directions."

"Helen, I know these roads like the back of—"

"My Grandmother's hen house."

"Your grandmother never had a hen house."

"Exactly. And you never have a map. You're the only man I know who can get lost on a treadmill."

And that ends the discussion about the map, or lack thereof. We drive for another half hour along a seldom-used, narrow, winding road, which might have been paved in a previous life. Now alders scrape both sides of our ancient Dodge Spirit as we creep past, and weeds reach up from cracks in the asphalt, to rub our underbelly.

"Don't worry, Helen. The road has to come out somewhere."

It does: at a long-abandoned wharf, the timbers and pilings scattered by the endless pummelling of ocean waves on the rocky shore, and there's no place to turn around unless I want to mow down the alders and wild roses hugging the road and hiding the ditches. I shut my eyes to see if I can come up with a way out of our dilemma before Helen starts in on me.

"Arnold." Her voice is sweet. Something's wrong. "I think I saw an old house back there. Let's get out and take a look."

"Helen, the last time we 'took a look' at an old house, we almost got arrested."

My wife has an incurable addiction to empty houses. She can no more pass up a chance to explore an old deserted house than I can pass up chocolate peanut butter ice cream.

"Oh pooh," she says. "The Mountie was very nice, and the owners gave us a tour of the house and invited us for supper."

"Then tried to sell us the old dump. Supper was a pizza delivery and I got stuck with the bill. And the only reason the Mountie was nice was because you flirted with him."

"If it's a lady Mountie this time, I'll let you flirt with her. Come on. Let's go. Where's your spirit of adventure?"

How would I know? I don't have a map, remember? Only I don't say that out loud. Helen's happy, and it's always a good idea to keep her that way.

We get out of the car into a frigid drizzle. Someday I'm gonna invent a hooded T-shirt. The weather doesn't seem to bother Helen, and she favours me with a grin of childish excitement while I shiver. We start weaving our way through the alders, wild roses, and blackberry brambles, up a steep hill toward the old house. On the bright side, the alders at the bottom of the overgrown driveway aren't too thick to back over when it's time to leave.

After I suffer multiple life-threatening scratches on my arms and legs from the thorns and thistles, we come out onto what used to be a lawn. Smart-ass Helen is wearing a loose ankle-length summer dress with long sleeves and gets nary a scratch. "Be prepared" is her motto. "Be cool," is mine, and I have the bloody scars to prove it.

The house, atop a steep cliff overlooking crashing waves, is Edgar Allen Poe-ish in the extreme: imposing, dilapidated, and it scares the blue bejeebers outa me. I count the gables – seven. Not a good sign.

"Helen, maybe we—"

But she's already running through the chest high weeds, looking for a way in. When I catch up to her, she's standing proudly at the side of the old house, arms akimbo, in front of a broken basement window.

"Helen, I don't like the looks—"

She wraps an arm around my waist, leans affectionately against me, and squeezes. "Oh, Arnold, isn't this exciting? I love it! Just listen to those waves. What a wonderful adventure we're having!"

She unwraps herself and looks pointedly at the basement window. "Let's go in. You first."

"Why do I always have to go first?"

"Because you're braver than me," she lies.

So I get down on my belly and worm my way through the window feet-first. These old basements usually don't have much head room, I think, until I'm hanging by my fingers from the bottom of the window casing. Still no floor.

"I hope this isn't a coal mine," I mutter as I let go and drop—two inches to a dirt floor. A grimy window on the far side allows a shaft of dim light to penetrate the gloom. "It's pretty dark down here."

"Our eyes'll get used to it," she answers. "Now help me down."

The light disappears when she starts to slide in the basement window. As she shimmies down against me, my hands guide her ankles, her calves, her thighs, her hips, her bare waist...

"Just a minute. My dress is caught on a nail up here."

"I know." I kiss the exposed skin at the back of her leg.

"Arnold! Not now, silly."

"I'm just helping you, my darling."

Erotic thoughts cavort through my mind, temporarily replacing ghosts and zombies. Where's your spirit of adventure? I almost ask, but know better.

She untangles her dress and drops pleasantly into my arms, remains a second, sighs sweetly, then disengages herself. "Oooh! Look at everything!"

The "everything" is mere shadows at first, but as my eyes adjust I can make out a row of benches along the back wall, all different heights and moulded together by a solid rug of cobwebs. Thick curtains of the stuff drape from the rafters above us, and man-eating spiders join the ghosts and zombies.

"Let's go over there," she says, pointing to the benches. "You first."

"Why me first?"

"Because you're bigger than me, honey," she replies sweetly as she caresses my shoulder. "You'll do a better job clearing a trail through the cobwebs."

It's useless to argue, so I lead the way, parting the clinging drapes as I go, swiping the stuff away from my hair and face, wiping it off my bare arms. Helen remains close behind, her hands on my sides for encouragement, her head pressing against my back for protection from the gruesome cobwebs. We reach the benches along the far wall without incident, unless you consider choking on thick strands of spider spit an incident. Helen's in seventh Heaven, to match the seven gables, no doubt.

I poke among the shrouded treasures on the bench without enthusiasm: a folding ruler, a wooden mallet, an ancient plane, and other uninteresting obsolete tools. Helen, meanwhile, works along the lower shelves in my wake, examining Heaven knows what with boundless excitement. At the far end of the benches I find a rotted cardboard box of mummified vegetables; maybe turnips, maybe tomatoes.

"Ooh, Arnold! Look at this!" She holds up what looks like an old trophy of some sort, a large cup with a handle on each side.

"Better leave it there," I tell her. "It's probably important to somebody."

"I just want to wipe some of the dust and cobwebs off it, so we can see what it says." She hitches up the bottom of her dress and begins cleaning the thing off. "It's getting warm."

What looks like wisps of dust start to rise from the open top as Helen rubs it, and the thing begins to glow a deep gold. I don't like it.

"Put it back, Helen! Let's get outa here!"

But Helen isn't listening. She clamps the trophy between her thighs and rubs harder, her pretty pink tongue protruding from the corner of her mouth. The thing, now it's cleaner, looks like one of those magic lanterns from Arabian Nights.

Then it hits me. Helen has a *real* Arabian Nights magic lantern and the wisps of dust emerging from the lantern are gradually forming an image. But it's not an image of an old man with a long grey beard, a turban, a short vest, and pantaloons. Instead it seems to be wearing a Harley Davidson T-shirt, baggy shorts, and a Toronto Blue Jays baseball cap, the peak pointing north by northwest.

Now, I don't believe in genies. I don't believe in man-eating spiders, ghosts or zombies, either. But if there were such things, this is where you'd find them.

"Hiya, doll," the genie leers at my wife.

"It's a genie!" Helen gushes, in the same voice she uses when she sees a baby bunny.

"It doesn't look like a genie to me," I grumble.

The genie tears his eyes away from my wife long enough to snort, "This ain't eighteenth century Persia, pal. You been dreamin' o' too many scantily clad harem girls."

Helen turns on me abruptly. "Have you, Arnold?"

"No. It's never even occurred to me," I sputter. But now that it has, I might. I keep that thought to myself.

I find the genie disconcerting, even obnoxious, and I especially don't like the way he looks at my wife. I don't even know if he's a real genie. I tell myself to calm down, think things through, be analytical. Better still, grab Helen and get the hell outa here.

"Helen, put that thing down and let's get back to the car!"

"But I want my three wishes." She turns to the genie. "I get three wishes, right?"

"Only two wishes, I'm afraid, doll." He flashes his come-hither look. "But, perhaps if you come back another time. Without..." He tilts his head in my direction.

"It's supposed to be three wishes!" I argue. I'm becoming severely pissed with the genie's flagrant flirting with my wife.

The genie snaps back, "It's the off season, pal, and our inventory's down."

"That's two wishes each then."

"Did you rub my tummy?"

"No. I did," Helen says, a little too sweetly.

The genie floats closer to her and drapes a possessive wisp of an arm over her shoulder. "And it was delightful," he sighed.

"You never rub my tummy." I'm hurt, and feeling neglected.

"You never grant me two wishes." Helen's serious.

"Come on. Leave this fake genie and let's go. It's just a trick someone's playing on us with hollow-graphs. He's not real. Two wishes. Everybody knows it's supposed to be three wishes. Besides, genies don't put the make on attractive married women. Genies are eunuchs. Everybody knows that." That part gives me particular satisfaction. "He's a fake, a genuine fake. He doesn't even look like a genie. I'm gonna report him to the genie union as soon as we get home, then we'll find out—"

Helen turns on me then. "Oh, Arnold, I wish you'd shut up!"

"That's one wish, doll."

"Wait. That wasn't meant for you. I was speaking to my husband, Arnold, who never shuts up, has no spirit of adventure, never has a map, licks off the underside of the aluminum foil of the yogourt containers, and wants to leave as soon as I conjure up a genie who's going to grant me wishes, even if it is only two wishes when it's supposed to be three." She runs out of gas.

"One wish left, doll-face."

I try to protest, but my mouth won't open. I try till my face hurts. Nothing happens. Now I'm really scared. Early onset lockjaw. Good grief! I begin waving my arms around, pointing at my mouth and failing to make a noise, hoping all the time Helen won't wish I'd keep still.

"You have one wish remaining, cutie." The genie looks at his watch, "and I have a hot date in half an hour—with a scantily clad harem girl." This last part he addresses to me, with an 'eat your heart out' smirk on his face.

Helen looks at me, and I can see the wheels turning. I ignore the genie and plead with an expression I hope is a reasonable imitation of a forlorn puppy dog, pointing sadly at my shut mouth.

She ponders longer than necessary before she says in her most seductive voice, "Arnold, you know how I always wanted to go to Scotland and see the old deserted castles." She runs her hand over my shoulder and down my arm. "Do you think we could go this summer? Just nod your head 'yes,' honey."

What choice do I have? I heave an exaggerated exasperated sigh and reluctantly nod my head. Helen turns back to the genie, who's still leering seductively at her.

"I want my husband back to normal," she tells him.

"Sorry, doll. I can't return someone to someplace he's never been."

Helen pauses and places her pretty little finger on the tip of her pretty little chin. "I wish you would return my husband to the way he was an hour ago..."

Then she smiles sweetly at the genie and adds, "...tomorrow afternoon. Let's go, Arnold."

Negative Space

eloise comeau murray

It was loneliness that prompted Adam to sign up for the painting class. The ad made it sound easy enough: *Eight Wednesday evenings from seven to ten. Beginning level using acrylics. Materials provided. No previous experience needed.*

He thought it would be something to get him out of the house one night a week. There might be someone who would like to go for coffee or a beer after the class, someone to talk with.

If he did not like it, he could just drop out without losing much of an investment. He'd never dropped out of anything in his life that he could recall, but there might be a first time.

His kids—well, hardly kids since they were in their forties—had been urging him to find something, anything that he might take an interest in. Furthermore, that part about no experience meant he was eminently qualified. The only things he'd ever painted were walls and even then Janet had said it wasn't a very good job. Actually he agreed, but didn't tell her so; nor did he comment when he noticed she had repainted them one day when he was at work.

He was surprisingly nervous as he walked to the first class. What if he was the only man there with a bunch of yakking women? What if he simply couldn't make his seventy-year-old hands do what was required? What if the instructor delighted in making people feel stupid? Heaven knows with respect to painting, he already felt stupid enough.

He was pleasantly surprised. While there was no one he knew in the class, which he took to be a positive, there were five other men and eight women. He guessed he might be the oldest, but age differences didn't bother him.

The instructor was a soft-spoken woman named Tracey who looked as if she might have some First Nation ancestors. He liked her immediately.

The first night as they worked on a simple small canvas in an effort to learn about doing the background and the sequence of adding things to a painting, he was surprised when ten o'clock came. Tracey had walked among the group encouraging and suggesting options, but never telling anyone what to do.

She stated the goal of the class: "Everyone has their own style and part of the course is to discover what that style might be. Once we've covered some of the basics, the plan is to experiment with various approaches."

Adam was surprised when all the paintings were lined upon the edge of the chalkboard in the room. One would have thought they had all been at different classes. Individual style, indeed. He wasn't even ashamed of his own first effort.

Tracey suggested if they wanted to invest in some inexpensive materials they could try a similar painting of their own choice and bring it next week.

When he got home it was nearly eleven o'clock because Ned, who had been sitting next to him, asked if he'd like to go have a beer. They'd gone to the pub and chatted, beginning with why they were in the class.

Ned was very up-front about trying to meet a woman as his goal; however, he had wanted to try to paint and only now had the time. He was about forty, unmarried and working in information technology. Possibly a nerd—too soon to tell.

Adam allowed that he chose the course just to get out of the house with a purpose. His wife had passed away about a year ago and he realized that loneliness was overwhelming him at times. Ned was sympathetic.

When they left the pub Ned suggested, "Let's make this after class beer a habit. Maybe once we meet some of the women, we can ask them to join us."

Adam did not say that was not part of his agenda.

When he got home he looked at his phone and saw the light

blinking with a message. Before listening, he checked the display to see who might have called. His daughter Sandy had called five times.

What on Earth could be wrong? He dialed her number.

She answered with, "Papa, where have you been? Do you realize what time it is?"

"Whoa! I know what time it is. I am not on any curfew that I know of. I was at a class and then went out for a beer with one of the guys."

"A class! What kind of a class?"

"Introduction to working with acrylics."

"An art class. Now that would surprise Mum."

"No more than it surprises me, honey. It was fun. There's something soothing about the instructor. I think she's First Nation."

"So did you tell her about your DNA test results?"

"Surely you're kidding. The class is not about who our ancestors were."

"Maybe in the end people paint who they are, Papa."

The second art lesson was about shading and other ways to add perspective. Adam struggled with that one. His inclination was what he considered flat painting. He remembered reading a book about Maud Lewis called something about no shadows. There he was trying to make shadows in appropriate places.

Tracey came by a couple of times to make suggestions for approaches, but whether it was his brain or his hands, it just was not working to his satisfaction.

That night after the class, three of the women joined Ned and Adam at the pub. They were more Ned's contemporaries than his, but Adam enjoyed the repartee and having company.

One of the women, Sue, tried to interest him in a conversation about modern art, but he had to admit he knew little about it. She moved to the other side of the table to attempt that same conversation with Estelle. Adam became more observer than participant.

Ned was making a major play for Christina whom Adam surmised was way out of his league. He felt like he was watching a television reality show.

As much as Adam had considered the art class merely a reason to get out of his house, it became part of what he thought about as he went about his day. He started to look at things slightly differently. He wondered about some of the art work that Janet had hung in the house, art work that remained even though she was gone.

One night as he was falling asleep he tried to guess what he might have purchased as art for their house had he been asked. That had been Janet's domain.

It was the third class that really rattled Adam's cage.

"Welcome. Tonight we are going to consider the role of negative space in art. I've brought along pictures from various cultures to show you how it is used. Let's begin with those from Japan."

Tracey was talking and showing pictures, but Adam was stuck back at the term *negative space*. He was scarcely listening to her alternative definitions and how it worked in art, in rooms, even in advertising. He barely heard her say, "It is the space that surrounds an object in an image. Just as important as that object itself, negative space helps to define the boundaries of positive space and brings balance to a composition."

Vaguely through his own spinning thoughts he heard her talking about the peacock design of NBC and how the viewer's brain completed the empty spaces. He didn't know whether to sit and try to listen or to leave and attempt to sort out his thoughts.

When she had finished her remarks and made the night's assignment, Tracey came directly to Adam's table. "Are you having a problem with this concept? You looked a bit confused."

"I think I am, but not about the way you were describing it. I've never heard that term before and I think I way over-interpreted it. In fact, I don't think I can complete the assignment."

"Is there anything I could do to help you?"

"To tell you the truth, I have no idea. Could you suggest something else for me to do while I ponder all the things whirling in my head?"

"Let me see. How about you try to use paint to express, as you said, *all those things whirling in your head*?"

"Lord have mercy. It will be a mess. You realize I've only had two painting lessons in my life."

"Adam, I can deal with mess. I also have experience with art therapy. Just think for a few minutes. You can depict negative space or, if you prefer, the chaos that can come from the lack of it."

Tracey left Adam with a medium-size canvas and a range of colours. His first inclination was to walk out of the room and never come back.

Instead he closed his eyes and thought about what he wanted to show. Then he took the small piece of charcoal they each had been given and divided his canvas into six parts. They were not of equal size. Then he began selecting colours.

As he moved along he noticed the use of his paint brushes was changing from tight controlled dabs to strokes with greater movement.

At the end of the evening the boundaries of the spaces he had created had disappeared. Tracey walked by and quietly commented that she saw anger and sadness in his painting.

Adam nodded yes.

Pointing to the edge of the right side she said, "There's the good news piece. So glad it is there. Good job, Adam."

"Thank you for this."

He did not put his work up on the edge of the chalkboard. Before going out for beer with Ned and others, he put the painting in his car.

The next morning Adam sat in his chair and, instead of watching the morning news, which always seemed negative, he studied the painting he'd made the night before. He had no idea what he would do with it. Maybe hang it in his closet. He simply knew he should keep it for a while to remind him of things he had been unwilling to deal with since Janet's death.

When Tracey first used the term negative space, the only thing he could think of was the little room in palliative care where he spent hours sitting with his dying wife. At that time he would not let the anger enter his thinking. He had tried for decades to get her to stop smoking. There were times, even in that bare little room, when he wanted to say how much he wished she had listened to him. It was too late for that.

The next thing he thought about as negative space, by his initial definition, was the house. It had been Janet's parents' home, and Adam's sense was she had kept it as a memorial to them. They had been pack rats and Janet had the same tendency. It was cluttered with too much furniture, furniture he found overly ornamental. He liked plainer things, which he thought of as honest.

He did not like most of the paintings and objects on the walls and there were far too many. And those stupid frilly curtains swagged over the dining room window belonged in another age. He wondered when they had last been washed and thought if he smelled them they would still reek of Janet's cigarettes.

He could not change Janet's death, but by heavens he could change the house. And he knew in doing so he would be using Tracey's definition of negative space to make it his own place.

He would have to let his three children know of this impending transformation. Saturday they were all to be at a barbecue at Sandy's house, since her brother Jim and his partner Bruce were home from Montreal. He had a lot to do in the next couple of days.

The neighbours noticed Adam coming and going in a way they'd never seen before. No fewer than four tradesmen had been in and out. This radical change alleviated their concern for him. They had seen him slouching around being sad and lonely. As much as they tried to be kind to him, he seemed to have closed in on himself. They did wonder what had happened to instigate this change.

Saturday, after supper, the adults sat on the deck having coffee or a beer. The conversation was dancing around several topics. Jokes floated on the evening air.

Adam waited for a lull, took a deep breath and asked if he could have a few minutes to talk with them. "I wanted to have you all in one spot to tell you about some of my plans."

He nearly laughed out loud at the glances that flew back and forth among his children and their mates. *What the hell is he talking about.*

"I've been doing a lot of thinking over the past year. One of the conclusions I have come to is that I need to make the house my own. As it now seems like a memorial to your grandparents and, lately, to your Mother. I have no intention of trying to erase Janet from the house, as I have seen other people who were mourning a partner do. On the other hand, if I am to live there, it needs to have in it things I enjoy living with."

No one interrupted. He told them he had hired a painter to do all the walls and ceilings. The carpets would be removed and new flooring added where necessary. A supplier was going provide new doors for the kitchen cupboards and paint the interiors, but the layout would remain the same. Workers would update the bathrooms to better serve an older person. He went through all the details he had attended to so far.

Then he reached in a bag he'd brought out to the deck. "I've have gone through the house and put a blue dot on the things I would like to keep. I have not had time to shop for new furniture, but I do know what I am looking for.

"Each pair of you will have your own colour dots so you can mark the things you want. It would be nice if you could do that while Jim and Bruce are here so you can do any necessary horse trading. The floor contractor will begin work in ten days, so stuff you pick should go home with you before that time. I will donate things no one wants.

"You need to know I feel more alive than I have in over a year. I think your mother would be proud of me."

His family looked at him in surprise. Then they began asking questions. Foremost was where all this had come from.

"In my painting class last week, the instructor was talking about negative space and how it works in art. I misinterpreted the concept and thought it meant negative like awful, not merely empty. It was a rough night at that class for me, but I finally admitted what had been eating at me for a long time. I am so grateful. My intention is to apply the real meaning of negative space in the changes I make in the house – bare spaces that enhance whatever is there. It is very exciting. I hope you will support my plan."

Sandy spoke up, "Dad, I have a friend who is a decorator. Would you be interested in having some help from her?"

"I suppose it would help as long as she is not bossy or wants to make the place all full of frou fra."

"Well, I'm not sure exactly what that is, but she is known for listening before she gives advice. What colour are you having the kitchen cupboards and the walls painted?"

"White. When your mother painted the living room dark green and the dining room maroon, it felt like we had become a funeral home. We argued and she won."

Ben, the quiet one in the family, said, "Dad, was there anything other than that art lesson that prompted this burst of change? Which, by the way, I think is a great idea."

"You know I play Scrabble with Charlie Bent most every Monday afternoon. He's 90, but still sharp as a tack. Beats me most of the time. We sit in a living room he has kept like Mary used to have it. The curtains are drab and faded. She had collections of all sorts of useless things. I've never dared ask him if he likes any of the damn stuff. I am sure the person who cleans for him must dread coming there. I don't want to be like Charlie. It's not my plan to spend all of your inheritance; however, I'm looking forward to being in a place that brings me joy."

Everyone assured Adam he was doing the correct thing. Sandy expressed a hope that she could help him make choices about what to give away. He said he needed her help going through the kitchen cupboards. He was confident there were historic foods in them.

The next day his children came to put their stickers on things. He sat and observed the negotiations. In the end it seemed they were all content with the outcome and Adam was proud of how they had handled the few disagreements. He was surprised at some of the choices and the reasons they gave. They shared memories of grandparents and their mother. It was a poignant time.

The house was chaotic for a few weeks with workers, things torn apart, noise, and delays over materials. Adam helped where he could and otherwise stayed out of the way.

When it was done he found the result even better than he had imagined. Things he liked that had been obscured by so much stuff stood out like gems. The new floors matched the hardwood that had been hidden by scruffy carpet for decades. Adam was delighted, as were Ben and Sandy who lived nearby. They sent a large file of pictures to Jim so he could see the outcome.

Adam could hardly believe he was on his way to the last painting class. It was fun to greet people he now considered friends. They all wondered what Tracey had in mind for the finale. The canvases standing ready were larger than any they had done so far.

Tracey appeared and asked if people would help her bring in a few paintings. There were ten in total. She put them on the ledge of the blackboard. They were an astonishing range of styles and subjects: florals, two with boats, three still lifes, some outdoor scenes, one of water on the shore, a couple of the interior of houses.

"Tonight's class is about inspiration and being informed. It is not about copying. These paintings are all by artists who live less than fifty miles from this place. At the end of the class I will tell you who did what. I also have a listing of galleries and studios within the same distance that you may visit for inspiration after this class is over."

She talked a bit about the ways in which their paintings might differ from the ones they particularly liked. Then she told them to choose a painting and produce one inspired by that choice. At the end each one was to briefly describe what elements they had used from their chosen painting and what in particular inspired them about it. She said as usual if they needed help over a rough spot, she was there for that purpose.

Adam knew immediately which painting inspired him. It took some thinking to decide which aspects he wished to use. He knew his palette would differ from the one on the ledge because was bright colours and he preferred more muted ones. It would not be a boat, but a waterbird of some sort. It was the technique used to create the sense of water that he wished to emulate.

He gathered up the colours he wanted and set about the task.

Tracey passed by his table a few times. He merely looked up and smiled. She smiled and kept on going to the next person. At the end of two and a half hours he wondered where the time had gone.

"Okay. Take five more minutes and then we'll talk about your paintings and the artists who inspired you."

Adam was pleased with his painting. More than with any of the other exercises they had done, he felt a sense of satisfaction. He thought, *I might hang this one in the den.*

He listened to his classmates describing their work. When it was his time to speak he felt confident. "I picked the painting with the yellow boat. In particular I liked the form of the water. As you can see, my colours are more muted and the boat has become a loon. When we had our lesson about shading, it didn't feel like me. I've tried to do it as we went along. With this flat approach I feel like I've come home."

"You have certainly done your best work so far, Adam. It was a joy to watch you being confident. It is a wonderful picture. You should be proud. Now about the artist who did the original."

Tracey said a First Nation artist had created his inspiration piece. She told her background and where he could go to see her work.

When everyone had done their presentation Adam raised his hand. "I've just had my place remodelled and am anxious to show it to my family, friends and neighbours. So I'm holding a get-to-gether next Wednesday. It will be a simple affair. Come around seven for a glass of wine and some snacks, if you can."

Tracey and the whole class said they would be there. He was astonished and pleased. *Imagine me actually having a party.*

As he was leaving Tracey asked if he had minute. "I wanted to tell you about my background. I am part Mohawk and part Ojibway with some Scottish thrown in. My best advice to you, if you intend to keep painting, is to stick with the path you began tonight. It fits you."

"I feel that. There's something you might want know. A few years ago I had my DNA tested. For years people kept asking me if I was part Indian. It turns out I am about 25 percent Mi'qmaw. My parents always denied it. I guess they felt it was something to be ashamed of in their time."

"We can hope that times have changed, at least a little. Good luck, Adam. See you next week."

Go, Danny Boy, Go!

Kathy Brooks

The three boys stretched out on the railroad tracks, ears pressed to the rails.

"Listen," Sam said. "If there's a train coming, the tracks will vibrate."

"Yeah, I saw Tonto do that on the *Lone Ranger*," Derek said.

"I don't think it was Tonto," said Danny. "It was some cowboy movie."

"Shhh," Sam said. "We won't hear anything if you guys don't shut up."

They lay silently, concentrating. Derek and Danny sat up after a few moments, but Sam stayed with his ear to the rails.

Finally he jumped up. "Okay, let's go," he said.

Danny was to go first. The tunnel in front of them looked like a gaping black mouth. The drips off the top from the recent rain reminded Danny of saliva.

"Hurry up, Danny," Sam said, giving him a push.

They had watched trains come through the tunnel, blasting their way out of the blackness, barely clearing the tunnel walls. If a train came while he was in there, Danny knew he'd be squished.

The boys figured the tunnel was only a few hundred feet long. If it didn't curve, they would have been able to see the light at the far end. But it curved just enough that it was pitch black in the middle.

Danny took a deep breath, closed his eyes and walked forward. He held one arm out in front to ward off spider webs or any scaries that might jump out at him. He reached out his other arm and ran his hand along the tunnel wall as he walked.

He wanted to run, but he was afraid of falling on the uneven ground alongside the tracks. Sam had told him to walk on the ties, but Danny knew he wouldn't be able to touch the wall if he did that. Feeling the solid wall with his hand made him feel less alone in the tunnel.

His heart pounded. He stopped after ten steps, wanting to turn back. He swore he could hear a train coming.

Behind him Sam and Derek were yelling, "*Go, Danny Boy, go!*"

He plunged on, his nose filling with the moist air and the stale smell of diesel. His hand grazing the damp wall felt slime and crumbling dirt. The mucky ground seeped through his sneakers. The drip, drip of falling water echoed in the blackness.

He emerged from the tunnel, one hand covered with soot, the light blinding him for a moment. He gulped the fresh air. He sank down on the grassy bank beside the tracks and waited for Sam and Derek.

A few moments later, the sun caught Sam's red hair as he emerged. Sam looked as calm as if he was just out for a Sunday stroll.

Soon after, Derek came scrambling, his gangly legs flying. He ran for the grassy bank and collapsed beside Danny.

~

That summer, when they were twelve years old, they ran the tunnel a dozen times. Sam, being the tallest and looking older than his age, was the boss, and when he said they were going to the tunnel, Derek and Danny just nodded and followed him.

Many years later, Danny thought maybe Sam had craved a thrill, an escape from his boring life. His parents were both invalids after a car accident, and so Sam and his older sister had to cook, clean and do whatever parents usually did. Sam rarely had time for any fun.

Danny knew why he and Derek did it. They respected Sam and knew he had a tough life, and they wanted to please him.

Sam was super chatty after they ran the tunnel as if his system went into overdrive. The three of them would take a different route home through the woods, avoiding the tunnel, laughing, shouting and shoving each other. The black-mouthed tunnel would be forgotten for a few days.

~

When Dan graduated from high school, he moved two hundred kilometres away to go to college. His first day of classes, he hesitated outside the English 101 lecture hall. Through the open door he had caught a glimpse of a sloping bank of chairs with small desks attached. There must have been over a hundred seats in there.

He was tempted to turn around, but in his head, he heard the words, *"Go, Danny Boy, go."* He took a deep breath, closed his eyes for a moment and plunged in.

Dan's new life was absorbing and exciting. After a few futile attempts to keep in touch with Sam and Derek, he gave up. Before long, he realized that most people in his classes were new to the town and to college life, too, and he quickly made close friends.

Though he lived with his elderly Aunt Vivian, he managed to get out to the pub with his friends and get into a little trouble wandering home late at night, half-drunk. One time, they found some chalk and wrote rude words on the sidewalk outside Aunt V's house.

The next morning, she huffed and puffed as she scrubbed the profanities off with a brush. "I can't imagine the type of people who would do such a thing," she said. "Imagine the poor upbringing they must have had."

Dan pretended to sneeze to hide his smile.

His aunt nodded approvingly when she saw him writing or reading. He started to keep a notebook with him at all times to write down the new things he learned in biology or chemistry. He also found it useful when he wanted to avoid talking with Aunt Vivian, who was prone to lecturing rather than conversing.

Soon, he looked forward to the times when he could write in his notebook; it helped him clarify the day's lessons. When it was time for exams, Dan realized he only needed to review his notes to get top marks.

~

Four years later, Dan graduated with a Bachelor of Science and started looking for work. He'd had a summer job in the geology labs at the university, but he wasn't confident that this experience would count for much. He persevered, filling out applications and working on his resumé.

To his surprise, a local mining company asked him to come for an interview. He spent many hours in the library, making up mock questions and answers and studying books on interview skills, but nothing prepared him for what he confronted when he arrived at the company's office.

When he walked down the hallway to take a seat, he caught a glimpse inside the interview room. To his shock, there wasn't one interviewer but five of them, seated behind a long table.

As he waited in the hallway, his heart thumped. He held a copy of his resumé between his shaking fingers: his hands were so sweaty, he was afraid the resumé would be ruined.

He was tempted to run, but when his name was called he heard the words echo in his head, *"Go, Danny Boy, go."* He took a deep breath, closed his eyes for a moment, and plunged in.

~

Now in his late twenties, Dan was gaining seniority and feeling more confident in his job every day. He was travelling out to the mine sites, working with the microscope back in the office, even the report writing. He was starting to save money and had managed to buy a car. He was sharing a spiffy apartment with a good friend.

The one thing he hadn't found was a soulmate. There had been a few girls along the way, but no one he felt crazy about. Was he too optimistic to think that the right girl would come along? Or was he being too choosy?

He and his roommate discussed girls endlessly. Dan decided that the right girl would come along if he was patient.

His roommate disagreed. "You gotta get out there, Dan, and be assertive. If you see a girl who attracts you, ask her out."

Dan was hoping that a girl would come to him so he wouldn't have to go fishing for one, but he didn't forget his roommate's advice. Maybe he needed to pay more attention.

Shopping for a take-out roast chicken one day after work, he looked up to see a girl about his age examining the chickens. Dan thought her bright pink t-shirt contrasted nicely with her long, dark hair.

She smiled at him as she grabbed a plump chicken from right in front of him.

He started to turn toward the check-out and then stopped. He took a deep breath, closed his eyes for a moment, and took the plunge.

"Hey, your chicken looks bigger than mine," he said.

Go, Danny Boy, go!

Walk with Me

Angel Flanagan

"Why do we even have to go there?" Amie whined.

"Because I want to," Dot replied.

"Well, I don't."

"Doesn't matter. We're going. I am gonna prove that there is no ghost in that old house. Jay is full of shit," Dot said.

"I don't want to go." Amie turned back toward her house.

"Come on, don't be chicken shit. Come for a walk with me. It will be fun, like camping." She put her arm through Amie's arm and pulled Amie along with her.

"I don't even like camping, I will NOT enjoy spending the night in a rat-infested haunted house in the dark," Amie said.

They reached the end of the driveway and turned right on the road. Soon as they were out of sight of her parents' house she pulled away from Dot. "Gimme a smoke."

"You can't have any if you don't come with me." Dot stopped and fished a pack of cigarettes out of her backpack. Amie pulled a cigarette out of the pack and lit it up.

"Let's go now before dark. Then you can see there is nothing to be afraid of."

"Ghosts don't care if it's dark or not," Amie said as she trailed along behind Dot.

"For the last time: day or night, there are no ghosts!"

They walked along the cracked pavement for almost an hour and only saw one car. The car beeped; they both waved. They chattered on and on about school, boys, gossip and music. Everything and nothing.

As they walked farther from home, the pavement became jagged and broken. Big chunks had crumbled away from the edges.

Eventually, the road narrowed to a dirt lane. Fallen trees blocked their path. They walked among the tall grass and bushes that were thick enough in places to block the sun. The branches grabbed at their hair and clothes like bony fingers.

They walked up the overgrown driveway and stood in the shadow of the dilapidated building for a while before they dared to go inside. It had been this way for as long as Dot could remember. Nailed to the sagging corner was a faded sign that read "Keep Out! Rusty Nails and Large Snakes."

The house looked like the owners had just left for work one day and never came back. The broken windows stared out at a barren front yard. The once beautiful home was in shambles. A smashed kitchen table, broken chairs, and bottles littered the room. Rusty cans of soup were still in the pantry, and shattered sharp remains of plates in the corners.

Whatever teenagers over the decades had not wrecked, Mother Nature finished. Gnarled roots had grown through the floorboards. The ceiling caved in a few places where the roof had leaked. The wooden lathes were showing like bare bones behind the crumbling plaster and peeling wallpaper. It stank, a good sign that raccoons, rats and other wildlife had been living inside.

Dot's resolve faded. Even without ghosts, this place sucked.

~

Amie did not like this place. It didn't feel right. Dot didn't seem to notice anything. Amie wasn't surprised. If it wasn't about Dot, Dot didn't care.

Amie felt as delicate as a butterfly's wing. There was something that waited for them, something as dangerous as a knife in the dark. "I don't like it in here. Let's go."

Amie stepped towards the rotten doorway. Dot gabbed her arm. "No way. We just got here. We can't leave yet."

"This place is a dump. I am not sleeping here. It's ready to fall down, we shouldn't be anywhere near it. If the wind blows the whole place is going to fall down on our heads and crush us."

"Well, it is pretty bad. At least stay until dark, so we can say we did, and then we can walk back."

"Who cares if we stay except you?"

"I want to be able to tell Jay he's full of shit the next time he starts trying to scare people with his stories."

"It's only the dumb chicks he brings back here in his truck that he tells those stories to," Amie said. "Gets them all excited and easier to talk out of their clothes. Are ya jealous?"

"Never. He's not my type. Too tall. The dumb chicks are more his style, but you seem to know an awful lot about what goes in that old truck."

"I know nothing."

They both laughed. It sounded strange in the mouldy porch, kind of hollow.

"Let's go outside and think about what to do." Amie stepped across the door way and immediately felt better. Dot joined her and they went to sit under an old apple tree.

"That's much better. How do you feel?" Amie asked.

"Better, I didn't even know I was feeling bad until we came outside. Probably all the rotten shit making the air bad in there."

They couldn't see the ocean from this side of the property, but they could hear seagulls and smell the salt in the air.

"Let's go now before it gets dark out. It's a long walk back."

"No dice," Dot said. "We are staying here until after dark. I brought a deck of cards. Want to play for a bit?"

"Cards aren't going to distract me. What else you got in that bag?" Amie hoped there was more than stupid cards, cause this night sucked ass, she hoped things would get better. How did she let Dot get her into situations like this?

~

"Check this out, you old stick in the mud." Dot took a tightly folded blanket from her bag, snuggled in the middle of the quilt was a pint of clear liquid. "This should make things more fun."

"Looks like water."

"Not water: moonshine."

"Where did you get that?"

"My Dad and uncle made it. They have so many bottles, they won't miss one. It is powerful stuff. You can even light it on fire. Wanna see?"

Dorothy had brought a spoon along just for this little show. She poured a bit of the moonshine into the spoon and flicked the lighter. The clear liquid in the spoon lit right up in a pretty blue flame.

"See? It's real."

Amie sniffed at the bottle, crinkling her nose. "Man, it smells terrible. It's burning my eyes. Did you at least bring some pop for the mix?"

"Nope, no mix. Well, a bit of water, but we might need that later on after the shine is gone. Gonna have to be strong and drink it straight. I know you can do it, you are tough."

"I'm not drinking alone. So you are gonna have to suffer the taste too."

"I don't like the hard stuff, even with the mix. That's your thing."

"Too bad, you should have brought something else to drink."

"All right. I'll have two shots, but that's it."

"Fine, two it is. Then we start walking home."

"We don't have to hurry, we can smoke and drink all night, lets take our time. You know our folks are too drunk to even notice we're not home. After you have a shot or three of this magic juice, you'll feel better. The walk home will be a breeze. Let's play cards, loser drinks."

"We will play cards, and we will both drink. You aren't getting out of drinking, if I drink, you drink, or I start walking back alone. You know I'll do it, too. I mean it."

Dot knew she did mean it. "Okay, okay! You deal, what are we gonna play?"

"Something fast and easy and we don't have to keep score."

Dot didn't play many card games, war or crazy eights. War seemed easier. "War. Rules are simple. Highest card wins, we both drink."

Amie started to deal the cards.

~

Amie threw her cards on the old blanket they had spread on the ground. "You win. I quit. Gimme that bottle, I need another drink." She took a couple big swigs of the moonshine. She almost gagged on the second one, but kept it down. "That's it. I don't want any more, it's too dark to play cards now anyways. Let's go home."

"It's not that dark, no hurry. I have a flashlight for later. Come on have another drink."

"I'll puke if do."

"No, you won't. Drink a little water first."

Dot tossed over a half full bottle of water. Amie had a sip. "Now have some more shine, just drink it fast. I know you can handle it."

"No, I had enough." Amie hiccuped.

"I'll even drink more, too." Dot put the bottle to her mouth, took a small drink and grimaced. "Your turn. I am going to hold this bottle and you are going to drink. You don't want to waste it, do you?"

"I'll choke!" Amie pushed the bottle away, spilling a few drops.

"Don't spill it! There isn't that much left! You won't choke. It's the only way to get it all down. We're not taking it home with us. Can't have Dad figuring out I took some. Drink it or I won't talk to you anymore."

"Uggh. Fine, let's do this. Whatever makes you happy."

Dot put the bottle up to Amie lips and tipped it slowly. Once Amie started to drink, Dot held it and didn't pull it away until the bottle was empty.

Amie sputtered and choked. Her eyes were watering. "I knew you would do that."

"Didn't hurt ya none and the booze is all gone." Dot threw the empty bottle out into the woods.

Just then there was a loud snap. They both jumped about two feet in the air.

"What the fuck was that?" Dot said.

"Aw, that's nothing. Just a dead tree falling." Amie had shine courage. She wasn't feeling much fear right now.

"What made it fall?"

"Probably a bird settling in for the night or something."

"Must have been a big ass bird. It was probably a goddamned bear." Dot squeezed closer to Amie.

"Relax. It was probably Jay or his buddies. Did he know we were coming here? It was your idea to go looking for ghosts. Were you trying to get the boys to come here?"

"No one knew we were coming here. I didn't even tell my parents, I just left a note saying I was at your place. I left it on the outdoor fridge where they keep the beer, so they should at least see the paper."

There was a loud rustling in the woods, and then nothing.

"Well, guess maybe we can go before full dark. I knew there were no ghosts." Dot whispered.

"Why the whisper? I thought you wanted to stay the night. I bet you'd stay if the guys were here."

Dot cleared her throat and just about yelled, "We have to bring something from here with us, to prove to them we were here tonight. Is that loud enough for you?"

"Yes! That's loud enough, dammit. Even the dead could hear you. What do you want to bring? We probably have a hundred ticks on us to bring home. That should prove something."

"I want a little keepsake from the house."

"I'm not going in there. We can pull off an old shingle."

"No. We need something from inside. Should be able to find something in the kitchen."

"You can go inside and get whatever you want. I'll wait right here."

More branches snapped to their left. Then there was a loud crack as a heavier branch broke off to the right.

"Okay, let's go get your keepsake, before whatever is making that racket gets any closer."

~

As the girls walked toward the old house, there was a loud crash among the trees. They screamed and moved faster. Then there were a few thumps on the other side of the yard.

That was Kevin, right on time. The guys had split up for this to work. Jay threw a couple of old apples across the yard to make the noises come from everywhere. Kevin did the same.

The girls started to run even faster. They were going to piss their pants.

Jay decided it was time to get closer to the action. He did his best to stay hidden in the shadows until he could get close enough to jump out and grab one of them. That would be the best joke ever.

He snickered to himself. This should get some attention from Amie. She was the one he had his eye on. Dot did all the talking but Amie was the one he wanted.

He carefully made his way to where Kevin was waiting under a tree, smoking a joint.

"What took so long?"

"I didn't want the girls to see me yet," Jay whispered. "That would ruin the whole surprise."

"I think they are scared enough. They ran right inside the house to hide. We can't leave them in there: they will break their necks in the dark."

"They'll break our necks when they find out we've been messing with them."

"Oh I bet Amie will forgive you pretty fast," Kevin said. "Not too sure about Dot."

"Dorothy likes you, if we play this right we both might get lucky. We just have to jump out and scare them and then make them laugh. They will be wound right up."

~

Inside the old house was the only place they didn't hear strange noises. But it seemed to have changed since it had gotten dark.

The moon made the creaky ruin's shadows stretch long and hide some of the worst damage time had done. The roof had giant holes through which the moonlight shone. Instead of windows there were huge, gaping, black holes that were big enough to swallow you. Broken stairs to trip you.

Amie ran and hid behind what was left of a table. Dorothy cowered beside her.

"Grab whatever you want to bring and let's go home," Amie said. "Animals or ghosts don't make those kinds of noises. That was the boys."

"What the fuck is that?"

"What the fuck is what?"

"That red light. It's floating!"

"I don't see anything," Amie said. Stop fucking with me."

The red light was just floating there. Dottie didn't believe it was real. She knew the boys had to be screwing around.

But this didn't feel like it was fake. It seemed to want her to follow it. It called to her,

Follow me.

It was like she was on autopilot, she could not control here own feet. She started up the rickety stairs.

"Where are you going, Dot?"

Dorothy paused. She answered in a quiet, dreamy voice. "I am going to find the red light. It won't stop following me. Every time I think it's gone, I look back, and I can still see it. If I go find it, maybe it will leave me alone."

"I don't see any red light," Amie said. "If you do, it's just the guys with a laser pointer. Come on, let's just leave."

"Look behind you: it's there. I'm going to get that ghost light. I don't want it to follow me forever."

"It's just a trick. How can it be behind both of us at the same time? I thought you didn't believe in ghosts anyway."

"I don't. I don't know why you can't see it. It's right there." Dorothy turned and pointed behind Amie.

"I can't see it 'cause it ain't real. I can't believe you brought me here to mess with me. I'm leaving right now. You can come or stay. I don't care. Maybe you can get a ride home with the guys. I know they are out there waiting. I'm on to you all."

"Leave if you want. I'm going to turn off that light." Dot turned and went on up the stairs.

Amie stomped out the front door, and almost went through the rotted porch. She was so determined to leave and not look back, she didn't see Jay crouched by the door.

He jumped out and grabbed her from behind and swung her high in the air. She screamed and kicked, hitting the air, before one of her flailing elbows caught him on the jaw.

"Ow! Fuck! Settle down Am," Jay, shouted. "it's just me."

"I hate you. I fucking knew it."

"Aw, come on, I was just teasin'."

"Well, it's the last time you tease me. Put me down. Get your grubby hands off me."

"Don't be mad." Jay set Amie gently on the ground. She pushed him away.

Amie yelled at the house. "Come on out, Dot. I know you all planned this. I bet Kev is here, too. Jay can't go two feet without him being stuck up his ass."

Kevin stepped out of the shadows. "Fine, you caught us. It was just for fun."

"Not fun for me, you assholes," Amie yelled. "Dot get out here, I'm not going in to get you."

No answer.

"Fine. Stay there. Bye." She gave the house the finger, and gave the boys the double guns. She was done.

As she started to walk away, though, a red glow began to shine from the upstairs window of the old house. It was bright enough to cast her shadow in front of her.

Amie turned to see what it was. She started to doubt it was the guys with a laser.

The light got brighter and the shade of red deepened. Amie had to shield her eyes. Then it was gone. It puffed out like a candle, leaving Amie and the rest blind in the dark.

"What was that?" Jay asked.

"That was another trick you guys set up."

"No way. We had nothing to do with that. Our whole plan was just to make some noise and jumpscare you." He kind of looked sorry. "Hey, Dorothy, get out here. Joke's over."

Still no answer

"We better go get her," Kevin said. "Maybe she fell or something."

They crept inside the door. Even Jay was a little jumpy. They had done such a good job trying to scare the girls that they were scaring themselves.

"The last time I seen her, she said she was going upstairs to turn off the light." Amie whispered.

They looked up the ratty staircase. Dot stood at the top, staring at nothing. She had a big streak of white in her wavy brown hair that hadn't been there before.

"Dot, come on!"

Still no response. She just stood there staring.

Amie dashed up the stairs and grabbed Dot's hand. She pulled hard, but Dottie didn't move an inch. She didn't even look at Amie.

Amie pulled again and this time Dorothy took a small step. If she didn't start to walk, Amie would drag her.

Like a flash Kevin was beside Amie, scooping Dot up in his arms. Amie looked over Dot's shoulder and saw a red glow coming from the bedroom, it was pulsating and getting brighter.

They ran until they were outside. The stronger the throbbing angry red light became, the stronger Amie's feeling of dread grew. All the same, she sort of wanted to see what was making the light.

They all piled in Jay's blue truck. The half ton took off with the passenger door still hanging open, spinning clumps of dirt and grass behind it as it sped away from the house.

The red glow coming from the upstairs was still deepening, red light was surging from the windows.

They kept picking up speed. The old truck fishtailed and Amie almost fell out the open door. Kevin reached over and swung the door closed.

Dot just sat there, staring.

They almost crashed into one of the fallen trees, but at the last second Jay managed to avoid slamming into it and kept the truck on the path.

"Watch where you are going!" Amie screeched.

"I am trying!"

"Slow down at least."

"If I slow down the little red dot gets closer."

Amie resisted the urge to look back. She was afraid if she did that, she, too, would see a floating red light.

Walter's Mittens

eloise comeau murray

The members of the *Happy Hands* knitting group had been meeting regularly for nearly three years. Each Tuesday evening between seven and nine o'clock, ten to twenty women of all ages met in the local community hall. The members ranged in age from twelve to seventy-six.

The hall had recently been renovated and provided a welcoming place to share their interest in knitting. They sat around the newly painted tables in groups of five or six, having wide ranging conversations and sharing their lives as they worked on their current projects. There usually was plenty of laughter and, on a few occasions, a tear or two.

The women took turns bringing a snack and preparing coffee or tea. Among them there was little competition either about knitting projects or food. Those who were more skilled helped those who were there to learn. Older members shared treasured knitting books while the younger ones brought patterns downloaded from the web.

One October evening as they arrived, the women noticed a pickup they'd not seen there before sitting in the community hall yard. It was dusk so they couldn't tell if anyone was in that vehicle.

It wasn't alarming to anyone, but once inside they briefly discussed whose truck it could be. Someone suggested perhaps the truck's owner had been there earlier in the day and had had trouble starting it.

The matter was soon forgotten as knitting bags were opened and friends shared the progress they had made over the week. Two of the less skilled knitters had managed to get their work into major messes of dropped stitches and patterns gone awry. Two of the older women helped them sort out these problems. Coffee was brewing and Ada Baker had brought squares made with a new recipe.

"Oh, so we're going to be your guinea pigs tonight are we?"

"Not really. I had Tom eat a couple and he's still alive!"

The person in the truck was having a crisis of confidence. Sitting in the gathering darkness, Walter Maloney was having a stern talk with himself. He began by reviewing the two main reasons he was there.

First, he wanted to have a pair of fisherman's mittens like the ones his grandfather had knit for him. He'd been wearing them for a long time and they were at the end of their useful life with major holes and stains. The stains didn't bother him so much, but the holes were making them totally useless. Granddad had passed away over the summer so someone else would have to knit new ones. His wife did not know how to knit and since she was so engaged with hooking mats, she had absolutely no interest in learning. They'd had the "I need new mittens" conversation many times.

One day in total desperation at having the topic raised yet again Mary said, "For Pete's sake, Walter, why don't you learn to knit them yourself?"

"Who would teach me?"

"Join that knitting group at the hall. They meet every Tuesday evening."

"It'll just be a bunch of women."

"So!? When did you become intimidated by women?"

"They'd make fun of me."

"I seriously doubt it. Fishermen have been knitting mittens around here for years. Granted no one does it much now, but I'm sure they're not going to call you a sissy."

The second reason he wanted to learn to knit was that he was giving up smoking and needed something to do with his hands. He'd tried a variety of things, but so far none of them had been satisfactory. He had the nicotine patch on and wasn't smoking, he just felt his hands were twitchy. Sitting in the truck in the dark he sure wanted a cigarette, but none were available.

Those two reasons he could share with the women he'd seen entering the hall. The third one had only come into existence last Friday. That was an evening of beer and darts at the Legion. He'd been telling the boys about wanting new natural wool mittens and that Mary'd suggested he join the knitting group to learn to make them himself. No one laughed, but that darn Tom Baker had reached into his pocket and put some money on the table.

"I got $50 that says you haven't got the gumption to go to that knitting group Ada goes to."

The boys had laughed then, by golly.

Walter thought for a minute before replying, "So how long do I have to claim that money?"

"Take as long as you need, I suppose. I've no idea how complicated knitting is."

The other three each added $50 to the pot. However, they were less generous with the matter of time and told Walter he had three months to bring mittens he had knit to the Legion if he wanted the $200.

Walter shook everyone's hand and the bet was on. It had been easy with the beer and the companionship of the Legion to accept that challenge.

Now, sitting in the truck, he wondered what he'd been thinking. He figured Tom had told Ada about the bet. He'd seen her go into the hall carrying a basket and her knitting bag. Whether he had told her or not, though, when she got home Tom would know; and if Tom knew, so would the other three.

He'd already tried to decipher the knitting instructions with the help of the computer, but that proved to be hopeless. As scary as it was, going into the hall was his only hope of learning to knit. Why did things have to be so tough?

As he passed the kitchen on his way into the meeting, Walter smelled the coffee brewing and saw two plates of squares sitting on the counter. He heard the buzz of women's voices. He hesitated a bit and stepped into the hall.

Several of the women looked up. One of his neighbours said,

"Good evening, Walter. What brings you here?"

"I've come to learn to knit. I want to make mittens."

No one laughed or even smiled. However, there are some statements, regardless of how brief, that change how others see a person. Those two short sentences were pivotal in having the sixteen women of the *Happy Hands* group revise their view of Walter Maloney, fisherman.

There he stood, all six feet of him. At fifty-three he was a well-built man with greying hair, cleanly shaven for the occasion, wearing clean jeans and a plaid shirt.

All eyes shifted to his hands, the huge hands of a working man dangling at the ends of his long arms. Each of them tried to imagine those hands with knitting needles. It was going to be an interesting process.

To Walter it seemed like a long time, but Leona Ritchie was the quick to speak. "Walter, why don't you come sit by me? I can't tell you how many people I've taught to knit, including my fifth grade classes for nearly twenty years."

"I need to buy some needles and yarn, I guess."

"We don't sell that sort of thing here. I've got few spare needles in my bag and a couple balls of yarn you can use to begin with."

"What I really want is to make mittens of that untreated wool that my grandfather used to use."

"There are couple of places that sell it. I'd advise you get the brand that comes from Prince Edward Island. It has more lanolin in it. Knitting mittens requires four needles, but first you have to learn to knit with two. Let's get started."

Leona cast on ten stitches and showed Walter the process of simple knitting. Like most beginners, he dropped stitches, forgot to slide the knitted stitches off and started going in the wrong direction. She was a no-nonsense person, but she was patient. Walter tried hard. At one point Leona calmly suggested he not stick out his tongue as he concentrated as he might bite it off.

Walter could hardly believe it was nearly the end of the meeting when Ada brought out the squares and coffee. Where had the time gone? Sure took his mind of that cigarette he had wanted in the truck.

Before he left, Leona asked him to bring the old mittens to next week's meeting.

"Oh my soul, woman! They're full of holes and all stained. And they stink of fish."

"Well, wash them at least, but I need them as a pattern. For now, I'll give you your homework."

"Does everyone have homework?"

"No, just those who are learning. I've cast on twenty stitches for you. I want you to knit evenly for at least six inches. If you make mistakes, just keep going so I can figure out what your problems are. Remember how I showed you to wrap the yarn around your fingers to keep the tension correct. Next time we'll tackle purling and maybe casting on stitches."

When he got home, Mary's first question was, "Well, how'd it go?"

"The good news is no one laughed when I said I wanted to learn to knit. The bad news is, it's harder than I thought."

"Anything's hard when you're learning. But it'll get easier, I'm sure."

"Some of them sit there talking and hardly look at what they're doing, but they're going a mile a minute. It's Leona who's teaching me. I have homework, plus I have to find needles and the right kind of yarn."

"Did she tell you what size needles?"

"Needles have sizes? So, I guess I better wait. She's going to use Granddad's mittens as a pattern for me."

Mary thought the conversation was over, but a few minutes later Walter began again.

"I'm not used to being around women, except you, of course. Having four brothers and three sons and always working with men is why, I guess. That group went along so smoothly. No one seemed in charge, but everyone did things as if there was a big chart on the wall. Ada served her squares—you should ask her for that recipe, they're good—then a couple got up and served the coffee. When we were done, people just started cleaning up without someone yelling about it. Amazing, really!"

"So you had a good time?"

"I'd say so. Never thought I'd join a women's group or that it would be enjoyable."

"I hate to tell you, Walter, that group has never been limited to women. It's just until you, no man dared go there."

By the third time Walter went to *Happy Hands* he had his own knitting needles, some skeins of the same natural knitting yarn his grandfather had used, and, with Leona's help, enough courage to tackle knitting with four needles. She had written out the directions he should follow, and supervised him as he cast on the stitches.

"How'd you know how to write those directions?"

"By counting the stitches in your Grandfather's mittens. That and having knit dozens of mitten over the years."

Friday nights at the Legion his buddies didn't say a word about the bet. He thought that Ada would have told Tom, but he acted as if the whole matter had been forgotten. Furthermore, Walter had never told them he was attending the knitting club. Most assuredly he didn't let on a couple of times he'd had to call Leona to ask to come down so she could get him out of a knitting malfunction. She was patient and helpful.

Walter had already asked Mary what sort of a gift he should buy for all her help. Her suggestion was to ask the members of the group. That's when Ada commented that Leona really wanted a few sets of bamboo needles as they would be easier on her hands. She even told him what sizes to get.

The first mitten was not a thing of beauty. The thumb gusset was too short for his hand. There were missed stitches and the tension was all over the map.

Leona said, "Just keep that mitten to remind yourself of your progress. Now let's start again."

Walter had given up the nicotine patch, and the knitting was helping with his fidgety hands. Finally, he finished two reasonably knit mittens. He couldn't remember being so satisfied with any project in his life.

Mary told him how proud she was he'd stuck to his goal. The members of the club praised him and said they hoped he'd keep coming. Next Friday would be bet collection day!

It was early December and Friday night was very cold and windy. As usual Walter met his friends met at the Legion for a few beers and darts.

When it was time to leave, Walter said, "Well, I best be going. Cold night out there."

With that, he took his mittens from his pocket and slowly put them on his big hands, which he held up in front of the astonished faces of the other four.

"Come on, now, did you knit those mittens?"

"Sure did. What you think of them? They're just like Granddad's. Seems to me there was a bet about them."

"How do we know you knit them yourself?"

"Tom, call Ada and ask her. Didn't she tell you I was at the knitting club?"

"Not one word. I trust you. Okay guys, I'm sure he did it. We need to pay up."

"Anyone need any mittens? I'll make a pair for you. I'm kinda into that knitting club. Nice people and good eats. You should come sometime."

The Curling Game

Connie Jodrey

On a gray afternoon in late January, Max stopped at the library to pick up Diane's books. It was anybody's guess if the snow would come, but the wind had started up and Charley, the librarian, was standing outside in her shirt sleeves, tossing handfuls of salt onto the sidewalk. She tugged the heavy door open for Max and followed him inside.

"I hear the house next door to you has finally sold," she said.

"It has?" This surprised Max. "Any idea who bought it?"

"A funny name. Goo-shoe?" she said, dragging out the word. "Something like that."

"Gushue?" Max said. "As in Brad Gushue?"

"Brad. I think that's it." She pulled Diane's stack of books from the holds shelf and started scanning them.

"Brad Gushue the curler?" asked Max, excited now.

"I haven't a clue." Her eyes flicked back and forth from the scanner to Max.

"You know who Brad Gushue is, don't you, Charley?"

"Nope."

Max was practically dancing. "Anyone who doesn't know who Brad Gushue is should be ashamed to call themselves Canadian! Brad Gushue won the Olympics with Russ Howard. He's won every major tournament in the country including the Brier. He's a curling icon, and if you're a Newfoundlander, Brad Gushue is nearer to God than God himself."

"Well it can't be him, then. If he's as great as all that, why would he be moving here?"

"Good question," Max said, watching Charley's hands as they slid another book under the scanner. "But if it is...and I know it probably isn't...but if it is the real Brad Gushue, I need to get my hands on him before Wallace Dempsey does."

"You have a problem with Wallace?"

"A big one. Wallace Dempsey darn near killed my brother."

Charley shoved Diane's heavy stack of books across the desk. "I thought Danny had a heart attack."

"Caused by Dempsey."

"That's quite an accusation. What did he do?"

"He might as well have shoved a knife straight into Danny's heart. I was there that day, helping Danny stack wood in his garage when Dempsey gives a thump on the door and struts in like he's king of the world and announces to Danny that he's off the team. Danny's been on that curling team from the beginning, and just when they're getting good, when there's a possibility of getting into the provincials, Dempsey tells him he's out."

"Why?"

"Turns out Dempsey got his hands on a young guy, one of those muscle types who can throw a torpedo and sweep the whole length of the ice without breaking a sweat. Danny might be getting up there in years, but he can shoot and sweep just fine. And anyway, curling is not just about physical strength, Charley, it's a game of strategy and precision."

"Is that what Wallace told Danny? That he was too old?"

"Not in so many words. He mumbled a bit of an apology, I guess, but it didn't mean anything. I told Danny he should go talk to the other guys on the team, but Danny said it wasn't worth it. He said —and it's true—he said there'd be no joy playing on a team with a skipper that didn't want you."

"So Danny did nothing?"

"He went back to stacking wood and whistling through his teeth the way he does. And I went back to helping him. But Nancy—you know Nancy, don't you? Danny's wife?"

Charley nodded. "She's in here all the time."

"Nancy told me later that Danny went out and brought down another whole load of wood afterwards and sawed it up and stacked it outside, practically enough for the whole of next winter. That wasn't Danny. That was pure annoyance. Danny was never the sort to push himself like that."

~

Max had driven Danny to the hospital that night. He and Diane had just finished supper—Diane's fried chicken with milk gravy, made only the way Diane can make it—when Nancy came running over in a panic. They loaded Danny into the car and clocked a hundred and twenty on the 101 all the way to the hospital.

The hardest part was coming home after leaving Danny back there in the hospital. Max remembered standing at the kitchen window, looking out into the pitch-black yard, while Diane scraped gluey old gravy into the garbage.

Danny was still in the hospital on Tuesday when Nancy called Max to come over and help her get the back door unstuck. A January thaw had sent the temperatures from cold to hot in a single day, and Danny's back door always needed adjusting when the frost started to lift.

Danny wasn't out of the woods yet, but things were looking hopeful. Nancy put the coffeepot on while Max worked away at the door. When he was finished, he sat down at the table, the sun warming a spot on the back of his neck. The warmth felt nice. Reassuring somehow after the difficulty of the past few days.

Out of the blue, Nancy said, "I want you to enter the charity tournament this year, Max. I want you to beat Wallace Dempsey."

Max couldn't help but wonder if Nancy had lost her mind. This was the big event of the year at the curling club, and Dempsey, with Danny throwing third, had won that tournament three years running.

How the heck was he supposed to beat Dempsey when he didn't even have a team?

~

Max managed to recruit the Sherman brothers, Harve and Gary, but he couldn't nail down a fourth—nor did he want to. He was pinning his hopes on the new fellow, Brad Gushue, when he arrived. Max figured with a name like Gushue he had to be a curler, even if he wasn't the real deal.

He couldn't have been more wrong. This Brad Gushue was a chubby little guy with a wife and two small kids and another one on the way. They were barely out of their car when Max was over there with a basket of blueberry muffins and a plate of macaroni and cheese that Diane had made as a welcome gift.

"Never tried it," Brad said when Max asked him if he curled. "With my name? In Newfoundland? Can you imagine?"

Max could see what he meant. It would be a lot like living in the United States if your name was Donald Trump—but for different reasons, of course.

He was probably related somewhere along the line to famous Brad, he said, but he didn't know him except to see him on TV like everyone else. He'd moved from Carbonear to manage the fish plant in Delaps Cove.

"Are you hooked up? Electric?" Max asked, handing him the macaroni. "This needs to be warmed up."

"Yep, we're good," Brad said.

Famous last words though. An hour later a Nor-Easter swept in and took out the power in communities all up and down the Bay of Fundy, and there's nothing you can do with cold macaroni and cheese during a power outage except eat it cold...unless you happen to have a wood cook stove and a generator.

Within ten minutes of losing power, Max was over at the Gushue's inviting them for supper. "Bring the macaroni," he said.

During supper, Max set about trying to convince Brad to take up curling. There wasn't a single athletic thing about him: short legs and arms, oversized gut, big clumsy feet. But to be honest, it wasn't the man's ability he was after. What chance of winning did they have anyway?

What Max was after was the name. Brad Gushue. To see that name in big letters on the board in the rink right next to his own name? Now that would be worth a photograph and a frame. It might even end up in *The Spectator.*

Max cracked open another Keith's and tipped the bottle over Brad's glass. "Drink up," he said. And then he spooned another load of macaroni onto Brad's plate.

The way the wind was shaking the house and piling snow up against the windows, Max figured the power wouldn't be on until morning, and that's if they were lucky. "Crews won't be out working in this mess." he said after supper. "You folks had better spend the night. There's no sense going home to a cold, dark house when we have a perfectly good spare bed upstairs and air mattresses for the kids."

Diane stood up and started clearing the table. "Grab the glasses," she said to Max, and when they were in the kitchen, she put down her stack of plates none too gently and gave him a look.

"We took that bed apart to make room for my sewing table, remember? And the air mattresses went to the silent auction for the Syrian refugee family." She opened the dishwasher and dumped in a load of silverware. "You could've talked to me first," she said.

But by then it was too late. And Max knew the outcome would have been the same, anyway. Diane would never send them home on a night like this no matter what she said.

Max slept on the recliner and Diane slept on the couch, and Brad and Marlene slept in Max and Diane's queen with their two little kids...and Max nabbed himself a fourth player for his curling team.

~

Harve and Gary were waiting on the ice on Wednesday when Max and Brad arrived. The sidewalks had been cleared but there was still a foot or more of snow in the parking lot and they had to park at the Legion across the street.

Max helped Brad settle himself in the hack and Harve slid a rock over. "Let's see what you're made of," Harve said. "What would you normally play anyway? Lead? Second?"

"Lead," Max said, answering quickly for Brad.

"A master of the tick shot, are you?" Harve said. "I've seen that shot done a hundred times and I still can't manage it myself."

Brad gave the rock a casual spin like the pros do on TV. Then he grabbed the handle and tried to flip it on its edge to clean its surface, but the rock shot sideways and sent him sprawling.

Harve walked away, muttering a single word to Max under his breath. "Idiot." He jerked his head toward the lounge upstairs and said to Gary, "C'mon. I could use a beer."

"Don't mind Harve," Max said, nudging Brad out of the hack. He stooped to take hold of the rock. "Watch how I do it."

He heaved the rock backwards in a wide arc and swung it down onto the surface, giving the handle a little twist as he let go. "I can't crouch down like some guys because of my knees. Just be careful when you bring the rock down that it doesn't crash on the ice."

He kicked a rock over to Brad and said, "Now you give it a try."

Brad took hold of the rock and gave it a hard shove. It came to a slow, wobbly stop halfway down the sheet.

By the time nine o'clock rolled around, Brad was starting to get the hang of Max's method, standing up and delivering the rock like a bowling ball. He'd even managed a couple of decent draws and a takeout.

"Let's see if you can make a double," Max called down the ice. He grabbed two rocks and planted them a few inches apart on the four-foot.

"Seriously?" shouted Brad.

"Sure! You call the turn. In or out?"

"In." Brad was grinning. He'd obviously started to feel the confidence—or recklessness—that comes with a little bit of success.

Brad flipped the rock over and wiped the surface with his hand. Then he gave a little wiggle and propped his broom under his left arm for stability. Harve and Gary had come down from the viewing area and were watching from the boards. The rink was deadly quiet.

Max positioned his broom on the ice. "Whenever you're ready," he shouted. "Aim for the broom."

Max kept his eyes on Brad, watching as he swung his arm backward with what looked like enough momentum to pull it straight around like a Ferris wheel. Max had to hand it to the kid. He was going to make this double takeout even if he ripped out all the tendons in his shoulder to do it.

At the apex of Brad's swing, the pivot point before the downward drive, Gary cleared his throat.

It wasn't a loud noise, but it was enough to stop Brad in midswing. Startled, Brad jerked his head around and the rock went flying backwards out of his hand. It missed Gary's head by an inch and crashed through the viewing window into the lounge. As Marty Price working the bar told them later, that rock landed on top of a table, slid off, scooped up a paper cup and some change on the floor, took out two chairs, and came to a stop by the men's restroom door.

Once all the hullabaloo had died down, they had a good laugh about Brad's reverse double takeout.

"Those chairs didn't have a chance," said Gary. "You'll make a helluva curler, once you get your directions straight."

~

Midweek, on his way home from the Superstore, Max decided to pop into Frenchys to look for a team uniform, matching polo shirts maybe, or jackets if he was lucky. Every time Max went into Frenchys, and it wasn't often, he lasted about a minute. He couldn't stand the mess and he hated the smell. It made him think of dead people lying in those sheets or wearing those shirts and pants and underwear when they'd keeled over. Underwear! Did anyone really buy used underwear?

He found a bin of shirts, a mishmash of shapes and sizes and colours, and plucked an olive-green tee-shirt from the pile. This didn't look too bad, if he could find three more.

He started digging, picking up speed as he ploughed through the pile, and when a clerk came around the corner, he held up the green shirt and said, "Have you got three more exactly like this one?"

She rolled her eyes at him and walked away.

Max tossed the shirt back in the bin. He hated this place.

As he was heading for the door, something in one of the bins stopped him, jazzy white pants with blue and red zigzag stripes like those crazy things worn by the curling team from Norway, Thomas Ulsrud's team. It would be ridiculous, but funny as anything if Max's team could pull it off. Jazzy pants.

Maybe they could! It would put Dempsey off his game, that's for sure.

He yanked the jazzy pants out of the pile and shoved them under his arm and went searching for more. He tossed aside a red stretchy thing with feet and something yellow and shimmery, grabbed hold of a bit of black lace, and then stopped and pulled himself upright.

This was stupid. Never in a million years would he be caught dead in pants like these. Or Harve. Or Gary. He couldn't say for sure about Brad, but he didn't think so.

The bit of lace in his hand, he saw now, was a brassiere. Good God! This thing wouldn't fit on a nose let alone a chest. He dropped it into the bin and tugged the jazzy pants out from under his arm just as the rude clerk from shirts came over with a fresh load.

"You won't find shirts here," she said to him. "This is ladies' lingerie." She pronounced lingerie as if this were a French boutique and not a stinking Frenchys.

"I don't care if it's shirts or not, so long as I can find four the same," he said. "It's a uniform I'm looking for, for my curling team."

She flashed him a grin. "You know those are pyjamas you're holding, don't you? Ladies' pyjamas?"

He glanced down and started to smile back to let her know it was a joke, that he wasn't stupid, of course he knew they were pyjamas even though he didn't, when he saw Wallace Dempsey, arms crossed, a big smirk on his face, staring right at him.

Max fired the pyjamas into the bin and headed for the door.

"McPherson, wait!" Dempsey shouted.

Max turned and saw Dempsey holding the flimsy black bra by its straps. "Did you forget something? With any luck this little number here might just fit Harve or Gary. It's way too big for you."

~

The day before the tournament, Max dropped a folder off at the library for Charley. The proceeds this year were going towards the library expansion fund and Charley was hanging on to the paperwork.

"Excited?" Charley asked.

"Nah." Max watched Charley thumb through the papers. "We don't stand a horse's chance in Hades of even making the final, three old guys who can hardly stand up and a new fellow who's so green he's still learning the rules."

Charley looked up at him. "Don't sell yourself short. You never know."

On the way home, Max thought about what Charley had said. You never know. She was right. The stars might line up and the gods might be smiling. His team might be on fire and Dempsey's might be off by a hair or two. You never know.

What if they won? Max could see it now, his team lined up on the red carpet—if someone remembered to bring it—holding the trophy up in the air while Dempsey stood there pretending to be happy with second place. Oh, how sweet....

And then a light bulb flipped on in Max's brain, one of those crazy-ass ideas like the ones he and Danny used to come up with when they were teenagers looking for something to do on a Saturday night. Max changed direction and walked across the street to the hardware store.

The bags of sand were by the door next to the snow shovels. A corner of one of the bags was open, Max saw, and a little hill of sand had dribbled out onto the floor. He scooped up a fistful and spilled it into his jacket pocket, grinning to himself. Sand and curling rocks are sworn enemies. A few grains lodged under a rock will make it skew off course, maybe a little, maybe a lot, but always enough to ruin a perfectly good curling shot.

As he left the store, Max saw Wallace Dempsey waiting to cross the street. He had a penknife in his hand, and he was wiping the blade on his sleeve. Max started to turn away, but he was too late.

"Hey McPherson!" Dempsey called. "Still looking for uniforms? You should take a peek in the V&S. They have a whole section of ladies' underwear." Then he snapped the blade shut, shoved the knife in his pocket, and stepped out onto the crosswalk.

Max wished he had words for moments like this, but he couldn't think of a single thing to say. He crossed the street and walked on home.

~

A handful of club members and friends came out on Friday night for the first game of the tournament, a halfway-decent cheering crowd but that's about it. Max couldn't blame them. He'd rather be at home himself, if it came right down to it, hollering at the Leafs on TV to stop messing around and do something for a change.

Max was tying his shoes when he looked up and saw Nancy and Danny in the doorway. Nancy ran over and handed him a brown paper package wrapped in twine.

"What's this?"

She was smiling at him. Excited like a kid.

Inside the package were four team sweaters, blue and gold, the players' names in big letters on the back: McPherson, Sherman, Sherman, Gushue.

"Did you do this?" Max ran a thumb over the shiny letters of his name. He was having a hard time finding his voice.

"We did," Nancy said, nodding towards Danny. "And Diane. Diane sewed all the names."

The jackets could have been measured and made, a perfect fit all around except Brad's. Brad's was a little too big. But with the sleeves rolled up it was fine.

~

To everyone's surprise, Max's most of all, Max's team won Friday's game and then the Saturday morning one, neither by a giveaway. Dempsey's team won both their games by landslides. No surprise there.

Game time for the final was two o'clock on Saturday afternoon, and at one-thirty, from his position in the hack, Max could see the lounge was already full of people elbowing for a spot at the viewing window. No wonder. It was the David and Goliath shocker of the century, Max McPherson versus the bully who'd fired his brother.

It threw him, all those faces staring down at him. He let go of his practice shot too early and watched with disgust as it came to a stop just this side of the hog line.

Dempsey called out from the other end, "Looks like you could use some help, McPherson!"

He wasn't altogether wrong about that, Max thought, stepping out of the hack on slow, stiff legs. What he could really use was a nap. He'd had more exercise in the past twenty-four hours than he'd totalled in the last two months.

At two o'clock, Andy Harrington, this year's chairman, lined up the teams and tossed a coin to see who would throw the first draw to the button for hammer. Dempsey called heads and heads it was.

Max's heart was thumping hard as he watched Dempsey's rock come to a stop on the four foot, just touching the button. Dempsey gave Max a wicked grin and said, "This game'll be over in six ends McPherson, and that's if you're lucky."

"We'll see about that," Max replied, trying to sound more confident than he felt.

He dug his fingers in his pocket, searching for the security of the sand he'd nabbed from the hardware store—not that he'd probably have the opportunity or the sneakiness to use it. But it wasn't there.

And then Max remembered. The sand was in the pocket of his red sweater, the sweater he'd given to Diane when he put on his new blue and gold curling jacket.

Max turned to see if he could spot Diane through the viewing window, maybe motion her to come down. But then suddenly the door flew open and there she was, jogging onto the ice, all out of breath. She couldn't be bringing him the sand, could she? Nah. How would she even know?

But it wasn't Max Diane was after. She was yelling at Brad, telling him Marlene was in labour.

"Go now!" she shouted, and Brad raced through the door, leaving the two teams, minus one player, standing there wondering what to do.

This was a blow, losing Brad just as the big game was about to begin. Max had been surprised at how well the young fellow had been doing. He'd been impressive really, unaffected by the pressure, ribbing the guys, keeping things light, making decent shots from time to time.

Dempsey turned to Max and said, "Your draw to the button."

"What are you talking about? We're down a man."

"You can play with three."

"We need a fourth," said Max, glancing around to see who might be available.

"Not allowed."

"Who says? There's no rule book for this tournament. What do you think this is, the Brier?"

Max couldn't figure out why Dempsey would even care. Dempsey knew the odds were stacked in his favour, full team or not. Was it possible that Dempsey was a bit worried? The idea gave Max a jolt of pleasure.

Pete Ryland, Dempsey's new third, shot an apologetic grin at Max and told Dempsey he saw nothing wrong with Max recruiting another player. But Dempsey was fired up, a big overgrown kid throwing a tantrum, and there was nothing anyone could say to get him out of it.

Eventually the organizing committee came over and told Max to go ahead and choose a fourth player but do it in a hurry, they didn't want to delay the game any longer.

Dempsey threw his slider on the ice and stomped away a few feet and then he turned around and came back. "If you're gonna pick a player, pick one now, McPherson. I have a game to win."

Just then the door at the back of the rink opened and in came a man Max had never seen before, at least not in person.

"Am I too late?" the fellow said, looking around. "I had a rough time finding this place."

Max recognized him right away, tall and slim, short sandy hair, smiling eyes. Max had seen that face a hundred times on TV, the raised eyebrows as he shot a look at the big screen to check the position of a rock, the tilt of his head when he spoke a word or two to his sweepers as he settled himself in the hack, his appreciative nod to the cheering crowd after executing a raise double takeout to win a game.

It was Brad Gushue. Real Brad. In the flesh.

"I pick him," Max said.

~

Max was stuffing his gear into the trunk of his car when he saw Charley drive in.

She pulled up beside him and cracked open her window. "Did you win?"

"Pretty hard to lose with Brad Gushue on your team."

"Ha ha funny," said Charley. "You won? Really? With the new guy?"

"Nah, we won without the new guy," Max said. "He went off and had a baby."

Then Max told Charley how the real Brad Gushue had arrived just in the nick of time.

"That's crazy! What was he doing here?"

"It was a promotional appearance. When you win the Brier, you get money for promotional appearances."

"How come nobody knew about it?"

"That's the funniest thing. Apparently, someone from the Canadian Curling Association called Brad about our tournament. Only thing I can think is they must have come across fake Brad's name on the list of players somewhere. In the *Spectator* maybe, or it could have been on the internet. Real Brad checked with the club and they confirmed his name was up on the board. You know what it's like. Anybody and everybody answers the phone around here when it rings."

"I'm surprised they allowed him to play. Wasn't Wallace cheesed? It seems like an unfair advantage."

"He started to put up a fight, but when the crowd went wild, he knew it was hopeless. Think about it, Charley. When would these folks ever get a chance to watch the real deal, the real Brad Gushue, play a game in their rink, in their town, right in front of their own eyes?"

"So, you beat Wallace."

"Fair and square. Brad held back a little, you could tell. He made some dandy shots, but he's way too nice a guy to walk all over Dempsey without giving him a fighting chance."

Max chuckled. "You wouldn't believe it, but it actually came down to the very last shot. Dempsey had a chance, but it was tough. An angle raise. He had to hit his own guard a smidge off centre and raise it to the button. The line was good, but Dempsey knew right away he was light and he came scooting out of the hack to sweep. All four of them were out there sweeping like crazy. But then the rock caught something and made a sharp right turn and stopped dead just like that. When the boys went down after to take a look, they found a bit of sand on the ice.

"How would sand get there?"

Max shrugged. "Who knows?"

But Max was pretty sure he knew. On his way to the car to fetch his wallet after the game—Max owed the guys a round, that's for sure—he saw Dempsey lighting a smoke outside the door.

"That game was ours, McPherson!" Dempsey called out as Max walked past. "We shoulda won, you know. Woulda won for sure if my rock hadn't got burnt!"

Max could only shake his head and walk away, especially when he realized what Dempsey was doing out there. He wasn't just sucking on a cigarette. He was dumping something out of his pocket and it wasn't shreds of tobacco. It was something that looked suspiciously like sand. Dempsey had sabotaged his own shot when he'd been out there sweeping like a maniac.

Charley started to roll up her window, but then she stopped and said, "Where is he now? Real Brad?"

"On his way to the airport. He's flying out tonight for a big money tournament in Toronto." He pushed the trunk closed and straightened up slowly, stretching his back. "You know what's almost as good as beating Dempsey?"

"No. What?"

"Pete Ryland quit Dempsey's team."

Charlie let out a laugh. "Good one. How come?"

"Besides the fact that Dempsey is a number one a-hole? He quit because Brad wants to work with him.

"What?"

"That's right," Max said, hauling his keys out of his pocket. "Brad wants Pete to spend some time with him in Newfoundland. He thinks Pete has potential."

Rags to Riches

Vernon Oickle

The gurgling and tightening in the pit of his stomach remind Henry that he hasn't eaten in almost three days. The smell of the deep-fried chicken wafting from the fast-food joint down the street assaults his nostrils, driving his senses into a frenzy, but he knows he can't eat. He can't afford to. He doesn't have the money to buy groceries, let alone take-out food. It's been months since he's had a decent meal, or anything that he would consider a treat, like a hamburger or pizza.

These have been hard times for Henry. He's a good man, lived a clean life and helps others when he can; but ever since he lost his job at the local sawmill due to "down-sizing", he's been struggling to make ends meet. His unemployment insurance benefits have long since run out and his welfare cheque doesn't go far. After paying the rent for his tiny apartment, giving his ex-wife money for child support, coughing up the cash to pay his electrical bill so his heat and lights aren't disconnected, scraping together enough pennies to cover his car payment and to buy fuel so that he can continue his job search, he doesn't have money for food or for the medication he needs to keep his high blood pressure under control. If he doesn't die of starvation first, he fears he'll conk out from a stroke or a heart attack.

He often thinks a quick death would be more merciful than a slow, lingering demise from starvation, with his body feeding off its own fat. Going to the grocery store is a thing of the past, so he relies on charities such as the Salvation Army and the local food bank to help get him over the bumps.

But times are tough even for these services. Now the charities have had to put a limit to how much food you can get, as donations have dropped off and government funds have all but dried up. The food bank has limited users to visiting twice a month, and if donations don't soon pick up, that rate may have to drop to once a month.

That would be tough, he thinks, but he hopes soon he won't have to rely so heavily on these charities.

Today, as he rummages through the Loonie bin at a secondhand store he hasn't visited for a long time, Henry is searching for a decent-looking shirt he can wear to the job interview he's managed to line up for tomorrow. Waiting tables at the coffee shop will only pay him minimum wage and maybe tips, but he's desperate and he'd take anything he can get. He's become the ultimate example of that old adage, beggars can't be choosers. The money will be a far cry from the payday he enjoyed at the mill, but at this point he'll take anything. He'd even clean toilets if there were a few dollars to be made.

"Help you find something?" asks the short, plump woman. It's been awhile, but he recognizes her as a clerk he's seen in the past. "You look like you're on a mission," she adds, watching Henry dig through the piles of wrinkled and discoloured-shirts, T-shirts, sweaters and odds and ends in the dollar bin.

"I'm looking for a shirt," Henry says.

The woman has black hair streaked with hints of silver pulled to the back of her head in a tight ponytail. He smiles politely at her. He likes her. She has friendly eyes, he thinks.

"Need it for something special?" She starts digging into the pile of clothes. "What size are you?"

"Small," he answers. "And yes, something very special. I want to look my best. I'm hoping I can find something that will make me look professional."

"Good for you," the woman beams. He doesn't know her name and he doesn't feel comfortable asking her what it is.

He's always been shy around woman and often wondered how he ever managed to find a wife, even though that didn't work out so well for him. She left him for another man about three years ago, right around the time he lost his job.

"Yes, good for me," he sighs. "I really need this job. Times are tough."

She nods. "There's more people looking for jobs than there are jobs these days, so I hope it works out for you."

"Thanks," he smiles, carefully sorting through the piles of clothes that mostly resemble discarded rags.

"Keep looking," the woman encourages him. "I'm sure there must be something in here that will suit you. You just gotta dig through the pile, but you can sometimes find a hidden treasure if you don't give up."

"I don't know," Henry shrugs. "It's not looking good."

Finally, the clerk agrees. "You know what? I think you're right. I don't see anything in here that's good enough for a gentleman like you. A man going on a mission as important as the one you face must be dressed properly."

She pauses in thought, then heads into the store's back storage area. "You stay right here and keep looking. I think I've got something back here that will be just perfect for you."

"Don't go to any trouble. I'm sure I have something at home that will do."

"Nonsense," the woman replies just before she disappears into the back room. "I'll be back in a jiffy."

"Okay," Henry shrugs. He examines a white shirt with large, vertical mint-green stripes. "Not for me," he decides, tossing it back in the bin.

"All right," the woman says several minutes later, reemerging with a powder-blue dress shirt in her right hand. It looks almost new to Henry. "I think this will be perfect for you, and it's just your size." She smiles at him. "You did say small, didn't you?"

"I did," he nods. "That is very nice, but I'm sure I can't afford it. That's why I was looking in the discount bin."

He picks up the green stripe shirt again and shows it to her. "See? This is more my speed. With a little bit of love and tenderness this shirt will look all right."

"I don't think so," the woman says, suppressing a cringe. "That one's ready for the recycling bin."

Snatching the older shirt from Henry, she tosses it aside and hands him the blue shirt. "This one is more like it."

"I can't afford that."

"Sure you can. It's only two dollars."

"That shirt looks almost brand new," he says. "It must be worth at least five, and I don't have that much on me right now."

"Nope. It's your lucky day," she smiles. "It's on special today for only two dollars. So if you've got two bucks on you, it's yours."

"I don't know," Henry hesitates.

"What's your problem?" the plump woman asks. "I'm telling you what it costs. Do you want it? I think you'll look really sharp in it. It's important to make a good first impression, isn't it?"

"Well," he stalls.

Then he digs into his pocket and pulls out a handful of pennies, nickels and dimes. "You drive a hard bargain, but okay. I'll take it, but do you think I should try it on first?"

"Nah," the woman shrugs. "I'm sure it will fit just fine. It looks like it was made just for you."

Henry thrusts the change toward her. "I'll take it, but you better make sure I have enough to pay for it."

"It's enough."

"You better count it just to be sure."

"It's enough. Let me put it in a bag for you," the woman offers. She takes the change and puts it in the cash register without counting it.

"Thank you," Henry smiles. "This shirt will be perfect."

"No need to thank to me," she winks. "Just knock their socks off tomorrow."

Hurrying home, Henry thinks about the upcoming interview and wonders what it would be like to have a job and a steady income once again. It's a modest job, but he's not proud. If he can earn an honest pay and slowly work his way out of the system that has him trapped in this oppressive level of poverty that's slowly killing him, then he'll be happy. He'll go to work every day and hold his head up, for he knows he has nothing to be ashamed of. He didn't ask to be thrust into this predicament, and he's determined to pull himself out of this rut, inch by inch if he has to.

Remembering the nice woman at the thrift store as he pulls the blue shirt from the bag, Henry wonders who she is. He can't recall ever seeing her any other place except in the store, which he thinks is rather strange since this is a small community and he believes he knows most people around here.

"Whatever," he shrugs. Doesn't really matter who she is.

He peels off his well-worn black T-shirt. All that matters is that she found him this fantastic shirt, although he's convinced she gave him a great discount to help him out. He's positive she could have gotten more than two dollars for it from someone else.

"Nice," he sighs, sliding his arms through the sleeves and buttoning up the front. "Sharp," he thinks, looking at his reflection in the glass of the front door, his gaunt frame reminding him just how far he's sunk into poverty. He doesn't have a full-length mirror so this will have to do, but he can see enough to confirm the shirt looks good on him.

Turning sideways and looking at his reflection one more time, he decides he should rinse the shirt in the sink and hang it up to dry so that it looks fresh for the interview tomorrow. Slowly running his hands down the front, he suddenly pauses at the breast pocket when he feels something inside.

"What's this?" He slips his right hand into the pocket and pulls out what looks like a lottery ticket.

"Hum," he sighs, quickly scanning the white paper with blue and red printing on it. There's no question it's a lottery ticket. He doesn't buy them, as he doesn't have money to gamble, but he certainly knows what they look like.

"Garbage," he decides and starts to crumple it up. He's sure that whoever owned the shirt before him must have checked the numbers and then forgot to throw the ticket away.

He's about to toss it into the trashcan when he stops. "Still," he thinks, "maybe I should have it checked, just on the off chance."

He pulls off the shirt and slips back into his black T-shirt. "You never know."

Henry makes his way to the nearest corner store and hands the clerk the ticket. "Can you please check this for me?"

"Sure thing," the young man nods. He takes the ticket and slides it into the computer terminal. He then presses several buttons.

Immediately, a loud ringing breaks the silence in the store. The clerk beams. "You're a winner," he yells with excitement. "You've won!"

"No way," Henry says.

"Yes way."

"How much?"

"One *million* dollars," the young man smiles broadly. "You've just won one million dollars."

"Oh my God," Henry cries. "You are kidding. This is a joke, right?"

"No sir," the clerk says, pointing to the computer screen. "It says right here that this ticket is worth one million dollar. And you're in luck because it was drawn in the lottery two years ago. If no one had claimed the prize by the end of today, the ticket would be void and the money would go back into the pot."

"Seriously?" Henry can't believe what he's hearing.

"Seriously. It's says so right here. We get these notices all the time from the lottery. If people don't collect their prize, the money eventually goes back into the pot."

"Why wouldn't anyone claim his winnings?"

"Different reasons, I suppose," the clerk says. "Tickets get lost or thrown out by accident." He shrugs. "People die and the tickets are never seen again. Lots of reasons, I guess."

Henry pauses for a second to gather his thoughts, then says, "May I have the ticket, please?"

"Sure." The clerk pulls the ticket from the terminal and hands it back. "It's yours. What are you going to do with your new fortune?"

"I'd like to say I'm going to keep it," Henry says as he slips the valuable piece of paper into his jeans pocket. "But it's not mine and the money doesn't belong to me."

Leaving the corner store, Henry makes a beeline for the thrift shop where he hopes to find the plump woman who generously helped him buy the shirt. He was tempted to keep the ticket and cash in on the prize, but he knows the money isn't rightfully his. The ticket belongs either to the shirt's former owner or to the operators of the thrift store, but he's sure, in all good conscience, he can't keep it.

When he gets to the thrift store, he's surprised to see the place in complete darkness. Odd, he thinks. It's only mid-afternoon and he believes the store should still be open.

He knocks on the door and waits, but no one answers. Cupping his hands on the window he places his face close to the glass and peers inside. He's shocked to find the place completely empty.

"What the…?"

"Can I help you?" a man asks from behind him.

Spinning around, he comes face to face with a tall man in a navy suit. "Can I help you with something?" the man asks again.

"I was trying to get into the thrift store," Henry stutters. "But it's closed."

"It is," the man nods. "It's been closed for over a year."

"What?" Henry answers, his breath catching in his throat. "But I was just in there not more than an hour ago and that place was filled with all kinds of stuff."

"I don't think so." The man shakes his head. "I work in the office next door and I can tell you for a fact that store hasn't been open for a long time, not since the owner died."

"The owner died?" Henry asks, trying to gather his thoughts. "Who was that?"

"Nice woman," the man says. "Chubby with black hair that she always kept pulled back in a ponytail. Always friendly and smiling, and always wanting to chat. Really generous, too. I'm sure she'd literally give a stranger the shirt off her back."

They stand looking at the store for a moment. Then the man in the suit adds, "She died of cancer about a year ago. Had a real tough time in the end, but once it took hold of her, she went quickly. That was a God-send, I'm sure."

"That's really sad," Henry says.

"Her name was Pearl," the man says. "I didn't know much about her, but I don't think she had any family. She left everything she owned to the local Salvation Army."

"Wow," Henry says, trying to assimilate what he's just heard.

"And you say you were just in her store today?" the man asks. "I don't know how that could have been. The place has been sitting empty since they cleaned it out and got rid of all the stuff."

"No," Henry stutters, backing away from the door. "I guess I was mistaken. I've never been to this place before."

The Assassin

Bob Bent

Natalya Larosova parked the buttercup-yellow Chevrolet Camaro convertible next to a dark SUV outside the elegant Queen Anne Inn in Annapolis Royal, Nova Scotia. She removed her sunglasses and slid from behind the wheel; her dress, the same yellow as the Camaro, was offset by a shiny black belt to match her long black hair. The purse slung over her left shoulder was also black.

She walked around to the passenger side of the rented car, unfastened the seat belt holding her cello case, and carried it to the trunk, where she stopped to admire the extensive green lawn and the scattering of large trees in front of the inn. In the process she noted the absence of other guests, or even people passing by on the sidewalk. Nevertheless, she shielded the contents of the trunk as well as she could with her slim body as she removed a small suitcase, leaving a second cello case hidden beneath her navy blue raincoat. She carried the first cello case and the suitcase up the wooden steps to the front door.

"Good afternoon." The young man at the front desk greeted her with a smile as he glanced at his watch. It was twelve-fifteen and he'd almost said good morning.

"Welcome to the Queen Anne Inn. Miss Larosova, right?" She appeared too young to be an accomplished musician, and was even more attractive than her picture on the brochure he'd been staring at all morning.

"That's right." She returned his smile. "Have the other members of the Glazunov Quartet arrived?" Unlike the three male members of her quartet, she spoke with no trace of accent. But then she was much younger.

"Yes. A few hours ago." The smile had not left his face. Her long dark hair, dark rimmed glasses and innocent beauty were as much a ray of sunshine as her brilliant yellow dress. And her easy manner made her seem like someone he might have gone to school with.

Natalya Larosova filled in her name, address and vehicle license number on the form provided, received her key for room three, and headed for the stairway with her cello case and suitcase.

The young man rushed around the desk. "Let me help you with those."

She smiled at him, a very natural smile. "Thank you. I'll carry my cello. It's not heavy. Besides, musicians never let their instruments out of their sight, or their hands." Her voice was casual and friendly. "If it weren't so big, I'd sleep with it under my pillow."

The young man laughed, took her suitcase, led Miss Larosova up the wide carpeted stairway, opened the door to room three, and then stood aside.

Natalya gazed around the room, smiling contentedly, then moved dreamily to the nearest window, eased the lace curtains aside, and looked out over the front lawn at the sidewalk and street beyond.

"This will do nicely," she said. "Thank you."

The young man bowed and left. The warmth from his close encounter with the accomplished young cellist lasted for the remainder of the summer and into the fall.

Natalya Larosova locked the door, placed the black cello case on the white covering of the canopied bed, returned to the window, and peered through the lace curtains more intently. The large maples and oaks on the deep front lawn obstructed her view of only a small portion of the sidewalk, and the screen could easily be removed and quickly reinserted.

Satisfied, she returned to the cello case, opened it, and examined the Dragunov SVDK sniper rifle, taking as much care with it as she did with her cello. Nothing had been harmed on the drive from the warehouse adjoining the container port, along Highway 101 through the lush and peaceful Annapolis Valley, to the charming

Queen Anne Inn in Annapolis Royal.

Tonight the Glazunov Quartet would perform Ivan Petrov's new string quartet, Borodin's Second String Quartet and Shostakovich's String Quartet Number Eight at King's Theatre. The melodic calm of Borodin's Second, the frantic energy of Shostakovich's Eighth, and the familiarity of both made them favourites with North American audiences.

She had passed King's Theatre on her brief cruise around the small town; roof down, sunglasses on, smiling like the happy teenager she had been only five years before. Those who recognized her from the posters, and even the males who did not, smiled back. Some waved, and she timidly returned their waves. To all appearances, she and her cello, strapped in the passenger seat, were delighted to be in Annapolis Royal.

Tomorrow morning she would terminate the traitor Zmurchuck. Then in the afternoon the quartet would repeat their performance in the Historic Gardens across the street from the Queen Anne Inn, after which she would quickly leave under the pretext of wanting to see some of Eastern Canada before returning to Moscow. Instead of visiting Peggy's Cove and Lunenburg, she would drive directly to the Halifax warehouse, return the sniper rifle, and then fly Air Canada Express to Montreal and Aeroflot to Moscow.

She returned the Dragunov to its case, closed it and slid it to the other side of the king size bed, where a lover would lie down beside her, if she had one. She had almost an hour and a half before their rehearsal at the King's Theatre.

~

Zmurchuck. Anatoly Vladimirovich Zmurchuck. Former secretary to the Assistant Deputy Director of the SVR. Defected to the Americans five years ago. Sixteen deep cover agents, one of them a woman her age, terminated as a result. Given a new identity and a new life by the CIA. Finally traced to this tiny tourist town in Eastern Canada.

Nicolai Leonov had been one of the sixteen. He had been her

professor at the Moscow State Tchaikovsky Conservatory, and like her, a cellist; a kind man, tall, much too thin, with a bald head, a full white beard and a slight stoop. He had taken a special interest in her and refined and polished her talents until, so he said, she played the cello better than he did. He could have retired to a dacha on the Black Sea, but he continued to play, and to teach. He loved his work, he loved his music, and he loved his students. And his students loved him, thinking of him as a kindly old uncle with no children of his own. Everyone at the school, even fellow musicians, referred to him as Uncle Nicolai. Natalya had admired him more than most.

Now he was dead. She remembered the day she learned he'd been killed.

~

The heavy set man in the expensive dark suit of a bureaucrat watched her walk toward him in the hallway of the Conservatory late that August afternoon.

"Miss Larosova." It was not a question. Although his hardened face did not smile, there was a slight trace of sadness in his eyes.

"Yes?"

"Would you come with me, please?"

Natalya's heart fluttered. The fluttering spread to her fingertips and she almost dropped her cello case.

She followed half a step behind him, her mind racing. This man was more than just a policeman, possibly an agent of state security. She desperately tried to recall some transgression she had committed, something she had done or said, but came up with nothing. She was not interested in things political. Her young life was composed only of music. Perhaps she had inadvertently said something that gave the impression of a mild criticism of the government, although she could not think what it might be.

He walked briskly along the sidewalk and she hurried to keep up, still slightly behind him and to his left. The cello case in her right hand gradually began to strain her shoulder, so she shifted it to her other hand.

"Do you want me to carry your case, Miss Larosova?" His voice was politely businesslike.

Afraid to say anything, Natalya merely shook her head.

They crossed the northbound lanes of Nikitsky Boulevard and he led her to a long wooden bench in the shade of a linden tree.

"Please sit down."

She sat down.

The bureaucrat waited as two female office workers walked past, his eyes not leaving the traffic heading south on Nikitsky Boulevard. When he spoke, he continued watching the cars, trucks and people passing by.

"Last evening Nicolai Alexandrovich Leonov was killed in a traffic accident in New York State, in America." He waited for her gasp before he continued. "He suffered a heart attack and went off the road in a wooded area and struck a tree." He paused again before delivering the final life-changing blow. "The heart attack was caused by a bullet hole in the head."

Finally, he looked at her. She had turned pale and her fingers and lower lip were trembling. The tears would soon follow. "The media, of course, will not mention the bullet hole in the head."

She was shaking now, so he placed his hand on her shoulder with unexpected kindness, and the tears began. Embarrassed by her emotion, she hid her face in her hands, folding forward in dreadful pain.

After a workman strolled past, glancing at her with questioning eyes, the man continued, "He was killed by the American CIA."

She sat up and turned to face him. The shaking had subsided, although the tears continued running silently down her pale cheeks.

"Nikolai Alexandrovich was a patriot. He worked behind the scenes in foreign countries to protect his homeland. My homeland. Your homeland. Mother Russia."

She was looking in his eyes now, which was what he wanted. The shaking and trembling had ceased. Even the tears were subsiding, being replaced by the rumblings of rage.

"He was betrayed by one Anatoly Vladimirovich Zmurchuck, a

man who defected to the Americans two months ago."

He watched the storm of anger and hatred grow, then break.

"I want to kill him!"

"So do I," he said softly, "but they know me."

She rose from the bench, the hatred of a man she knew only by name a fierce thunderstorm inside her. Anatoly Vladimirovich Zmurchuck. She stared at the southbound traffic without seeing it, clenching her fists, stamping to the rhythm of "no, no, no, no, no!", trying to destroy the grass as she wanted to destroy this Zmurchuck, as Zmurchuck had destroyed a part of her.

The bureaucrat watched her. She was barely eighteen. He had seen her perform. She had passion, a passion that was very evident as she uttered curses that, although outrageously violent for her, were tepid compared to what he used himself. She would be good. He was certain of that.

He took her by the shoulders and she fell against him, beating his chest with small, impotent fists. The tears were back, tears of anger now.

"Do you want revenge?" he asked softly.

"Yes!" Her answer was sharp and hard.

"Then meet me here tomorrow afternoon. At four o'clock."

~

She kept the appointment, and began her recruitment into the SVR and her training as a sniper. The bureaucrat, whose name she never learned, found in her an eager student with excellent skills. Over the period of her training she lost her schoolgirl timidity, replacing it with self-confidence; but the shy schoolgirl persona remained as a cover for her burning hatred of Zmurchuck and her work as an SVR assassin.

The death of Nikolai Leonov left a vacancy for a cellist in the Glazunov Quartet, a vacancy she filled through the unknown influence of the man whose name she never knew. But she had fit in easily: her talent, passion and dedication soon convinced the three older men who made up the rest of the quartet that she was a worthy replacement for Uncle Nicolai. And her picture on the brochures and posters did not hurt their popularity.

Under the cover of the quartet's international tours she had eliminated four enemies of Mother Russia: in New York, San Francisco, Toronto and London. Although the man with no name convinced her each one had to die, they were not Zmurchuck. It was Zmurchuck she wanted. The others were merely practise for the day she would have Zmurchuck in the sights of her sniper rifle and would pull the trigger with all the hatred built up over the past five years for the man who had deprived the world, and her, of such a wonderful teacher.

Dmitri, Andrei and Vladimir still talked about him; of his kindness, his unwavering optimism, and the sense of humour she was just beginning to discover when Zmurchuck had murdered him.

Now, after five years, Zmurchuck had been found, in this pretty little town, on a pretty little river, on the east coast of Canada. This is where he would be executed tomorrow morning, on the sidewalk in front of the Queen Anne Inn.

An agent she knew only as Grossman, whom she had met in the warehouse near the container terminal in the port of Halifax, had been the one to track down Zmurchuck. Posing as a tourist from Manitoba, he had watched their prey for nearly two weeks; had learned his habits, his routines, his acquaintances. Grossman had taken photos of Zmurchuck, and a video which she had watched many times in the dim light of the warehouse before driving to Annapolis Royal.

She had seen earlier photos of him, shortly after she was recruited, and kept one stuck in the top corner of her mirror, as if it were her lover. Each night, before she turned out the lights, she pointed her finger at him—and pulled the trigger while she whispered, "Bang!"

It took a long time for her to recognize the Zmurchuck she executed nightly as the man in Grossman's photos and video. The picture on her mirror was of a younger man, a slim, sophisticated man; a man her few friends called handsome. Only she could see the evil in his eyes.

The new Zmurchuck, the hidden Zmurchuck, the condemned Zmurchuck was a slovenly middle-aged man whose loose shorts drooped below a large belly, a grey shirttail hanging beneath a tattered black sweater, sloppy running shoes with the laces undone, and a cigarette stuck perpetually to the corner of his lower lip. Somehow that odious creature had attracted a slim, not-unattractive single mother called Bonnie, who gave Taekwondo classes on the wharf and worked part-time as a waitress in Leo's Café.

They shared a small apartment on Upper St. George Street, and six mornings a week, at eight-fifteen precisely, he would walk along the sidewalk in front of the inn on his way to meet Bonnie when her class ended. Then they would go to Leo's for breakfast before her shift started, after which he would stroll about the town, doing whatever errands he had to do, before slouching back along Upper St. George Street to their small apartment.

Because the time of his return trip depended on the number and duration of his errands, he would pass the inn any time between nine-thirty and noon; occasionally later if his errands kept him downtown long enough to justify stopping for lunch at Leo's. That would provide a second, but less secure, opportunity, should the first have to be aborted.

~

Before she left for rehearsal she looked out the window again, at the sidewalk Zmurchuck would walk down tomorrow morning at eight-fifteen. The line of sight was not perfect, but close enough; certainly an easier shot than the one in Toronto.

She nodded to herself and placed the cello case carefully in the corner of the closet, obscuring it with a long white nightgown and the black blouse and pants she would wear that evening and tomorrow afternoon. Satisfied, she bounced down the stairs to the lobby, flashed a friendly smile at the young man at the front desk, and waltzed out to the buttercup-yellow convertible.

She drove casually along St. George Street, the roof down, the breeze floating her loose dark curls about her face, her right hand on the steering wheel, the fingers of her left hand tapping a Borodin melody on the side mirror.

She passed the police station, town police, and the tapping changed to Shostakovich. The police were only a few minutes from the inn and a shooting on the quiet streets of Annapolis Royal would cause an immediate reaction. They would call the Royal Canadian Mounted Police for backup; but the closest detachments, in Digby and Bridgetown, were almost half an hour away. The blaring sirens would no doubt interfere with the Shostakovich sonata she would be practising loud enough to be heard throughout the inn, with the piano accompaniment on a CD.

~

After a satisfactory rehearsal, the quartet locked their instruments in their vehicles and enjoyed supper at the pub across the street from the theatre. Natalya then left the three men, who, in the tradition of Glazunov himself, remained to continue drinking.

She paced up and down the small wharf and along the boardwalk, looking at the mirrored image of the tiny village of Granville Ferry on the opposite shore. It was such a quiet place, Annapolis Royal, although she could sense its melancholy past. It was a town more suited to Borodin than Shostakovich, but she knew it would be the Shostakovich people would talk about afterwards

Quiet people are attracted by violence. Perhaps that is why a pleasant little town like Annapolis Royal could tolerate a person like Anatoly Zmurchuck.

Maybe the reverse was also true, and violent people preferred quiet towns like Annapolis Royal, and soothing music, like Borodin. And which category did she fit in? Was she a violent person looking for calm? Or was she a quiet person looking for violent excitement? Did she prefer Borodin, or Shostakovich?

She wondered what the reaction of this quiet town would be if they knew they harboured a killer, that the man they knew as Alf Zimmer had caused the death of sixteen people, including one of the finest cellists the world had ever heard. How many other young musicians would Nicolai Leonov have inspired to greatness if the traitor Zmurchuck had not murdered him?

~

Looking out over the full house at King's Theatre, Natalya Larosova was pleased so many people in such a small, rural town had come to hear a classical string quartet. It made her smile, and many in the front rows of the audience smiled back.

As always, she was dressed conservatively: a black blouse, buttoned modestly; black pants, freshly pressed; and black high-heeled shoes, all matching the black rims of her glasses and her long black hair. She joined her fellow musicians and tuned her instrument.

The lights dimmed, and she began Petrov's String Quartet with intensity, concentrating on the music. It was not an easy piece, and this tour was its first exposure in North America. Thus far the reviews had been mostly favourable. When it ended, the applause was politely enthusiastic.

Borodin's Second String Quartet was one of her favourites and she drifted away from the audience into a world of baubles, bangles and bright shiny beads. The applause after the Borodin was immense, and the quartet nodded smiles at the audience.

During the intermission Natalya sat by herself in a quiet corner, as was her custom. The Borodin melodies, both cheery and melancholy, gradually faded. When they were gone she stood and stretched her arms high above her head and turned her mind to Shostakovich's Eighth, and to Zmurchuck. She was ready.

Early in the relative calm of the first movement, a *largo*, an old man near the aisle in the ninth row, who had spent the warm afternoon working in his garden, dozed off. He was jolted awake when the second movement began.

Natalya Larosova was no longer in a world of music, although the frantic driving rhythm of the quartet still controlled her. Now it was Zmurchuck trapped between her knees, and her bow was a butcher knife. She no longer saw her music sheets, nor the dim shapes in the darkened audience. She was no longer connected to Dmitri and Andrei on violin, nor Vladimir on viola. She was connected only to her butcher knife bow as she stabbed Zmurchuck again and again and again and dug her fingernails into the frets of his neck and face until the blood gushed from him and ran down her arms off her elbows and pooled around her black high-heeled shoes.

The two and a half minutes of the *allegro molto* left her shaken, her violent visualization of Zmurchuck's death glistening on her flushed skin as perspiration clearly visible to an audience in a state of shock.

In that fraction of a moment between the second and third movements, as Natalya took a mental and emotional deep breath to partially decompress, she caught a glimpse of the three older men looking at her with an "Are you all right?" expression on their red faces. Yes. She was all right. She would be better tomorrow morning, after her duty was fulfilled, and her revenge extracted.

But she would not stab Zmurchuck with a butcher knife, even though her intense hatred called for such violence. She would remove him cleanly, clinically, with a bullet through the head, the same way Zmurchuck's treachery had enabled the American CIA to kill Uncle Nicolai.

An eye for an eye, a tooth for a tooth, a bullet in the head for a bullet in the head. Those were the rules of the game.

She regretted Zmurchuck would not see her face as he died, would not know it was a mere girl who avenged Nicolai Alexandrovich's death. She regretted she would not see the blood as she had seen it in her mind, nor the shock in his eyes as he died. But that was the way the game was played; clean, clinical, no mess to deal with afterwards. Someone else would handle that.

The intensity of the second movement carried into the *allegretto* as the violent stabbing gradually subsided in her mind, and early in the fourth movement she felt the sniper rifle's three shots, much louder than the slight "piff" of her silenced Dragunov. She would only need one shot. Three would be more satisfying, but also an unprofessional extravagance.

The final movement, another *largo*, brought back the memory of Uncle Nicolai's funeral, when her youth and innocence had been buried with him.

After the final notes faded, the audience sat in stunned silence before rising with explosive applause. Natalya smiled shyly as she bowed.

Offstage, Vladimir approached her, Andrei and Dmitri close behind. "Tonight, Natalya Andreevna, especially in the *allegro molto*, you made each of us exceed our abilities. Each of us found something in ourselves we had not known was there. Even Nicolai Alexandrovich did not reach such heights."

He bowed, gallantly took her hand and brought it to his lips in homage. The violinists did the same and Natalya blushed.

~

Natalya spent a fitful night, waking almost hourly to look at the glaring red numbers on the clock radio beside her bed, afraid she would oversleep. She did not.

She awoke for the last time shortly after six and lay in bed, reviewing her plans for the morning. At seven she got up and removed the screen from the window looking out on Upper St. George Street. She had a hot shower, dried and brushed her long, dark curls, then took the cello case from the closet and assembled the sniper rifle, attaching the stock, sights, magazine and silencer.

At eight o'clock she took a small CD player from her suitcase and at five minutes after eight inserted a CD of the Shostakovich Sonata for Cello and Piano. She turned up the volume to concert hall level, loud enough to cover the quiet "piff" of the silenced Dragunov.

Beside the CD player she placed a second CD, this one with only the piano portion of the Sonata. She would replace the first CD with it at the end of the first movement, at eight-eighteen, after she had terminated Anatoly Zmurchuck, replaced the screen in the window, and returned the rifle in its case to the closet. Then she would accompany the piano with her own cello, lying ready on the bed.

No one would notice the difference. No one would question her. Everyone in the inn would know the young Russian cellist was practising when the scruffy old man was shot. They had heard her.

Natalya knelt in front of the window; the lace curtain pinned to the heavy green drapes so the light breeze would not cause it to drift across her vision and interfere with her clear view of the sidewalk. At eight fourteen he appeared, just as Grossman had described him; belly bulging over droopy camouflage shorts, shirttail hanging below a rough dark jacket, and the perennial cigarette dangling from the corner of his mouth.

She followed his head with the sights of the Dragunov, waiting until he would emerge from behind the oak tree. That would be the easiest shot.

He was moving slowly, smiling, talking to himself it seemed, the cigarette bobbing up and down in his mouth, occasional wisps of smoke drifting behind him. He was approaching the oak. When he appeared on the other side, she would gently squeeze the trigger with all the hatred in her soul. And that would be the end of Anatoly Vladimirovich Zmurchuck. Uncle Nicolai would be avenged.

Just before he reached the oak tree, Anatoly Zmurchuck turned his head away and down, then began walking across the lawn toward the inn. He reached behind his back, but instead of removing a handgun from his belt he merely yanked up his sagging shorts by the loops.

Had he seen her? No. That was impossible. Had he sensed her? Maybe. If he continued toward her she would shoot him in the middle of the forehead. Zmurchuck was the epitome of evil. Zmurchuck had killed Uncle Nikolai. Zmurchuck must die.

She took her eye away from the sights and looked through the lace curtains. Zmurchuck was walking toward the sign for the Queen Anne Inn.

Then she saw something she had missed when she had Zmurchuck in her sights: a little girl, perhaps four years old, with golden curls, wearing a pink dress, waited anxiously on the sidewalk. Zmurchuck stopped in front of the sign, bent down with some difficulty, and plucked a solitary daisy from among the flowers. With a big grin he turned and headed back toward the little golden-haired girl on the sidewalk, who was laughing and clapping her hands.

Yes, Zmurchuck must die—but not today.

A Cure for Allergies

Grace Keating

Dean looked through the kitchen window, his eyes resting on the crab apple tree across the open field. One whole half filled with apples, not a leaf in sight, lit up by a mid-winter sun. Branches pulled down by the weight in a loop that almost touched the ground. Frozen apples of deep red, glossed with frost, long past their best. Hard to know if they hung on or if the tree wouldn't let go.

Holly came to mind. Holly from his city life, dressed in her cool colours. Even in summer she was winter. Cold and frozen in fear, clinging on and not able to let go at the same time. She sat alone in her ice world, made up cold stories and kept them to herself. Whenever Dean tried to reach her, she'd recoil.

She hadn't started out that way. She'd once been loving and warm but somewhere along the way, everything Dean did began to frustrate her. It got to be that arguing was what they did best. Each argument became like a new coating of frost on apples. And all their dreams, one crystal at a time, became frozen. Dreams to see and never to touch, long past their best.

Was it Dean or was it Holly who hung on?

After Holly, he dated Hannah for a short time, but she seemed far too young. Not her age but her life. It wasn't so much that she and Dean didn't get along, it was just that there was so little to share.

She came with a set of friends who were obsessed with things Dean wasn't interested in and found quite boring. If they went to a restaurant in their neighbourhood, there'd soon be four or five others at the table and the discussion would change to the latest version of some video game he hadn't played.

Hannah and her gang liked to party, and although it was fun for a short time, for Dean that lifestyle soon lost its appeal. As did Hannah.

After the break-ups with Holly and Hannah, there was Heather. Ah, Heather. He actually proposed to her. They'd been living together for over five years and dated for two years before then. Her parents were coming to visit from California, and he thought it was what she wanted, a proposal. She kept hinting and dropping clues, saying things like how nice it would be for her parents to know she was finally settled and how they were looking forward to becoming grandparents.

Maybe he read it all wrong. When he popped the question, she said she needed to think about it. Think about it!

And then it sort of hit him: they weren't right for each other. She had a career she wanted to follow as a junior designer for a mid-sized clothing company. She wanted to branch off on her own. She wanted to travel, to go places and not be tied down with a family or stuck in some small city.

They both thought of each other as great people and thought they'd remain friends. But when they split, they drifted apart and, for Dean, Heather became just a fond memory.

Dean had done well with investments. By all accounts, he was successful. But the thing about success, he found, is that it's a moving target. There was no 'there' to get to. 'There' always changed places. Once you hit success, you wanted more, you acquired this insatiable need to keep going.

Dean tired of the whole thing: he'd had enough of it all. Enough of women, enough of always having to be more successful than the guy next to him and enough of the fast pace of the city life.

He managed to opt out and walk away, but that didn't mean he knew where he was going. Then his mother became ill and it was during that time when he was home more, spending time with family and with his dad, he made the decision to move back.

After his mother passed away, he moved in with his dad, Charlie, at the old farmstead at Turtle Ridge on the outskirts of town. it was a comfortable half hour walk to the stores, which he sometimes did. But more often than not, he drove.

He drove mainly to take his dad to town. More than once, Dean found Charlie driving the tractor at a snail's pace, smack in the middle of the road, on his way to Vern's Diner or the supermarket.

Charlie, having lost his licence the year earlier, figured he'd found a way round the rules. "Nothin' wrong with taking the tractor to town, they can't stop me driving that ol' thing."

His castle on wheels, Charlie called it, on account of being so high up looking down at the world. A few times Dean had driven into town with him, sitting high off the ground in the castle on wheels.

Riding along, he could see into the living rooms and kitchens of school friends and neighbours. Into the worlds of Don and Martha, Phil and Kimberly, Steve and Helen, and others. Couples. Couples and families.

Somehow he got left behind. Not that he'd intended to. Seven years with Heather, another two with Holly. Time kept on.

Life tossed him the ball on Helen and he missed, let her slip on by. Too shy when he was younger, he guessed. It was only years later, when Steve was away and there was a party down at the hall when Dean was on a visit home from the city, that he and Helen danced and she told him she had thought of him in that way, too.

But he missed. It was Steve and Helen, not Dean and Helen. He was the single man back living with his father, looking after two cats and a barn.

More and more, Dean took to driving Charlie into town, to card games or a doctor's appointment, or to stop by Vern's Diner for a coffee or a meal. Mainly, he drove his dad into town to keep the tractor off the road.

It wasn't long, though, before Dean fell back into the swing of things. The slowed-down life of a small town, the idle talk over coffee at Vern's, of young locals who were away, old locals who had done well or not so well. Stories of who returned to live or to visit, who was set to retire and who was about to start a family. Talk of crops and seeds, deer, mice, flying squirrels and events at the church hall.

They became regulars at Vern's. Somewhere between 10:05 and 10:15 on just about every weekday morning, Dean and Charlie would push through the big glass door of the Diner.

Vern would call out, "Hello, Charlie. Dean. What'll you have? Coffees?"

And it was on one of these regular weekday mornings, with Vern asking about coffees, and Charlie saying in response, "Coffee'd be great," when Charlie, not hearing the usual reply in the usual length of time from Dean, looked over his shoulder and said, "Son?"

Then Charlie noticed things were different at Vern's. Dean had pulled his jacket off, hung it on the hook by the door, just like he'd always done. But it was as though he'd drifted into some sort of a spellbound world.

Vern mentioned it wasn't the first time it'd happened that day. In fact, it seemed just about everyone slowed down to double slow motion that morning.

What was different was that Vern had hired a new waitress, Hazel. The last time he'd had anyone working in the Diner with him, other than Pearl, was close to six years earlier. Then Stacey, who'd only been there a year, left for the city to work in a hair salon.

Vern was twenty-two when his uncle offered the diner to him almost thirty years earlier. Vern's Diner had always been Vern's Diner, but Vern hadn't always been Vern. Back then, he went by Matt. He was Matthew Vernon Slater, Vernon being a family name. But as soon as he inherited the Diner, everyone called him Vern. He's been Vern so long, Matt just didn't feel right anymore.

Pearl had already been at the Diner for years before he started and Pearl was overdue to retire. Her husband, Ray, was ready for her to retire, too. They had dreams of travelling and they'd planned out trips they wanted to take pretty much the whole of their married life. If Pearl wanted to take a day off, she'd take a day off. It was the only way Vern could keep her.

Vern's customers got used to days where Pearl wouldn't be

there and it'd just be Vern. So when Vern was busy, they helped themselves to coffee and even making it. They'd find their own cutlery, fill up the creamers and the sugar bowls. Those days when Pearl wasn't there, they'd toss their money in a jar on the counter, most times they'd even have to figure out how much they owed. Vern didn't keep track: took up too much of his time, he said. It was a town run on trust and a diner run on trust. The town was still small enough for that, he said. And if you didn't have the money for the jar, you could eat anyway and pay the next time you came in.

You could tell right away there was something special about the new waitress. Vern's Diner seemed almost transformed. It sparkled, and if someone could do that in just a few hours, then it was pretty clear that that someone was the right person for Vern's Diner and right for Serpent Bay.

Hazel had stepped off the bus the afternoon before. Walking into the Diner, she asked the whereabouts of her Uncle Jim. Vern hired her on the spot. Vern wasn't really listening when Hazel said she was looking for her uncle and she wasn't really looking for a job. When he stopped what he was doing and looked up at her to see that she was staring intently at him, everything just sort of fell into place.

She asked, "Did you just offer me a job?"

He nodded.

"Well, I accept."

Pearl came charging out of the kitchen and did a little dance in the middle of the restaurant. She was overjoyed. She pointed out where Uncle Jim's place was and said, "We'll get you something to eat. Then we'll get you settled in at your uncle's place and you can start tomorrow morning at 7:30. How's that sound?"

Pearl figured she would show Hazel the ropes over the next few weeks and help out when it got busy. Then Pearl and Ray planned to take off on their custom motorcycle with matching helmets, square-toed boots and matching gloves. They'd had a trip planned out for some time.

Vern said they were acting like they were back in high school, all fussy with each other.

Just about everyone was struck by the magical quality of Hazel, Dean certainly was. He couldn't keep from looking at her. Stealing a peek in the long mirrored wall behind the counter. Twisting his neck whenever she'd disappear into the kitchen while he was trying to carry on a conversation with his dad or with Vern.

This'd be all fine if Dean was interested in women, but he'd had enough of the species for a while. He'd signed off women forever, or for a few years anyway, at least that's the way he felt until sometime between 10:05 and 10:15 that morning when Hazel started at Vern's.

The way Dean and Charlie worked things on Martin's Road was that one evening a week they'd go off to Vern's and have an early supper. The other evenings they'd eat at the house, three nights cooking for each of them. They'd often stay up to watch the news or a game and have a few crackers and cheese. Sometimes Dean would put on a pot of tea.

But when Vern hired Hazel, things changed. That first night, Charlie suggested that maybe they could go down to the Diner and have a meal. Dean was quick to say that'd be a great idea. So father and son sat at a booth at the Diner and had pepper steaks and mash. The next evening, Dean and Charlie ate an early supper at Vern's again and had the chicken Parmesan.

For the next two weeks, they practically lived at the Diner. In between talk of the racetrack, in between Stu coming in to talk with Charlie about anything from sump pumps to carburettors, in between the updates on people's health, and on local news and sports, Dean would be looking at Hazel while trying not to, and making small talk between the shrimp cocktail, the spaghetti and ribs and the special dessert of the day.

Hazel introduced new dishes to the Diner which became the talk of the town. No one had tasted anything like shrimp cocktail at Vern's Diner for a very long time. In fact, no one remembered there being anything like shrimp cocktail anywhere in Serpent Bay.

Along with the shrimp cocktail with the sensational seafood sauce, she added pulled pork sandwiches served on a kaiser bun, chicken wings and twice baked stuffed potato jackets, and two new desserts: Aunt Betty's Four Layer Chocolate Tower Cake, which fast became a favourite, and Maid Marian's Marvellous Pecan Pie.

She had other ideas, but Vern said slow down a little, let people catch up. He was feeling a little out of breath. The Diner was becoming quite the popular spot and he'd soon have to find a second waitress.

One day, after Hazel had been at the Diner a few months and spring was just beginning to take shape in everyone's minds, Vern took Charlie aside and said, "This thing that's going on with your Dean and my Hazel is obvious to just about everyone in Serpent Bay. What's up with your boy, is he blind? When's he going to ask her out on a date?"

Charlie tried to hint at Dean, without being too blunt, but Dean didn't seem to be picking up any clues. So Vern and Charlie came up with a plan to help move things along a little.

Charlie needed some special parts for the ride-on lawn mower even though it was a little early in the season for mowing. He figured he could get the parts brought in and Dean probably wouldn't think anything of it.

He placed an order at the local hardware store and, when Jennifer called to say the parts were in, Charlie asked Dean to take a little walk down and pick them up.

Vern, at a signal from Charlie, called Jennifer and asked her to put aside a particular gasket for the coffee maker and sent Hazel down to the hardware store for it.

While Dean was waiting for Jennifer to sort through that week's orders, Hazel came rushing in for the gasket. His heart took a little skip and they immediately struck up a conversation.

By the time Jennifer found the orders, had the accounts sorted out and items signed for and Hazel and Dean were on their way back to the Diner, Dean had asked Hazel out on a date. Dean suggested they go to Elliottville, the larger town forty K or so to the west. He'd come by to pick her up mid-Saturday afternoon, so they might have a bit of time to go for a walk or take in a visit to a gallery before a nice dinner at the only fancy restaurant in that town.

On the Saturday afternoon, on a wooden walkway out along the beach dunes, and later, sitting across from each other at the restaurant, they got to talking about their past lives, past lovers, their insights, dreams, hopes and wishes. Hazel had been far too in love with Sid for far too long. He was far too not in love with her and, as it turned out, far too gay. She finally got over him and landed in the arms of Jeff. Another mistake but of a different sort. They'd lived together for four years and all the time he was having an affair on the side. When she found out, she decided their relationship wasn't worth fighting for. They grew apart. He was more surprised than upset when she left. There were others, but no one had been the right fit.

"I used to spend holidays and summers here with my grandmother," Hazel said. "At least until I was fifteen or so, when the visits petered out.

"I was manager of an internet cafe in Toronto, a pretty popular spot near the university, when it hit me. It came right out of the blue. There were these regulars playing some card game I hadn't seen before, and I asked them what the game was. Ophidian something, they called it. It took me right back into the kitchen of my grandma's house. I was maybe six or seven years old. My mom, my Aunt Sarah, and my grandma were making a special snake-shaped cake. And yes, I got to lick the icing. Anyway, there was a big celebration for the town's anniversary or something and the snake shape, they told me, was for the serpent in Serpent Bay. That's when I found out the word ophidian means snake. I love that word, ophidian.

"When the college kids said the name, I knew I needed to come back. I thought I could do with living an easier life in a smaller world. I guess I figured not knowing what I was doing here, in Serpent Bay, was better than not knowing what I was doing in the big city."

Dean told Hazel his theory of allergies. He'd heard about doctors who became allergic to latex gloves after years of use, and bakers who became allergic to flour. He'd even heard of a short-order cook who'd become allergic to eggs. And, as far as he could tell, there was every evidence to suggest he was allergic to women whose name began with the letter H: Helen, Holly, Hannah, Heather. He'd adored Helen in high school, had gone through hell with Holly, felt way too old for Hannah, and had almost married Heather.

"That," he said, "was why it took me so long to ask you out. I was almost paralyzed because your name started with H."

It wasn't until he'd heard her Uncle Frank walk in to Vern's and call out, "Betty Hazel Riley, where's my little girl? We heard you were in town. Look at how grown up you've become, spittin' image of your mother," that it all fell into place. That's the day he decided he would ask her out. Then, just minutes later, he ran into her at the hardware store.

What resonated most, Dean told her, was when Hazel said she'd wanted a smaller life. She wanted to live in a smaller pond. Not to be a big fish in a small pond, but to be who she is and to live in a smaller and less complicated pond. For Dean, her words seemed to fit with every reason he'd returned to Serpent Bay.

He might have said more, but that's when Hazel said, "My grandmother always says, a good cup of tea will cure just about anything. I'm wondering if a good cup of tea at my house might be a cure for your allergies."

Fester

Rhoda C. Hill

The first time Cleary sees him, the little green man is balancing on a shovel outside Cleary's kitchen window. He isn't doing anything in particular; just looks at Cleary and balances on the shovel. Cleary eats his oatmeal and toast, and sips hot black tea. His wife, Nancy, reads the paper across from him.

"New study says drinking black tea can improve your memory," she reads aloud.

"Oh yeah?" Cleary raises his cup to his mouth and sips. "Nancy, do you see anything on that shovel out there?"

Nancy looks out at the shovel. "Not a thing," she says and returns her attention to her paper.

Cleary tips his cup to the little green man and nods.

The next day the little green man is back. Only this time he balances right on the edge of the windowsill, inside the house, and he says his name is Fester in so low a voice that only Cleary hears.

"Did you hear that?"

"I didn't hear a thing."

"Right there," Cleary says pointing to the windowsill. "You don't see anything moving?"

"Not a thing."

Nancy's really losing her mind, Cleary thinks, and the little green man nods his head in agreement.

Cleary reaches for his cup, tips it at the little green man and nods. He doesn't see the creature dive into the cup until he tips it to his mouth, and the hot liquid sloshes onto his tongue. He slams the mug to the table and erupts into a fit of coughing.

Nancy jumps to her feet. "Are you okay?"

"I'm fine," he says, but he's not. He's scared. He's never swallowed a little green man before.

Nancy returns to her paper.

Minutes roll by.

"Nancy?"

"Yes, Cleary?"

"Do you think little green men can hurt you?"

Nancy laughs. "What little green men?"

"He was in my tea. I made a mistake and swallowed him."

Nancy laughs a different sort of laugh.

"I'm serious."

"Yes, that's what worries me," she says.

The tickle in the back of Cleary's throat persists until the little green man makes his way to the front door of his memory.

He knocks.

Rat-a-tat-tat. Tap-tap-tap. Rap-a-tap-tat.

Cleary's head aches.

~

The door opens and stuff spills out; nothing important. Fester, the little green man, kicks it aside. He stands in the middle of the over-stocked room and looks about. Where to be begin? He knows what he's come here for, but he can't see the box. Too much debris. Too much useless stuff that serves no purpose.

Fester picks up a box and peers inside at the contents. Thousands of words carefully filed and meticulously labelled. He gives them a shake and tosses them over his shoulder.

He pivots in the middle of the floor. Red box, where are you?

Something crunches under his foot and he stops to lift a hefty 'to do' list. Taking a few steps to the door he tosses it out and then turns back to the room and shakes his head. How could someone overcrowd a place this badly? He pulls up the sleeves of his little green jacket and delves into the piles of unorganized files.

Surely somewhere there's a shredder, Fester thinks, scanning the dirty room. He sees one stashed unused in a corner, and wipes the dust from its top. He flicks the switch, reaches out for a paper labelled "important dates" and swiftly runs it through the shredder.

Things are going to go a whole lot quicker with this nifty little gadget.

~

"Just a small bit of oatmeal in my milk this morning, Norma."

Nancy sets the oatmeal in front of him, and leaves the room to make a call. When she returns she says, "Cleary, the doctor wants to see you Tuesday."

"Great," he says. "Maybe he can tell me what these headaches are from." He eats half of the oatmeal and pushes the bowl away. "You want to go into town with me today, Norma?"

"No," she says. The crow's feet around her eyes deepen. "I've got a lot to do, but you can go on ahead if you'd like."

~

Fester can see the box. It motivates him, and he works even faster. In his haste to reach a stack of maps in the corner he trips on a couple of wires and pulls them from their sockets. Quickly, because he didn't come to totally rewire the place, he grabs their ends and jabs them into what he assumes is their rightful places. He feels the room jar, but then everything is calm and he resumes his cleaning.

~

Cleary had meant to go home. The flashing lights are shining in his car windows and a police officer opens his door and takes him by the arm.

"Where are you taking me?"

"Your wife is coming to get you. You're lost."

Lost? Cleary looks around. Nothing is familiar.

"How did I get here?"

"You drove."

~

Fester stands back and admires his work. This is as it should be. All cheery and bright, with a red box in the corner. Now he can find the info he needs. He goes to the box and reaches inside to remove a photo album.

The glue that holds the film over the pictures has lost its tack. The pages fan open and the pictures fall out.

Fester collects the fallen papers and begins to reattach them in no particular order.

~

Cleary sees a woman coming toward the police car.

"Oh, look," he tells the officer. "That's my sister, Jean, all the way from Ontario. She didn't tell me she was coming to Nova Scotia."

Nancy stops at the car and the police officer gets out.

"Are you his sister, Jean?"

"No, I'm his wife Nancy." It takes all the strength she has to holds back her tears, but she has to be strong, so she smiles at the officer.

The smile works and he relinquishes Cleary into her care. As she walks away, a complete picture of strength, she is weak.

She leads the man who was once her strength to the passenger side of his car and slips behind the steering wheel, taking him home with her where she will be alone.

~

Fester rummages in the box and finds the personal identification folder. His stomach rumbles, and he eyes the paper hungrily. He crumples it in his small green fist and shoves it into his mouth.

Leaving the lid up on the red box, he opens a nearby window and watches as the remaining information blows away.

~

Cleary is staring at his reflection in the window. He doesn't know who is looking at him, but he can see a little green man dancing on the stranger's tongue. He wants to nod, but he can't remember how.

No End to It

Gary Lovett

When Lawrence Whalen sees the car go past the gates and on into town, where the access road to the new highway will take Miss Walters to Halifax, he quickly puts the lawnmower in the tool shed and, after picking up his lunch bucket, heads for his truck, parked in the shade behind the garage. She's already paid him for the week and he sees no point in putting in any more time than necessary. What she doesn't know, won't hurt her, he thinks.

But he sits in the cab of the truck eating a sandwich, and lets fifteen minutes go by in case she returns, before he starts the truck and heads into town. If by chance she sees him, he'll say he's just in to check the mail. Always be prepared!

He knows it's more of a game now with him, the shirking of work that began years before when he worked at the fish plant. But he doesn't remember exactly when it started. Maybe it evolved slowly, like the realization that, no matter how hard he works, it will never amount to anything. Unless you call being a straw boss something, which he didn't. He knows that his life will end just where it began, right here in this small town he often refers to as 'Nowhere, N.S.'

Even Clarey Morrison, who sucked up to the bosses for twelve years before he got the straw-boss job, got it up the ass when the low fish quotas came in from Ottawa and the company packed up without so much as a 'thank you' and headed for greener pastures. The whole damn town, he thinks, took a screwing from them bastards.

He feels a sense of righteousness in the playing of his game. Why bust a gut to get something when you can get it for nothing.

He chuckles to himself, remembering the time he worked construction, building the new shopping mall. He spent two weeks, *two damn weeks!* walking around the job site carrying a two-by-four on his shoulder, stopping to chat with the boys here and there, sometimes replacing the two-by-four with a shovel, drinking his coffee and eating his lunch right under the boss's nose, and the dumb shit had no idea who the hell Lawrence was, thought he worked for another contractor. When it came time for the first pay, the look on that man's face when Lawrence picked up his cheque! "Well, sir. I was just trying to help out as much as I could, seeing as how no one seemed to want to *tell* me what to do," he said.

Despite getting fired, Lawrence had felt, as he walked away with the cheque in his pocket, that he was on top in the game. And now he was pulling in $250 a week in cash from Miss Walters with her not wanting any receipts or anything, and drawing the welfare too, because what they didn't know wouldn't hurt them either. Besides, lots of fellas are doing the odd job here and there under the table while collecting unemployment or welfare, with nobody thinking too much about that, it being the only way to stay ahead of the bills and keep food on the table. Let those bastards up at County Welfare try to feed seven kids and put shoes on their feet with what they doled out. They wouldn't be so goddamn tight with the money then, no way!

Yes, he feels well on top of the game, but only because he makes up his own rules as he goes along. He drives through town searching for the grey Volvo and, not finding it, makes a U-turn and heads for the tavern.

Lawrence pauses for a moment inside the door, letting his eyes adjust to the dim interior. Nobody calls out to him, which doesn't surprise him. He is not a sought-after drinking companion, being tight with his money. When it comes time for him to buy a round it is not unusual for him to be in the washroom or on the way out the door on one pretext or another.

But he remains convinced that, although his cheapness is well known, people still enjoy having him around because he is funny. Like the time he danced a jig on the table, beer slopping over everyone, but nobody caring. He remembers the unbelieving looks on their faces and being the centre of attention was something he enjoyed.

As he surveys the tavern, looking for a friendly face, he notices Clarey Morrison sitting off by himself in the corner, nursing a beer. I'll stay away from that son of a bitch today, Lawrence thinks.

Clarey scowls at him, then waves for the waiter to bring more beer.

Six men are seated at tables. Two more are at the pool table near the back wall. They look like Department of Highways workers, both wearing scuffed work boots and overalls. Two yellow hardhats lie on the floor under a table that has two pints of beer on it. The boys are having a late lunch. Highways: more like the Department of Holidays, he thinks.

He looks at the others seated at two tables pulled together, recognizes two of them. They work the draggers and are probably bar-hopping up the coast with their shipmates. But first they have an ocean of beer on the table to swim through.

Lawrence looks over towards Clarey, who appears lost in thought, as he walks past the bar towards the other corner table where he can sit with his back to the wall.

"Drop a couple draft over there, Charlie," he says.

"You eatin' today, Lawrence?"

"Maybe. Give me a menu. Pretty quiet for a Friday, ain't it?"

"She'll liven up before too long, buddy. Enjoy the quiet while you can."

Lawrence sits at the table, keeping a watchful eye on Clarey as he pretends to scrutinize the menu. He thinks, I should have gone to the Legion, but it's a little early yet. Just my luck to run into Clarey when he's in a sour mood. I'll just throw back a couple of beers and head to the Legion before things get too rowdy here. After all, it is Friday night and the shit always hits the fan on Friday. I don't want to be around when those goddamn hams that Clarey calls fists start flying.

He hates my guts, anyway. Many a time I made him look foolish up at the plant. He deserved it though, always walking around with his chest pumped up and full of himself, as if he didn't wear the same fish stink as every other man in the place. He wore that white hat like it was a friggin' crown, even back and forth to work. And kept it up by the back window of his car all weekend, like one of those stupid white dogs some folks had when he was a kid, with the eyes that light up when you touch the brakes.

Well, he must of gotten the shock of his life when they told him he was going down the road like every one else, when the company put the lock on the gate and Clarey looked around and saw that all those years of sucking up to the bosses didn't get him any further ahead than any one else. But at least most people still have their dignity, a sense of pride in who they are and what they've accomplished over the years.

Maybe if Clarey had some kids along the way that would have given him something to be proud of, something to hope for down the road. With two kids up in Halifax at Dalhousie University, Lawrence knows about hope, that at least his kids will get out of this shit-hole of a town and make something of their lives. Something to make the old man proud, he thinks.

But Clarey has none of that. Everyone in town knows Clarey and how he got to be straw boss. He's like that idiot Lawrence had seen on the TV who was bitching about not getting any respect. Well, respect is something you earn, not something you have a right to. Yes, if Clarey Morrison had a few kids he might have turned out to be all right, instead of becoming such an asshole.

At four o'clock Lawrence finishes his sixth glass of beer, drops a loonie on the table and leaves the tavern. He had watched Clarey all afternoon, sipping away but drinking little. Maybe the money is getting real tight for him, Lawrence thinks. Usually Clarey drank with a vengeance.

Lawrence takes a backward glance as he leaves the tavern, notices the beet red face and bulging veins in Clarey's neck and is glad to be heading home to his family. Liquored up or not, Clarey's got a bug up his ass about something, he thinks. Someone's going to cross him tonight. Then there'll be hell to pay.

~

Clarey Morrison is only faintly aware of Lawrence's departure. He watches the men at the other table, listening to their conversation. Their raucous laughter deepens the scowl on his face. Those bastards are to blame for the goddamn mess we're in, he thinks, selling their catches over the side to the Russian factory ships so they can stay out longer, double their profits and appease the Department of Fisheries' regulations and quotas. Clarey hates the Russians and the fishermen who have killed the fish stocks. He hates the Fisheries Department, who have no bite to their policing of Canadian waters, chasing the foreigners off when they should be hauling them into port and confiscating the ships and catches.

That would set the tone. We'd all be working still, content with our lives and none of this bullshit going on with plant closures all over the eastern seaboard. The Fisheries quotas are killing off small towns all over, up and down the coast where fishing is a way of life and the people know nothing else.

Even over in Newfoundland, where it always seemed that the sea's harvest would go on forever, the plants are closing. The times are long gone when he was a boy, fishing with his uncle on the Grand Banks and coming home with the holds so damn full you'd think the boat would come apart at the seams if you hit rough seas.

What's a man to do when they pull the rug out from under him and sitting there flat on his arse with no idea how he got there because he'd never thought to look beyond the way things get done, to see how or why they are done? There was never any need to know. But when a man is flat on his arse, he needs to know what put him there.

Clarey had always thought of himself as a big fish in a little pond, but now he realizes that the pond is bigger than he ever imagined and he isn't so big after all, not even close to what he thought before he was out of work and worrying about the future. Remembering what he'd been told these past few months by the government and others only served to confuse him even more. *You've got to understand, Mr. Morrison, with no marketable skills the work just can't be found.* Those pen-pushers at the unemployment treated him like he was a child.

For a while talk circulated about how the company was just using the promise of jobs as a way of getting government money to modernize the plant. But two months after the plant closed, when the manager's home was sold to that rich bitch Walters, he knew they'd never re-open. And everyone else knew it, too. You didn't need a college degree to figure that one out.

If Mavis hadn't gone to work for that Walters woman, she'd be home cooking his goddamn dinner like a wife's supposed to be doing. He feels the hatred welling up inside him for this woman he's never met. But he knows all about her. From Mavis, who at first couldn't stop talking about how *sweet* she is, how *kind* she is. But after a while Mavis got the message loud and clear that if he wanted to know anything about *sweet, kind Miss Walters*, he'd ask. But that wasn't the end of it altogether. He heard plenty from the boys who did renovations up at the Lawson place. She paid them all in cash, too, American money, just to show everyone what a rich bitch she is. All of the boys coming in here after getting paid, making a big show of the American money. *What's the exchange rate today, Charlie?*

Over at the Legion Clarey finally got so fed up with listening to them bragging about all this work they were getting under the table, he almost decided to give the Unemployment a call. Instead, gave Ken Langston a punch in the face and said if that didn't shut him up there was plenty more where that came from. That shut him up and all the others too.

Clarey knows they talk about him behind his back, but that doesn't bother him. What's said to a man's face is the only thing that counts.

He has a few things he'd like to say to Geraldine Walters' face. He isn't exactly sure what they are, but he knows he'll feel a hell of a lot better once they're said. That always has been the way things work best for me, he thinks. No sense wasting time thinking about what you'll say until the time comes to say it.

And as Clarey sits in his corner of the tavern, as he combs the shadowy spaces deep inside himself where things, even the most absurd, make sense, his hatred begins to fill those spaces. When Clarey comes to his feet that hatred explodes and he heaves the table away from him, sending the glasses crashing to the floor.

~

"She has no husband?" Clarey asks, reaching for the cup of tea on the corner of the table.

"It's not my business to ask," Mavis replies. "I clean and cook. That's what she pays me to do. I don't stick my nose where it doesn't belong."

She stands at the kitchen sink, washing up after a late supper. She is a short woman with a once-shapely figure. Her rounded features are far removed from those of the young girl who was crowned Queen of the Pageant and dreamed of running off to Hollywood and becoming a movie star. She looks tired and knows that dragging all this excess weight around will kill her someday.

"Damn!" Clarey jumps up with the hot tea soaking his shirt front, trying to pull it away from his skin. "Throw me a dish rag there, Mavis. I think I must of scalded myself. Jesus Christ! Look at this now."

His shirt is open, revealing a long, red burn stretching from his chest down past the navel.

She hesitates before passing the towel, fearful of what might come if she gets within arm's reach of him. "I'll get some ointment to put on that," she says.

She hurriedly leaves the kitchen and climbs the stairs to the bathroom, pausing for a moment at the top to catch her breath. She feels as if she doesn't breathe right around Clarey anymore. It doesn't take much to set him off these days. With the fish plant closed and no work for these past eight months, he's wired up from the time he crawls out of bed in the morning until when he goes to sleep. It's only then, when his breathing has become deep and regular, that Mavis can relax around him, come down from the tightrope that her life has become.

For a while in early spring, when politicians talked of ways to re-open the plant, making all kinds of promises to the townsfolk, It had looked as if things might improve. But that was three months ago, and those politicians up in Halifax weren't making promises about anything now.

Mavis thought things might improve when she started working for the summer, doing housework and cooking at the Lawson place. She enjoyed the old estate. But her working just seemed to make things worse between her and Clarey. It is as if he resents her working more than not working himself.

True, he still has the unemployment coming in. But having a few dollars in your pocket doesn't make up for having no job to go to in the morning, and all the day stretched out in front of you with nothing to occupy your time except a trip to the tavern, where a fellow might talk things over with the boys and enjoy a few beers before checking the post office box to see what would come of that.

Since she's been working and not getting home until almost seven o'clock most nights, so tired it's a job just to stand up let alone cook another meal, things have gotten much worse. Most days he doesn't bother to go to the post, unless his cheque is due. He stays at the tavern long after his friends have gone home to supper, sometimes getting a bite to eat there, more often than not coming home fit to be tied because a man needs his supper on the table when he's hungry, not when he's ready for bed.

God knows she needed that job, though, so she could put some money aside. Once the unemployment runs out it will be a bleak winter, with nothing ahead but the welfare, which is feeding half the town already. With his seniority at the plant Clarey had been one of the last to go and so they were in better shape than most folks. But it was a great worry no matter which way you look at it.

Mr. Sheldon, who runs the grocery, had said the difference between an optimist and a pessimist was that the pessimist saw the bottle half-empty, while the optimist saw it half-full. Mavis thinks, when it's gone, it's gone. It may be all right to look at things that way when you have a good business. People got to eat no matter what, and whether the welfare is buying the food or it's coming out of a man's own pocket, what difference does it make to him, sitting there counting up his profit?

It is a sad thing to watch a proud man lashing out at those who love him because the ones who can change things are out of reach, sitting in some big fancy office somewhere with no concern for the working man at all. It broke her heart to see Clarey, who had never asked for anything he wasn't owed, being forced to crawl for those bastards at the unemployment, who hold the cheques out like carrots.

They said he must be ready, willing and able to work each day, but when there's no work to be had anywhere the bottle always looks half-empty.

"You gone to sleep up there, Mavis?" he says when she returns to the table.

"I couldn't find the rub. The last time we used it was when you pulled your back out at the plant."

"Jesus, woman! You don't put that stuff on burns. I need the Ozonal, not this crap." He storms out of the room, muttering under his breath.

Oh Lord! she thinks, be kind to me today.

She sits at the kitchen table, squeezing herself into one of the captain's chairs they bought during better times. She looks around the room, the frilly curtains, the new cushion flooring they put in two years ago, the microwave and the sideboard that matched the table and chairs; all remnants of better times. As she listens to his footsteps coming down the stairs, she knows that things can only get worse.

"So she got no man out there at all, then?" he asks as he walks into the kitchen, dabbing his chest and stomach with the ointment, a spot here, a spot lower, absently squeezing the tube and using more than necessary. "Rub this in for me now, Mavis. But be careful. Lord it feels like the skin's coming off me."

She takes the ointment and puts it in her apron pocket. He stands in front of her, a bear-like belly hanging low over his dungarees, hiding the belt buckle with the brass fish-head he got from the company for ten years without a lost-time accident.

She feels trapped in the chair, as tight as a straitjacket around her middle, and she is afraid of him. He could be mean at times, when he had a few too many at the tavern, or when his cheque was late. His whole world is caving in on him, she thinks.

"How's that feel, love?" she asks, gingerly trying to spread the ointment about. It is a nasty burn and might blister if she doesn't get it all moistened.

"That's good enough, Mavis. I think I'll live one more day. You say she's got no man up there at all, eh?"

"No, I didn't say that."

"Well how the hell does she keep up with the yard work? That place must be ten, twelve acres, with most of it lawn. And a house like that must always be needing some fixing of one sort. What's she doing about all that?"

"She has Lawrence Whalen in three days a week to see to anything that needs doing. If I see something I just tell her and she puts it on a list."

"Jesus Christ! The laziest son of a bitch that ever drew a breath, and she hires him. How the hell did he get the job, anyway?"

"He just walked up to the door and asked for work, about two weeks ago, I think it was. He seems to be working out all right."

After she says it, she knows that was the wrong thing to say, but it is out there now like a short fuse that has to be snuffed out. "I'm sorry, Clarey. If I thought for a minute that you were interested in working for Miss Walters, I would have said something to her."

"You thought! You *thought!* Jesus Christ, Mavis. You never *thought* about me at all, did you?"

"I'm sorry, Clarey," she says, looking down at the floor, beginning to shake uncontrollably as she sees his feet move and his weight shift back on his heels and she feels it coming long before the world explodes, knocking her and the chair over sideways, with Clarey's words echoing in her head as if they're coming down a long dark hallway.

"That's your problem, Mavis. You never *think* at all!"

~

Mavis slowly walks past the gate and the guest cottage, where the driveway takes a dip and forks off to the right down towards the water, where early morning mist shrouds the power-boat she knows lies moored to the wharf. Normally, she enjoys the order of the old Lawson estate: everything in its place, like the dream home in the Hospital Lottery. But this morning she is simply trying to put one foot in front of the other, trying to cope with the pain in the left side of her head.

She had looked at herself in the mirror this morning and her reflection scared her. Her eye was almost swollen shut and her face was badly bruised down to the jaw-line. When she opened her mouth the pain snaked out from behind her ear and raced to her eye and began to pound, like some one beating on an empty oil drum with a hammer, making her feel faint and woozy, like she might throw up.

She sat in her kitchen holding a cold cloth to her face most of the night. Gradually the throbbing stopped and she got dressed as quietly as possible and left the house at six o'clock without even a cup of tea for fear of waking Clarey, the thought of which makes her eye begin to throb again as she follows the drive and feels the jarring shock of the dip that caught her off guard, drifting between the bright, early morning sun starting to burn off the fog and some dark place inside herself where the pain couldn't find her.

Her full weight comes down on her left foot, past where the pavement should have been and then just as she feels like she is going to fall forward, a jolt as the ground comes up to meet the ball of her foot and the pain erupts in her face again like it is about to split open.

~

Lawrence looks out the window and sees the ambulance coming down the highway, lights flashing but no siren. He turns to his wife sitting beside him on the couch, where they're watching the morning news. "Pretty early for them to be out."

"Shush! The mayor and a busload of people went up to Halifax yesterday to see the Premier. I want to hear what happened."

"You know what happened: sweet fuck-all, that's what."

"Watch your tongue! The kids are in the kitchen."

"You know as well as I do that all they'll get is a song and dance and a pat on the head for all their trouble."

"I don't know any such thing."

"Come on, Ellen. There's no end to the bullshit those politicians keep shovelling at us. Those guys—"

"Shush! Here it is now."

Lawrence gets up and stomps into the kitchen. A moment later, through the window above the sink, he sees the ambulance silently coming back down the highway on its way to the hospital in Bridgewater.

He winces as Ellen turns up the volume on the TV. Two of his children leave the table to watch the news with their mother. He listens as the newscaster describes the Premier's response to the delegation "...take time to resolve this issue..."

The ambulance passes the house and he returns to the living room to watch as the flashing lights slowly disappear into the fog. He looks at the calm, almost benevolent face of the Premier on the screen.

The Fall

Debra Whittall

"It's not the fall that kills you," Tom Rafuse always used to say. "It's the landing!" He'd lift his florid face toward the sun or the ceiling, depending on his location, and laugh and laugh at his own joke. Tom had an easygoing manner, a penchant for pocket protectors, and the meaty paunch and polyester wardrobe of a much-beloved high school shop teacher, which he was.

Millicent Robar lived next door with her cats, Mister Mittens, Princess Poo and Sir Scratchalot. She had seen and heard Tom tell his fall gag many, many times, and those around Tom when he told it never failed to chuckle along. Even those who, like Millie, had heard it many, many times. Tom was that kind of guy. Jovial and a bit obtuse. You couldn't help laughing at his stupid, repetitive jokes.

Millie didn't ponder long on her own feelings for Tom, but she often wished that she had a man like him in her life. His wife, Rose, was downright dim, Millie thought. She was always at his side, looking up adoringly at him as he held court on their back porch, a goofy grilling apron across his girth and a spatula in his hand. Their backyard barbecues were such fun affairs: Tom's monster hamburgers; Rose's exquisite potato salad and chilled cherry cheesecake. Children and adults alike squealed with delight, and Tom most of all.

Of course, the laughter stopped when Rose Rafuse was found dead at the bottom of the cellar stairs, her neck snapped and her blood pooling under shelves of homemade raspberry jelly and pickled beets. Millie watched first the fire trucks, then the RCMP and, finally, the coroner's van pull into the driveway or park along the curb across from her kitchen window. It was all she could do not to fly right through the window to find out what had happened.

When she saw Tom emerge from his home, hiccuping with sobs, she ran to him.

"My Rose," he cried. "She's gone, Millie. She's gone!"

It was, indeed, the landing and not the fall that killed her. The coroner ruled the cause of death blunt force trauma. The *manner* of death she left undetermined.

Millie watched as the tall detective with the odd moustache came to question Tom, carting bulky, space-age devices into the basement to measure angles and gather evidence. These visits were daily and lasted for hours during the first few weeks after Rose took her tumble, but their frequency and intensity eased as autumn leaves fluttered to the ground.

Millie was among the neighbours, friends and relatives who enveloped Tom with support and casseroles in the early days. She was briefly confused when she saw Candy Krauss bounce up the driveway within a week of the accident. *Empty handed and empty headed*, Millie thought.

Candy chewed gum vigorously and wore a midriff baring blouse that barely contained her perky, 16-year-old breasts. Her cut off jeans rode so high that her left butt cheek was exposed as she stepped up on the back porch, spit her gum into Rose's prized begonia and knocked on Tom's door. *He must be tutoring the poor girl,* Millie decided, *to take his mind off his troubles.*

Millie redoubled her efforts to ease Tom's pain. She made it her job to return the green bin from the side of the road even before she returned her own, within minutes of the truck rumbling by. She dead-headed the begonias, weeded the walkway and mulched Rose's roses. When she offered to wash and fold his laundry, Tom happily handed her a key to the back door.

With access to the house she tackled his sink full of dirty dishes, ran a vacuum over the gold carpet in the front room and mopped the cellar floor with bleach. She reined in her instinct to straighten the entire house, setting a goal of just one casserole and one extra chore per week. She didn't want to overwhelm poor Tom. Not when he was grieving so and keeping up such a hectic tutoring schedule.

Millie didn't believe Wanda Wentzel, the cashier at the Super Store in town. While scanning Millie's cases of Whiskas, she whispered in not-so-hushed tones that Tom had been seen holding hands with Candy at the Boston Pizza out by the Walmart.

"No!" Millie cried with a bit more vehemence than she'd intended.

"It's true," whisper-shouted Wanda. "They're an *item*."

Poppycock, Millie thought. She refused to believe that Tom would replace his Rose so quickly. And, if he did, she thought, surely, he would look across the driveway and not to the hallways of Parkview Collegiate. Hadn't they exchanged a significant look that horrible day of the accident? Hadn't she been tenderly folding his underwear since Thanksgiving? Hadn't he told her just last week that he didn't know what he'd do without her? Millie pushed the trash talk about Candy Krauss from her mind.

But Detective Al Himmelman of the RCMP did not. He was very interested in Tom's relationship with Candy. That's what he called it when he knocked on Millie's door the day after Remembrance Day, a "*relationship*."

"Mrs. Robar," he started.

"Miss," Millicent corrected him. She did not like this smirking man who reeked of cheap aftershave and condescension. Good breeding, however, dictated she offer him a seat and a beverage.

She led him to her front room and pointed to the pink patterned chesterfield, noting the tilt of his moustache when its plastic cover crinkled as he sat.

Millie remembered the first time she'd met Detective Himmelman. It was shortly after she and Tom had shared their first embrace. He must have seen it, since he seemed fixated on Tom and Rose's love life. "How was their marriage?" he'd asked. "Any signs of trouble...fights? Other women?"

Millie was horrified by these questions and her disdain for the detective had not abated since then. She was secretly pleased when Princess Poo rubbed up against this leg and then jumped into his lap, spreading her white fur across his navy suit.

"*Miss* Robar, we have reason to believe that your neighbour, Mr. Rafuse, is having an affair," he said.

Millie felt the heat rise to her face and hoped the detective didn't notice. *How could he know*? She had not told anyone of her growing feelings for Tom, nor of the obvious signals that he had sent her, clearly reciprocating. This smelly man, his obscene moustache and his prurient questions were an affront to decency.

Mister Mittens, perhaps mistaking the facial hair for another cat, jumped up on the couch and took a swipe at the detective's face.

"An affair?" Millie echoed weakly.

He must have seen her blush. He continued to smirk as he calmly moved Princess Poo from his lap and then set Mister Mittens on the floor beside her. Brushing ineffectually at his pants leg, he said, "We know for a fact that Mr. Robar is in a *relationship* with Candy Krauss."

"What?" Millie sputtered. She couldn't be sure whether she'd said it in her head or out loud; and, if the latter, how loudly. She saw white. Her mind went blank. Princess Poo jumped back onto the detective's lap.

"Miss Krauss has confirmed for us that she and Mr. Rafuse are romantically involved. I would like you, Miss Robar, to think back to this past summer and the behaviour of your neighbour. Is it possible—?"

"That can't be! Candy is a child—"

"—possible the affair began before Mrs. Rafuse's unfortunate fall?"

"No...no...*no*. No! N-n-n-n-n-n-no! No!"

Princess Poo and Mister Mittens turned slowly to look at her, reacting to the shouted word in the same way they always did, which was not at all. Sir Scratchalot appeared from thin air on the back of the chesterfield and hissed at the detective.

"Miss Robar, I don't mean to upset you, but—" The man obviously did want to upset her, he was taking such delight. "—there is some evidence that Mrs. Rafuse was pushed down the stairs, and I believe that Mr. Rafuse did it. If he was having an affair with Miss

Krauss before his wife's passing, that would be the motive we've been looking for."

Millie ignored the dangling preposition. Rage overtook reason and grammar. "Tom did not push Rose down the stairs, and I can prove it!"

Millie surprised herself with those words. She was speaking and acting on instinct. She had no idea how to prove Tom's innocence, but she focused on doing so, so that she wouldn't have to think about Candy Krauss. Her mind simply could not process that!

What happened next would ensure that Tom's name would be forever linked to Millie's, even if he was not.

In a fury she rose, beckoning the detective to follow her through her immaculate kitchen, where she grabbed the key to Tom's house from a hook by the back door. She'd attached it to a heart shaped fob encrusted with fake rubies that she'd received as a gift from a niece at Christmas.

She led the detective across the driveway, through the back door and into Tom's kitchen. The cellar door was to the left of the refrigerator where, gathering snow in the freezer compartment, sat a lasagna, two tuna casseroles, a meatloaf and a Tupperware container of chicken and dumplings.

Millie opened the cellar door and Detective Himmelman entered. At the third step, he turned, looking up.

"This is where it hap—"

Unable to look at his misaligned moustache one more minute, Millicent Robar wielded the broom with which she'd so lovingly swept these steps just last week. Jousting with all her might, she shoved the disbelieving detective down.

It wasn't the fall that killed him.

The cause of death was blunt force trauma from the landing. And, this time, there was no question about the manner of death. It was murder, and the culprit was clear. Detective Himmelman's body was covered in cat hair.

Millicent Robar and Tom Rafuse were found guilty, in separate trials. Millicent sold her home to pay for her legal bills.

Candy Krauss moved into Tom's house. There she waited patiently for him to get out of prison while doting on her new companions, Mister Mittens, Princess Poo and Sir Scratchalot.

The Course

Daniel R. Lillford

Gracie Cheeseman believed that her husband went off the rails the night that Bundle died. Though she was at a loss to explain why, convinced as she was that he'd never really liked the cat. So why would the cat's death send an elderly man like Barney Cheeseman over the edge? She did not know. And neither did their few remaining friends in the dwindling St. James Anglican Church congregation, fellow members of the bowling club, and best friend Clementine, the Bridgetown librarian.

Most were genuinely shocked by Barney's bizarre criminal behaviour. Gossip reigned as gossip does, but remained as vacuous as a Facebook conversation. The truth was that nobody really knew anything.

One month, and one week before his 77th birthday, Barney was sitting in his small study next to the bathroom. He was trying to read but could not concentrate. Bundle's intermittent cries were distracting and distressing him. Barney knew that the little tabby was dying, and he figured that tonight was going to be her last stand.

He put the Graham Greene novel down, took off his spectacles and pinched the bridge of his nose, then slowly stood up, making sure not to put his back out. He walked quietly into the bathroom to look in on the emaciated cat lying in her box behind the bathtub.

She hadn't moved from the last time he'd looked. She lay flat, breathing heavily, and her eyes remained glassy, vacant. He crouched for a closer look. His right knee cracked, and he grimaced.

He thought of his father, a man who would not have given a

second thought about putting a sick cat in a sack with a brick in the river: "Putting it out of its misery," he'd have said. But Barney could not do that.

A sound he'd heard before, and not so long ago, started to peal from the cat. The death-rattle. He stood up, turned away and stared out of the small bathroom window that looked out upon the golf course. Bundle rattled on for a few minutes more, then a sad kind of high-pitched sigh ended it.

Barney felt his eyes moisten, but he kept his gaze on the 9th hole where a limp red flag clutched at its pole in the moonlight. "God speed, cat," he whispered.

Minutes later he bent down and reached out, touching the cat's fur. Her little body was still warm, but her eyes were without light. The cat, that had always lived in their bathroom, ever since Gracie had found it, bleeding from a head wound and half-dead, on Granville Street five years before was gone.

He walked out of the bathroom, through his study, down the stairs to the kitchen, then into the laundry. On the middle shelf he found a box of latex gloves.

Gracie was in bed reading when Barney's presence made her look up. He stood in the doorway, not venturing over the threshold.

"Cat's dead," he said.

She put her book down and stared at her husband, whose face was half-hidden in shadow, unable to read him.

"I'll bury her near the lilacs in the morning. It was quick...she didn't linger."

His voice sounded different. Slightly choked.

"Oh, dear...I should have stayed up with her, Barney. I thought she'd see the morning..."

"Makes no difference now. Besides, you said your goodbyes, so don't go all catholic on me. Just a cat."

He left the shadows of the doorway and she heard him go into the bathroom and run a tap.

"It was our cat, Barney! Our cat!" She didn't really believe he could be so hardhearted. That wasn't him. No, he was being flippant because that's how he dealt with unhappiness, with death.

~

At breakfast they exchanged few words. It was the routine. Gracie ate her Weetabix cereal while reading The *Chronicle-Herald;* Barney drank his coffee and listened to the local breakfast program on CBC radio.

The discussion today centred around an infestation of rats in downtown Halifax. He guffawed at the host's concerns about the possibility of disease being spread in the downtown core, then switched the radio off.

Gracie folded the paper and sighed. "No news in the paper today. Very slim."

"Yup. Nothin' interestin' on the radio either. Cat's in the laundry, if you want a final look before..."

He left the sentence hanging and stared out of the window.

"Will you make a little cross for her?"

Barney nodded. "Already have. Made it a few days back."

She followed her husband into the laundry. A small black and white Adidas shoe box sat on top of the washing machine. He took the lid off the box. The cat rested among what looked like scrunched-up balls of tissue paper.

Gracie stared at the tabby. She ran her fingers over the little body, then started to cry.

He put his large gnarled hands on her shoulders and held her close to him. He could smell the tea tree shampoo she used.

~

As he planted the shovel into the earth, he heard the first golf cart of the day approach the 9th green. He watched quietly from under the lilac trees as two obese men dressed in brightly coloured v-neck sweaters, one yellow, the other fuchsia, lumbered out of their cart and started searching for their balls. Mr. Fuchsia found his in the bunker and cursed openly at the lie. Mr. Yellow, who was also wearing an alarmingly tight pair of tartan shorts, found his ball in the rough just off the green.

As Barney dug the small grave for the cat, he recalled a gentler era when the golf course didn't have carts, when young boys made a few dollars caddying for the rich, when it used to be called a walking game and, above all, a gentleman's game. His father had been the head groundskeeper throughout the 1930s and into the Korean war years. As a boy Barney used to sit on the tractor with his father, who would let him steer the Massey-Ferguson down the big fairways, cutting the grass with the gang-mowers clanking behind. After school he'd wade into the water traps collecting golf balls in a net, to resell at the clubhouse for pocket money, money he diligently saved that would one day help pay for his first car, a '54 Olds.

The small shoe box went snugly into the hole he had dug beneath the lilacs. He heaped earth upon it. When he was done, a small pyramid of dirt lay at his feet. He patted the dirt down with the shovel, then walked off toward the shed.

He was about to open the old red door when a golf ball flew past his head and smashed into the shingles, chipped paint off the building, and bounced onto the lawn. Some clown had overshot their fairway drive. Not an unusual occurrence on this hole, a par three, which had deceived many a professional and legions of rank amateurs. He picked up the ball, a Callaway, and pocketed it.

A small wooden cross lay on his workbench among shavings and tools. In the middle of the cross he'd carved the cat's name, 'Bundle'. He picked up some sandpaper and took the cross off the bench. The maple wood felt smooth to his touch, but he gave it a gentle sand while thinking about the stain he'd use. Something red, he thought.

Old, unvarnished persimmon drivers and woods heads sat in a line like a collection of Peterson pipes, waiting for their hickory shafts. His father's work, from another age, when his father made his own wooden drivers during the long winter months, often filling for his small but growing boutique mail-order business with golfers who lived in the States. He remembered helping his father most winter nights, sanding and sanding. Always sanding.

Now he sat in what used to be his father's chair, and the apple box beside the bench was where he'd sat as a boy. The old valve radio, long dead now, waited on a shelf above the bench, and he recalled the warmth of its light, always a yellow hue, and the hum it made before it came on. It had kept them company with Don Messer's CBC show when the snow was three feet deep outside the shed door, and the small wood stove had kept them warm.

His father never spoke much when he was working, but he smiled a lot. Barney could still see the old man's crinkly blue eyes, called 'dancing eyes' by family and friends...Yup, another age.

He thought about how everything was made of steel now, from golf drivers to baseball bats. All cold, unwelcoming to the touch. He wondered about the world he lived in, the hardness he felt around him, the changing manufacturing mores. An old Gil Elvgrin calendar from 1957 still hung above the unvarnished drivers, faded and crumbling away at the edges. Miss June. Yesteryear's model. Beautiful. Gone.

He finished sanding the cross, and after giving it a once over, decided it was ready for staining. Remembering the golf ball in his pocket, he took it out and tossed it into a four-gallon bucket that was already half-full of lost balls.

As he stepped outside he heard the sound of a tractor. The head grounds keeper, Donald Hamilton, a man he did not like, parked the big blue Holland tractor most mornings on a blind rise where the trees met the rough. There he would take a break, sometimes a nap, for about 40 minutes. Then he'd wake up just in time for lunch.

Barney had watched 'old Mudguts', as he referred to Hamilton, and his sly ways for many years. He knew that the small crew of men that worked under him did all the real work; Hamilton merely coasted on their sweat and effort, scooping up the credit from the owners in the process. Barney had tried to tell the new English owners a few hard facts, being the elder retired grounds keeper living almost on the course, as he did, but they appeared uninterested, dismissive. It was clear to Barney that they thought that the sun shone out of Donald Hamilton's ass. 'Old Mudguts' had certainly pulled the wool over their eyes.

Not that Barney cared, but he hated seeing people duped by lazy scoundrels like Hamilton, even if these English owners smacked of Cumbrian peasantry trying ever so hard to be landed gentry. Some might be taken in by their accent, but not Barney.

Well, more fools they, he thought. Let Hamilton bleed you, because sure as hell I know he will.

~

They say you can tell a helluva lot about a business, about the boss, by the staff turnover rate. Since Donald Hamilton had wrangled the job as head grounds keeper some ten years back, Barney had counted 23 different grounds-men under his charge who had moved on after the golfing season was over for another year. They never came back. In his day, and in his father's time, the small crews remained the same groups of men year in, year out. They became fixtures at the course, seasonal friends to the regulars.

As Barney chewed on a tuna sandwich, he stared out the kitchen window at the half-hidden tractor, and the outlined lump of Hamilton asleep at the wheel. He spoke his mind: "Cream always rises to the top...so do turds."

~

Perhaps it was the sacrilege at the cat's grave later that week that finally tipped the balance, and something just snapped...Gracie could never be certain. She had come home from working at the St. James ACW salad plate luncheon to find Barney standing by the lilac trees, beside himself in fury. His face was the colour of beetroot, blotched, and he could hardly contain the spittle that was dribbling from the corners of his mouth. His fists were clenched and his whole body was as rigid as a steel pole.

Gracie approached him quickly with a sense of growing alarm. She'd never seen him like this before. She touched his arm. "Barney, what, what's wrong? What is it?"

Barney made noises, but no words formed. He pointed at the

cat's grave.

The mound of earth had been trampled over. Clear spike marks from a pair of golf shoes marked the earth where a deep weight had stood and hacked out a golf ball from below the lilacs. Some branches were bent in on themselves, as if they'd been pushed that way. The small wooden cross was broken and lying lopsided against the tree; placed there like a guilty afterthought.

It wasn't uncommon for golf balls to fly into the Cheesemans' back garden, but in all their years of living beside the course, no golfer had ever disrespected their private property by playing a shot from the garden to get back onto the green. Gracie was at a loss for words. It was like an ancient law had been violated.

She recalled a similar feeling when she'd lived in the city while studying to be a nurse, and had come back to her apartment one night to find it had been burgled. She felt that sick feeling again now, as she clutched at Barney's arm.

~

A Bard owl hooted. Gracie looked out into the garden, to the shed, and saw that the light was still burning strong. Barney was working on the new cross for the cat's grave.

She'd thought about asking him if he wanted a cup of hot chocolate, but decided against it. He was being uncommunicative, and she knew her husband well enough by now to just let him alone.

She made her hot drink and went upstairs to bed.

Barney stared at the new cross. He wasn't happy with it, and he knew why. He'd worked quickly, in anger, in haste, to right a wrong. And all he had accomplished was a second-rate job. His father would have looked at him in that way of his, and he would know by the look in his eyes that he was disappointed...as disappointed as Barney was with himself right now.

He threw the mallet across the room. "Shit...! Shit!"

He stabbed the chisel into the wood and left it there.

~

It was a muggy night. The air was heavy, pregnant with the perfumes of summer.

Barney decided to go for a walk around the course, to help drown out those voices inside his head. Walking the course was something he had done all his life, in all seasons; walking had always managed to clear the cobwebs away.

He made his way along the fairway and then cut through a stand of pines alongside the 7th tee. An owl hooted close by; its call was answered further afield. The gravel track that led to the maintenance sheds took him through an open steel gate. He was surprised it wasn't locked.

As he moved closer toward the main shed, intending to cut across the fairway that led to the 10th green, a dim light spilled from the workshop window, stopping him in his tracks. It was after 10 pm. Nobody should be around here now.

Curious, he decided to investigate. From the safety of the shadows, looking through the workshop window, he saw Donald Hamilton filling up gas cans out of the 44-gallon shop drum. Hamilton then put the gas cans in the back of his truck, which was parked alongside the tractors and the greens lawnmowers. Hamilton was helping himself to his employer's gasoline.

"You lowdown dirty bastard," Barney muttered. He wished he had a camera.

He watched Hamilton open the doors quietly, then drive his truck out into the yard without headlights. Hamilton lumbered out of the truck, locked up the shed, then placed the key where it was always kept, under a rock near the door. Then he got back into his truck and quietly drove away, still without lights on.

He won't put his lights on until he closes the gate, Barney thought, to keep those English fools up at the big house from noticing anything suspicious.

He held the shed key in his hand, a key to a padlock that hadn't been changed in over 30 years. He clicked open the lock and stood in the doorway of the shop.

The silhouettes of machinery, the smell of cut grass, gasoline, oil, mingled with greens chemicals and paint thinners. Quite the cocktail, one that still brought a smile to his face. There would be paint brushes resting in thinner on the large stained industrial sink, cleaning out the green enamel paint used for the numerous gates around the course.

He walked through the past, his past. The small office, a partition really, was quite bare. Gone were all the black and white photographs that he used to have on the walls there.

Paperwork lay on the oak desk, receipts stabbed on a spike, a telephone, scribble pad. Hamilton's coveralls hung from a hook near an army green metal filing cabinet.

A buxom young woman lying on the hood of a motor car stared temptingly at him from a calendar. Barney grimaced at the tattoos covering her arms.

The old Massey-Ferguson was still there. That made him smile. He ran a hand over the faded and chipped red mudguard. Everything else was relatively new, from the bright orange Kubota greens mowers to the big blue Holland tractor that towered over all. This was the one Hamilton used exclusively. An arrogant-looking machine, he thought. Imperious.

~

When the RCMP arrived at the golf course the following morning, there was a show of universal head-scratching. The Cooks, the English owners, were in a state of shock. Mr Cook was reported to have taken to his bed heavily sedated.

Some vandal had driven the big blue Holland tractor on quite the spree the night before. All the golf carts had been flattened, driven over. Complete write-offs. The greens on seven, nine, 10, 12, 13, 15 and 18 were ruined. Massive ruts crisscrossing each green's surface.

The tractor was half-submerged in the water trap on the 16th fairway.

Constable Laval stared at the tractor. "Whoever did this sure hates golf...Any ideas, Mr. Hamilton?"

Hamilton glanced briefly into the dark eyes of the police officer. He shook his head. "Kids, I expect. Goddamn vandals, I know that! Whole season's ruined. Ruined!"

Constable Laval consulted her map of the course, and the rough route of the tractor. "Kids, eh? Well, if they were kids, then they knew this course very well."

She pointed out to where the tractor had come from, where it went through, how each green had been approached and wrecked, and then how the tractor had gone by the fastest route to the next green, often bypassing the fairways. "There was no luck involved here. Whoever did this knew exactly what they were doing. And the maintenance shed was unlocked, so someone knew where to find the key to get at the tractor. Any ex-employees come to mind who might hold a grudge, Mr. Hamilton?"

Hamilton tried to laugh off her question, but he felt perspiration form on his temples. His neck started to go red. Ex-employees... where would he start? He remembered some who wouldn't think twice about punching him in the nose, given the opportunity.

The police officer did not drop her gaze. She was used to questioning the guilty, and there was something about Donald Hamilton that irked her, and she did not trust him. His furtive glances creeped her out.

"Perhaps we should start by going through the records of the past employees, eh?"

~

Later that morning, Gracie was nervously watching a police officer inspecting the damage on the 9th green. Constable Laval looked up, smiled, waved, and walked toward her.

"He...he's in the shed..."

The policewoman looked quizzically.

"My husband, Barney. In the shed." She pointed, a little offhandedly.

"Do you think I should speak to your husband, Mrs...?"

Gracie nodded, she reached for a handkerchief from her apron, dabbed at her eyes.

"Mrs. Cheeseman. I'm Mrs. Grace Cheeseman. This way, officer."

Gracie's birdlike frame moved quickly away from the lilac trees.

"Mrs. Cheeseman, do you know anything about what happened on the golf course last night?"

Gracie glanced at the constable. "It's, it's best you talk to my husband, officer. You see, he's not, not been himself since the cat died. I don't know what's happened to him."

Constable Laval wasn't quite sure if she'd heard right, but the sight of this frail old lady, obviously upset, left her hanging between knocking on the shed door and giving the old lady a hug.

The faint sound of music could be heard coming from within the shed. She thumped on the door. "Mr. Cheeseman, it's the police!"

A voice called from inside: "Door's unlocked, come in!"

The policewoman instinctively placed her right hand on her holster as she lifted the latch on the door and opened it.

Barney Cheeseman was standing beside the wood stove. He was wearing golfing attire from the late 1930s: forest Tweeds, plus fours, Argyle socks and two-tone leather shoes. They had once been his father's clothes. The RCMP officer from Quebec thought he looked like an elderly version of Tin Tin.

The music she had heard was coming from a small tape recorder. Julie London was singing about a cottage for sale. Barney turned the tape off.

"Ah, Mr. Cheeseman, I just want to ask—"

"I did it...I'm your man."

Constable Laval stared, mildly intrigued.

Gracie stood in the doorway, her face red from crying. "Oh, Barney..."

"I see. Could you tell me exactly what it is you have done, Mr. Cheeseman?"

"Certainly. I destroyed half the greens on the course, and I flattened those lousy, rhino-butt carryin' golf carts. Oh, and sent that lazy, thievin' sonofabitch's big tractor into the water trap on the 16th. I think that about covers it."

"Okay...Would you care to, to tell me why you did it?"

Barney shrugged, glanced at Gracie. He moved toward the workbench and picked up some sandpaper. A small wooden cross lay on the bench, the name 'Bundle' carved out in the middle. He gently sanded the edges. When he spoke, it was in a quiet and measured tone.

"It used to be a walkin' game, you know. A gentleman's game... Ladies', too. That was a long time ago. Nowadays it's populated by the fat men. Slobs in carts. Rushin' all over the place like lunatics, an' seein' nothin' in the process. You can't see the beauty of the landscape like that. I doubt they'd even notice a cardinal singin', or the chickadees chirrupin', dartin' between the trees, as the sun starts to rise over the putting greens. Such a wonderful time of day...No, sir. No style. Just loud. Too goddamn lazy to walk, too fat to exercise. Too rich to care. The course is nothin' but a blur to them, an exercise in killing time, a seasonal status symbol. There is no love of the world, what we created here, what my father helped create...No love of the game neither, not really, not as it was meant to be played. Blind ignorance never did appreciate truth nor beauty."

He stopped sanding, put the cross down, then looked at a black and white photograph on the shelf where the old valve radio was. The photograph depicted a crew of grounds men from the 1930s, all dressed it shirts, ties, vests, cloth caps and plus fours. They were smiling, happy.

"I guess it's just a different world...And I guess I hate it."

Constable Laval looked at the cross. "Who was Bundle?"

Tears slid gently down Barney Cheeseman's face. "The cat. She used to live in the bathroom..."

Gracie made her way to stand by her husband. She rested her head on his shoulder.

Constable Laval took a good look around the shed, and considered the old-world charm of Mr. Barney Cheeseman. This morning, this summer's morning, she wished she wasn't a cop.

Mrs. Weasley and the Red Dress

Kathy Brooks

Mrs. Weasley inserted the key, then pulled the door knob as she simultaneously pushed the bottom of the door with her foot. The key made a satisfying click.

As she entered, she could smell the faint scent of lavender that lingered in the shop. She took a quick look around, admiring the polished floor and the rainbow of coloured dresses hanging neatly on the racks. The window display needed a dusting, but the bright green evening dresses and the mustard-yellow scarves she had displayed still looked fresh and inviting.

As Mrs. Weasley hung up her coat in the back room, the door of the shop opened and Genie bounced in. "Good morning, Mrs. Weasley. Am I late? I don't think I'm late. But the bus seemed awfully slow today. I'll get to work right away. Let me just put my lunch in the fridge."

"I hope you didn't bring any more of that salami in your sandwiches. That made quite the odour the other day."

"No, no, Mrs. Weasley. I won't do that again. Today is just cheese and lettuce. You won't smell a thing."

Genie went into the back room to hang up her coat and put her lunch in the fridge. "What would you like me to do today?" she called. "I could do some dusting or sort out the paperwork."

"Please, Genie, don't shout to me from another room. It's so unladylike."

"Sorry, Mrs. Weasley," Genie said as she came out of the back room. "I won't do it again. What would you like me to start on today?"

Mrs. Weasley glanced around the shop. "The dust can wait.

Tuesdays are usually quiet. I think we should start on the inventory."

"Right-o, Mrs. Weasley. Good idea."

"But if a customer arrives, make sure they don't realize what we're doing. I find my ladies don't like to think they're interrupting us."

"Yes, I've noticed that, too. They seem to worry they'll mess up our system."

Mrs. Weasley pulled out a sheaf of papers from under the counter, affixed them to a clipboard and searched for a red pen. Genie stood ready at the first row of dresses hanging by the door. "No, we don't start there, Genie. We always start with the scarves. Okay, count the blue floral ones. Let's see, there should be—"

"Seven! There's seven here."

"Genie, wait until I tell you how many there should be or we'll get mixed up!"

"Sure, Mrs. Weasley, sure. I understand,"

"Okay, there should be six mustard-coloured scarfs."

"Mustard, mustard. I love that colour. Whoops, there's only five of them."

"What! Count them again."

"One, two, three, four, five..."

Just then the door to the shop opened. Mrs. Weasley expertly placed the clipboard behind her back and Genie refolded the scarves. A large, well-dressed woman bustled in.

"Good morning, Miss Evans. So good to see you again," Mrs. Weasley said. "How's your cousin, Emily doing? You said she was suffering horribly from chilblains last time you were in."

"Oh, you remembered. You're so sweet. That's why I came in today. She's improving, but I thought she could use a little treat so I thought I'd buy her a scarf to cheer her up."

"Lovely idea!" Mrs. Weasley slipped the clipboard out of sight behind the counter. "Genie, lay out an assortment of scarves for Miss Evans, please."

After much indecision and discussion about colours and textures, Mrs. Weasley convinced her customer that the purple-striped scarf would be best. "It's muted enough to go with many outfits but just colourful enough to make a statement, don't you think?"

Genie wrapped it up, including a small sprig of lavender in the package. Mrs. Weasley knew every time her clients caught the scent of lavender, they would think of her dress shop.

Miss Evans trotted off, smiling.

Genie looked at Mrs. Weasley after the door shut. "Is there really such a thing as chilblains?"

"Now, Genie, we never even think to question our customers. If she said chilblains, then chilblains it is."

Mrs. Weasley and Genie returned to their inventory. Genie pointed out the reason there weren't six mustard-coloured scarfs on the shelf was that one was on the dress in the window display.

"Of course. Good work, Genie."

They finished the scarves and moved on to the dresses. "Let's start with the green print dresses over there. There should be two small, one medium and three large."

"Check, check, check," said Genie.

"Genie, please, there's no room for error here. Please give me the numbers."

"Two small, one medium and three large!"

"Thank you. Yellow florals...let's see...one small, one medium and one large."

"Exactly...I mean one small, one medium and one large," Genie said. She held one of the yellow dresses up in front of her. "What do you think of this colour on me, Mrs. Weasley?"

"Yellow is definitely not your colour. And besides. where would you ever wear a dress like that?"

"Remember, I mentioned my sister is getting married soon? I was hoping to get a new dress for the wedding. I've been saving and saving. I thought I had enough but then my stupid tooth started aching. I had to dip into my savings for that dumb dentist."

"Yes, well, teeth are more important than new dresses."

"I know. I guess I'll have to wear my old pink dress again. It's been to quite a few weddings."

"Enough chatter: let's continue. Okay...the red dresses now. Let's see, there should be only one left in size small."

Genie shuffled through the rack, then went back and looked carefully through the rack again. "I'm not seeing any red dresses at all."

"Look again. It's hard to lose a bright red dress."

They both looked thoroughly through the clothes racks but there was no red dress.

"I'm sure it's here somewhere," Mrs. Weasley said. "I think I would have remembered if we'd sold the last one."

"Do you want me to go through the receipts?"

"Yes, check to see if we sold it. I need to take a little stroll."

About this time of morning Mrs. Weasley would take a break. She couldn't bring herself to say 'toilet' or 'bathroom' so she always referred to her 'little stroll'.

Genie took one last look around the shop while Mrs. Weasley went into the back room to the toilet. This time Genie looked on the shelves and under the dress racks.

To her surprise, crumpled on the floor underneath the long robes, she caught a glimpse of red. She reached in and pulled out the wrinkled, but still lovely, red silky dress. She held it out in front of her and stared at it in amazement.

"How did you ever get there?" She asked the dress.

Just then she caught a glimpse of herself and the red dress in the mirror. She moved closer. She held the dress in front of her and stared at her reflection.

With only a moment's hesitation she moved to the counter, wrapped the dress in tissue and stuffed it in her large bag.

When Mrs. Weasley returned from her little stroll, Genie was carefully going through the sales receipts.

~

That evening Genie rushed home, climbed the stairs to her one-room flat, and closed and locked the door. She pulled the red silky dress from her bag and held it out in front of her. She moved to her full-length mirror. With a big smile, she began sashaying around the room, then dancing to a tune in her head. She thought the dress swirled and swung just beautifully. She danced faster and faster, a blur of red.

Breathing heavily, she stopped and hung the dress on her closet door where she could admire it. The light from the street seemed to focus right on the dress; everything else in the room was muted as the daylight ebbed away. Still she stood staring at the dress.

Then her smile faded as if an inner switch had turned off. She sunk to her knees and buried her face in her hands. She knelt like that for a few minutes, glancing from time to time at the dress that now looked like it was in a spotlight from the street lights.

A knock on the door made Genie jump. She lurched to her feet and flicked on the light switch.

Her sister's familiar voice called out, "Are you going to let me in or not?"

Genie rushed to open the door and her sister Eloise came in, all business as usual. "Did you forget that I told you I was coming by after work? I want your opinion on these two veils. Which one do you think will go best with my wedding dress?"

As Eloise turned to the mirror to hold up the veils, the silky red dress caught her eye. "My goodness, Genie! However could you afford such a gorgeous dress? Mrs. Weasley must have given you a good deal!"

Genie was silent just a second too long and Eloise turned to look at her directly. "Why, what's the problem?"

"I...I'm thinking, well, I've decided...yes, I've decided not to keep the dress. I can't really afford it."

"Well, you would have to buy a pair of heels to go with it. I told you not to buy pink shoes. Now you're stuck. You'll have to wear your old pink dress. Quite honestly, I'm a bit tired of that dress, but what can you do?"

After Eloise left, Genie had a bowl of tomato soup with saltines, all the time staring at the dress. When she climbed into bed, the dress still glowed from the streetlight. After twenty minutes of tossing and turning, she got up, folded the dress in the tissue and placed it back in her large bag.

~

The next day at work, Mrs. Weasley was still fussing over the missing dress. "In all my years, I don't recall losing a dress or forgetting to note a sale." She kept sifting through the receipts and muttering angrily.

Mid-morning, she sighed loudly and announced she would take her morning stroll. When she went into the back room, Genie leapt into action, taking the dress from her bag and shaking it from the tissue. She quickly hung it on a hanger at the end of the nearest rack.

When Mrs. Weasley reappeared, Genie stood proudly in front of the dress. Mrs. Weasley stopped suddenly with her mouth hanging open in a very unladylike way.

"Look what I found!" Genie said. "I did another search of the dress racks and it had somehow fallen behind the display case over there. I just caught a glimpse of red while I was dusting."

Mrs. Weasley took the dress from the rack, and held it out in front of her, staring in amazement. "That has never happened in all my years in this shop. How could it possibly fall down and we wouldn't notice? I think, Genie, we must be getting a bit sloppy."

"I'm surprised too. It's only a bit wrinkled and it's not dusty, so it couldn't have been there long."

"I think I'll mark it down any way. We'll be getting a new shipment of dresses soon."

Mrs. Weasley busied herself adjusting the price, muttering to herself this time in a pleased manner.

Customers came and went, some admiring the red dress but no one buying it. Genie took a quick break to eat her cheese sandwich and Mrs. Weasley did the same a bit later.

The day passed quickly. Genie had learned to look busy moving around the shop, dusting, straightening the racks of dresses after a customer had gone through them. Refolding the already perfect piles of scarves. Mrs. Weasley didn't like to see her standing around idle. Between chores, Genie stole glances at the red dress. She straightened it so often on its hanger that Mrs. Weasley commented that the dress was just fine the way it was.

"Don't keep handling it. The oil from your fingers can leave marks!"

At six o'clock, Mrs. Weasley locked the shop door and flicked the open sign over. In her practised way, she expertly counted the cash and filed the receipts. Genie fetched her bag and coat and waited by the front door until Mrs. Weasley was finished. Mrs. Weasley liked Genie to wait until the cash drawer was empty and the float safely hidden under some old sales records in a box in the storage room.

As Mrs. Weasley came out of the storage room wiping her hands together she stopped in front of the red dress. "Genie, I've decided I want you to have this dress. The red will look beautiful on you at your sister's wedding."

Genie stood completely still with her hand on the door knob. She stared at Mrs. Weasley.

"Well, don't just stand there, Genie. Let's wrap it up for you." Mrs. Weasley carefully slipped the dress off the hanger and begin wrapping it in tissue.

Genie finally let go of the door knob. "But...but, Mrs. Weasley, that's a very expensive dress. You can't just give it to me!"

"Yes, I can. I've been thinking about it all day. You're a good worker, Genie. You deserve to wear something special to your sister's wedding."

"I don't know how I can ever thank you. This is too much! I never expected a gift like this from you."

"All right, all right, Genie." Mrs. Weasley laid the folded dress carefully in Genie's large bag. "Let's get going, I don't want to be here all night."

Again, Genie moved toward the door. Just as she reached for the door knob again Mrs. Weasley called out, "You and I have the same size feet, don't we?"

"Yes, we're both size seven."

"I thought so," said Mrs. Weasley. "That's just great. I have a pair of red strappy sandals—very flashy ones, if I do say so myself. I'll loan them to you."

Genie began to sputter a reply, but Mrs. Weasley shooed her out the door.

"Just be careful dancing! Don't let any of those clumsy boys step on the shoes."

Far and Wide

Being a writer in rural Nova Scotia does not mean writing only about the bright lupines along the highway exit, the visit to Frenchys, or the sound your canoe makes as it pushes through the reeds at the edge of Lake Joli. Although we write *here*, all the world is fair game to write about.

We are not content to accept the conventions of urban novels and Hollywood movies: we push back with our view, our stories, and our way of telling them.

The Family Business

P. E. R. Sprague

What is our family business, you ask? Well, it's complicated; and most people would say it ain't our business. You see, my family worked for Johnny Torrio's gang back in Brooklyn, and then Chicago. Johnny Torrio got shot and Al took over.

And that's where I came into the picture.

I missed out on the "good old days", as my father called them, back in the Home City. But things weren't too bad in Chicago. Coppers were in Al's pockets and he ran the place nice and neat-like. It was Hoover's boys we couldn't get off our backs. So, when things got too rough, Al moved north across the border until things cooled off.

He placed Pops in charge there in Moose Jaw. We were to keep the place neat and running for when Al needed to escape Chicago. And if that was all we did, it'd be a fine business.

I wasn't born under Johnny Torrio like my brothers were. All I'd known was Chicago. Life had grown calm once I came 'round. Especially once we moved to Moose Jaw. Too quiet. Flappers and booze kept my brothers busy for only so long. Al rarely showed up, and by this time it had been two years since we'd seen him.

It was the prohibition down in the States, and that was Pops' avenue. So he set up shop in them old steam tunnels that ran under the streets. Brewing booze for the rum-runners to haul below the border.

The "Chicago Connection", it came to be called. And it was boomin'. Miss Fanny's speakeasy was a perfect front and the booze flowed upstairs to her as well. Pops had built his own rule in Moose Jaw.

"Little Chicago" it came to be known, and the city thrived. And all under Al's nose, without him knowing, of course. Frank Nitti, Al's right hand man, ran Al's other bootlegging operations and would not look kindly on us moving in on his turf. Neither would Al, for that matter. So we kept it all hush-hush.

There were the dark corners, as there are in every city where there are businessmen such as my family's. But my brother Louie, "The Badger", dealt with the dirty jobs. Why "The Badger?" Well, you try sticking your bare toes in a badger hole and see what happens.

He was a short man, shorter even than me and I ain't no beanstalk, with a swinging temper. He was Pops' number two man. Number one being Luca, first born and all.

Giuseppe would have been second, but he was too much of a crooner to care about running the business. He did what he was asked, sure, but then ran to the very next doll's lap when the job was finished.

That was my family. Either it was all they wanted, or they did what was needed to keep Pops happy and enjoy their money and glad rags.

That's why I didn't fit with the family. I loved Pops, but I didn't want his life. I took a job as a typesetter for the newspapers. It wasn't glamorous, I wasn't lousy with dough or dames, but it was an honest living. And Pops knew that. So long as I continued to do a few jobs on the side, he'd leave me be.

Like Louie, I got a shameful nickname: Franky "Fingers". "Lightest fingers in the Chicagos," Luca used to say. I was a born dip, and Pops used me to his advantage.

And that was my life: typesetting by day and swiping pockets by night. I even found my own romance: Miss Trixie, one of Miss Fanny's girls. She was my life, I worshipped her. We often talked long hours about leaving Moose Jaw and heading west. Or maybe south.

But in the end, I couldn't abandon my family. Pops would take that as a slap to the face. He'd been good to me, and life was pleasant enough. A good job, a beautiful doll by my side, and a peaceful life.

Until Al returned.

One day during the height of Pop's bootlegging operation Miss Fanny gave him a ring. Heat was on in Chicago and Al was coming. In fact, he'd already arrived. The slice of freedom I had carved out for myself was taken away. The family was in need, and you don't turn your back on your family.

Pops, Louie, Giuseppe, Sonny, and myself sat cramped around a card table in a filthy tunnel. Luca paced in front of the Victrola; Count Basie, of course. There was always music down there. I don't think Luca could concentrate without jazz filling the tunnels.

"You said he'd never come!" Luca poured us a draft of his rye whisky and finished off his bottle. "We'll be found out and we'll all be taking dirt naps by morning. If he's in a kind mood. He ain't blind."

"Calm down, Luca! It will be fine," Pops said. "I sent Johnny to Saskatoon on an errand." Johnny we'd nicknamed "The Squealer", for obvious reasons. It was best that he wasn't around. "We will get rid of the supplies."

Pops then gave us our duties. I was to head upstairs to Miss Fanny's and help get rid of the booze. Al was unaware that we were stocking a speakeasy, not to mention selling stuff by the barrel to bootleggers. It had to go. Load up the trucks and haul it all out of the city.

It was a Saturday night, Miss Fanny's was filled with smoke, and flappers filled the stage. Trixie was front and centre.

Any other night I'd be sitting front row. But my duty was to guard the door and keep an eye on Al's men. It was well into the evening, so most of the folks were half under. About this time my brothers would have been sorting out the riff-raff, threatening them or throwing them out. But that night we had to allow the boys their fun; we had too much to take care of.

The barrels were loaded and Sonny was pulling out of the yard when Frank came through the door. He was Al's right hand, as I said before. Pops said I was named after him. It was supposed to be an honour, but I didn't see any honour in it. But I put on a face.

"Mr. Nitti!" I said. "Things getting a little heavy south of the border?"

"Yes." He said it without even looking at me. Frank Nitti never spoke directly to people like me; we weren't worth the effort. "Everything is in good and working order, I expect?"

"Yes, sir."

And that was all he said. That was their way. We were the who's who of Moose Jaw, but according to Al and his boys we were nothing more than hotel management. My father was Salvatore Campione, for God's sake! We deserved better than that. But we were nobodies to Frank.

He moved on by and sat next to Jerome and Michael, the two biggest loose-lipped drunkards in the club. Being so busy getting rid of the booze, we never thought to get of them; and they knew far too much.

"Where are they taking the booze?" Michael asked nobody.

"Big boys must be in town," Jerome said.

"Quiet."

"No need to be quiet for my sake, gentlemen," Frank said.

"Nothing to say, good man."

"I'll buy you a round."

Silence.

"I'll pay your tab."

And that was all it took. Michael spilled like a tipped barrel. "Well, it's the Campiones, you see. They may run the city, but they're run by a bigger crowd."

"They run the city, you say?"

"Where are you from, son, not to know who the Campiones are?"

"From Chicago, I'm afraid. Whisky, please, barkeep."

I couldn't believe my ears. Those damn drunks spilled everything. We were done for.

I headed to the tunnels, Pops would still be down there, waiting. And he was, drinking with Louie.

"What is it, Franky?" Louie said. He was a mean son-of-a-bitch, but he knew when his brother was in a panic.

I told them everything. Pops didn't say a word. He looked to

Louie and my brother was out the door.

"I need you to help Louie."

"Help him do what?"

"The rest of the boys gots their hands full. You're here, and I need you." He put his hand on my shoulder and squeezed, gentle but firm. "After this, I will never call on you again. Take Trixie and live your life."

"What is Louie going to do?"

"Go to the office and wait for him. He'll tell you what to do."

I didn't argue. There was no time. And what would I have said? You don't say no to Pops. I followed the familiar tunnels to what we called an office. It was a small room with a concrete floor, a desk, a switchboard, and a chair on wheels.

A man was sitting in the chair, bound to it with rope around his wrists and chest and a gag distorting his mouth. It was Michael, and Louie was finishing the knot. How he was able to make it to Fanny's and back in such a hurry I'll never know.

"What are you going to do to him?"

"I'm not doing nothing, I gotta head out and grab Jerome." Louie placed his Smith & Weston in my hand. "Bump this mick off and drag his body out to the river before he does more damage."

Louie left me with the revolver. Michael tried to cry out, but the gag choked him. It was wet from his tears.

I stared at him. His face red and puffy. He knew better, sure. But did this deserve death?

'Help Louie' Pops had said. This was his last request. If I shot him I'd be done with it, and could go on with my life with Trixie. Or refuse, and be looked down on by my family. What greater shame was there? Not much of a choice. I did what I had to do.

I dropped the revolver after the kick, after the echo, and while the blood poured down Michael's face. I'd done it, I'd become my family. It had to be done.

But the job wasn't done yet. Michael wasn't small, and I had to drag him to the river.

A dirt tunnel led to the river bank. Weights and chains were already waiting for us, not so much in preparation for this job, but as a constant precaution. But I wrapped the body in the chains and dragged it into the shallow water.

"What's all this?" a voice from the dark asked.

"Who's there?" All I saw was a flick of a match and burning end of a cigarette.

"Erasing evidence?"

"What do you want?" Louie said from behind me. He had come through the tunnel, too, dragging Jerome.

"Honestly, Louie. With your reputation I'd expect better," the voice said.

"I'll ask again—"

"Its not what *I* want." He stepped out of the shadows and I saw his face. His long, ugly face; Frank. "You all seem to have been busy while we were away. Al is not too pleased with you."

"We've been keeping the place running and ready for Al's return, like we were instructed," I said.

"Please. You don't think me that dumb-witted, do you, boy? You're cleaning up your mess."

Louie blurted, "Damned Scarface leaves us here to rot—"

"Watch your mouth. If Al hears that name....Come with me. He's waiting."

Two others stepped out of the darkness, Thompson machine guns in hand.

So Frank led us to our deaths. Down familiar streets and up familiar stairs and through familiar rooms. We knew where we were being led. This was to be my end. Even if I hadn't shot Michael and become my family this would be my end.

"Franky," Louie whispered to me. "You need to make a run for it."

"What?"

"You deserve better than this."

"Everyone's been saying that. You've all got a bad way of showing your concern."

"It's the family way."

"Fine excuse, Louie."

"It's too late for me; for us. But not for you. Go!"

Louie drew the revolver from his ankle holster. Before I could say "Bob's your uncle" he fired at the gunmen at our backs.

The two Tommy Guns unloaded into Louie's chest. He did it for me. They were distracted now, I could run for it. They were more interested in turning him into Swiss cheese.

So, I ran. I knew the tunnels well enough that I was able to keep ahead. I scrambled up the back stairs that led to Miss Fanny's. Should be a large enough crowd there for good cover.

I stopped at the top to listen for them running after me. Nothing. No footsteps; no voices; no gunshots. I turned the knob, but in my hurry I forgot which room that stairway led to before it reached Miss Fanny's club.

Al's chambers. A study meant for the boss alone. We were to leave it be. We didn't. A perfectly good study with unused quality cigars was a crime to my father. Pops was destined for greatness and he would not stay idle. But he should have.

For now my father and my brothers, except Louie of course, stood against the wall with a barrel aimed at each one. Luca's face was a bloody pulp; Sonny was of course drunk; and Giuseppe, clueless, stared at his shoes. Pops stared across the desk at the plump man sitting there.

Al's hat sat on the desk; a soggy stogie dangled from his lips. I had only seen him in person once before. I suppose it was the hype, the drama, but this man did not instill fear. I knew he was dangerous; everybody knew that. But he showered us with nothing but kindness when we were allies and he looked almost gentle. Like a loving uncle.

"Where is Louie?" Pops asked. I couldn't look him in the eye.

"No time to waste then. Salvatore," Al mouthed the words around his cigar, "I've been informed that you have been threatening my position."

"I haven't—"

"Quiet!" Al slammed his fat fist onto the desk. The fear was there now. "You've raised your own little rule. Fingers in every pocket, and everyone in your own. Who do you think you are? Is this your operation?"

Pops sat in silence. It was unsettling to see my father so submissive. But what could he possibly say?

"I'm not an unreasonable man," said Al. "Nor am I entirely un-caring. I've taken care of you, have I not?"

"You have, sir."

"Then I will give you one choice before the end. Your end will come shortly and each one of your sons is joining you...except one."

"One?"

"I can't allow all of you to be free. Everyone will think they can betray me. The next man I set in charge will be obedient. But I am not unreasonable. One of your boys will be spared. You choose."

This was worse than torture for my father. He was a hard man, but he loved his sons.

"Franky," he said without hesitation. My knees buckled and I nearly collapsed.

"The family traitor?"

"He is not a traitor." My father looked Al in the eyes for the first time. Like I said, he loved us, and he wouldn't allow anyone to speak ill of us. Not even Al Capone. "Franky is meant for greater things. That is my decision."

"All right, then." And that was it. Tommy guns, for the second time that evening, echoed off the walls and into my family. Guns clapped, blood sprayed, and heads rolled. In one single night my family was gone.

"Let him go." At Al's word they opened the door and pushed me out. "I suggest you leave town, boy."

"I will, sir."

"I wish you the best."

I think I said 'thank you" but I don't remember.

The door shut behind me and the next thing that I can remember is walking into Fanny's club, grabbing Trixie, and kissing her with everything I had. I remember weeping with her, but I don't remember where.

We lived out her desires. We moved west, to British Columbia, to start a new life. Once I reached the west coast the story about Moose Jaw and my family name had spread.

I set up shop, in honour of Pops, and soon it will be passed on to my own boys. We stay clear of Al, but he knows who we are and I'm sure he stays clear of us.

It is a gritty and dirty job; but, after all, it is the family business.

Off Camera

Grace Keating

"I took a deep breath and knocked on the door, Marj, just like you said."

"And...?"

"Well, nothing. Nobody said nothing, so I stepped in. And, just like you said, they were going at it like bunnies."

"Actors. Jeez, you'd think they'd have the decency to at least lock the door. What did you say, Tina?"

"I asked them to remove their wardrobe. Nicholas was still in his tux shirt from the wedding scene this morning and Sarah's gown was crumpled on the floor. I also mentioned that it's a damn unfair world, where by the simple chance of being born with good looks, 'cause lord knows you can't act, either of you, you get to fuck in your work day and make a lot of money doing it, while the rest of us get to do everything for you and treat you like gods and we make less money in a week that you make taking one single breath of air."

"You're kidding, right? You didn't say that!"

"Of course I'm kidding. I want to keep my job, don't I? I said, 'Oh, sorry. I did knock.'"

"What is it with actors that they can't wait till they get back to their hotel? Okay, then what?"

"I said, 'I'll hang your next change here. sir.' And I looked straight at Sarah and said, 'Yours is in your trailer, ma'am.' She just stared back at me, blank-eyed and all serious-like. So I added, 'Oh, and would you like me to hold on to your falsies? You wouldn't want them to slip out at some embarrassing moment.'"

"You did not! Very funny. She'll be out of that trailer in about ten minutes to make sure you're not posting something on Facebook. Nice job walking in on our two leads caught in the act. Watch, tomorrow our department will get a big bouquet of flowers and a bottle of red wine. It's always red. He won't want word of this getting out, either. She's the hot new flavour of the month and it would spread like wildfire."

"You know Annie's in love with him, don't you?"

"What? Back-up, back-up! Our Annie?"

"They've been seeing each other for a few weeks and he's telling her he's going to leave his wife. Shit, can I go home? I don't wanna talk to Sarah or Annie. What am I supposed to say?"

"Remind me, how many times have I said, 'Stay away from the cast, the director and the producers, they're out of our league'? He doesn't give a damn about Annie."

"What do I tell her? And what do I say to Sarah? What a shit she is."

"Wait a sec. First off, Sarah is not a shit, Nicholas is, and don't forget that. And second, what you say to Annie is the truth, that you walked in on him and Sarah and the sooner she forgets him the better. What you say to Sarah is, you know she's tense about the sex scene she has with him tomorrow. Today was just a rehearsal. That gives her an out."

"I don't blame either of them, though, Sarah or Annie. I wouldn't kick him out of bed."

"He's a manufactured image, that's all he is. And he has the brains to go with it, which is zero."

"That sounds a bit harsh. Let me guess, did you once fall for a star, Marj?"

"Yeah, I fell for a star. I flew to Los Angeles, rented a car and drove to the resort where we were supposed to meet, only he didn't show up. He wasn't there."

"What the hell did you do? I bet he didn't answer his cell either. What a shit. I'd wanna wring his neck, and that's not all I'd wanna do. I'd wanna do worse, far worse."

"This was in the days before cellphones, and the number I had for him was disconnected. So I drove to his house and parked across the street. I walked up the circular drive to the front door and rang the bell. A maid answered. I had the feeling it wasn't the first time she'd opened the door to a young woman in love. Some kid was chasing another kid across the hallway. My heart sank. I said to the maid, 'He's married, isn't he?' She nodded."

"Oh, Marj, I'm so sorry. What an asshole."

"It was a long time ago. I was sitting in the car with my head on the steering wheel, crying. Eight months, eight months we were together. I'd even followed him for a two-month shoot in Mexico, and then I was to meet him in LA."

"What happened? I don't know what I would've done."

"There was a knock on the passenger door window: his father, a big star himself. He sat in beside me, didn't look at me, didn't say much. My guy was still living in the family mansion and a scandal would've muddied his dad's name too. He handed me a cheque for fifty thousand dollars. Asked me if I would be decent about it. Go away quietly. And I don't know if he was being kind or mean when he told me I wasn't the first."

"I would've ripped it up and thrown it in his face."

"I think I really did love him, but at least I knew enough to hate him as well. And no, you wouldn't have ripped up the cheque. I was coming to tell him we were going to have a baby."

"That's Laurel?"

"That's my Laurel. She's the best thing that ever happened to me, but still, tell Annie to get out while she can, and shit-for-brains Nicholas doesn't love her."

Stricken

Rhoda C. Hill

The old farm house was stuffy and Lambert O'Malley had stepped out onto the porch, leaving his front door open in an effort to let the cool air enter and drive out the heat. He was the only person in town who dared open his doors and windows at all.

Mosquitoes gathered around the blue glow of his bug zapper and the occasional buzz sounded as their tiny bodies hit the wire mesh. Moths flocked to the porch light, flying sporadically as they mistook its glow for the navigational pull of the moon. The light was no substitute, but the crazy insects didn't have the God-given sense to realize that.

Canadian National Television's top Roborg, One-o-Ten, panned outward to take in the whole farm, land and dwelling. Lambert could see his eyes contract, to cover it all, and then enlarge and knew that it was zeroing in on the farm house, and on him.

One-o-Ten was standing directly in front of him, but its panorama vision let it stand up close and still take in all its surroundings.

Roborgs confused Lambert. They had super-human intelligence, and walked, just as fluidly as humans, on bionic limbs that never tired. Their temperature-controlled silicon-skin looked and felt as real as his own. So it was always hard to tell if he should greet them in the same manner that one would a human. It seemed polite to offer tea, but he wasn't certain they could consume anything at all, let alone a cup of tea, and up until now he had had no inclination to find out for sure.

For the most part, the world left him alone. People talked about what once was and marvelled over the old man who did not succumb. But for the most part everyone knew it would be pointless to waste time on him. He was just doing what he knew to do: eat, breathe, work, and live. There were no secrets to tell. Nothing special about him and his routine. He was as common and simple as baked beans and homemade bread.

But then, homemade anything wasn't considered simple anymore, so that wasn't as accurate an analogy as it would have once been. To Lambert it was simple, because he, unlike most people, still made his own bread and soaked lentils overnight before slowly letting them bake to perfection the next day.

Lambert was remembering the swine flu pandemic forty-four years earlier. Now with the strain of the VIM flu, the world wanted to know how people had managed during other pandemic times, and sadly those who had lived and could tell about it were few and far between.

"I remember they locked us in our house at first," Lambert recalled. "My mom was sick, and Dad tried to keep me, Lily, and Foster away from her as much as possible." He smiled a bitter-sweet smile, and ran a hand through the thick cloud of unkempt grey hair. "But Foster was a momma's boy, and one night he slipped into bed with her. She was so sick she didn't even notice him there until morning."

A few tweaking sounds indicated that One-o-ten was either panning out or zooming in on Lambert; no doubt the latter. It unsettled him, and he lifted his mug to sip in an effort to hide his face.

"When Foster took sick, mom took a turn for the worse."

"And how did your mother contract the flu?"

Lambert knew where this was headed. They blamed his dad. He'd been jeered at about it in the past. But that was years ago. The world had finally pointed its blame elsewhere, or found something new to scoff at.

With the VIM on the rise, people were remembering him again. He had wondered if this would happen. Had hoped it wouldn't, but a nagging suspicion warned him it would. And no doubt exposure on CNT would bring the crazies out of the woodwork.

He looked at One-o-Ten, and smiled despite the burning desire to sock him one between his shifty eyes. "My dad worked for a special drug enforcement team with the RCMP, and went Mexico to train their police in search and seizure. When he came back he was fine, but he was carrying the bug. Within a couple of days he was sick. He started to feel better just as my mother started to get symptoms."

Lambert shifted uneasily as the Roborg panned up from his feet to his face. He didn't wear a face mask like most of the residents on Vancouver Island, and it made him self-conscious. He didn't want the world to see him on CNT and think him presumptuous. If he'd known One-o-Ten was coming, he'd have purchased a face mask or fashioned one from scratch to give the illusion of doubt: let the world see he was not as self-assured as he seemed to be.

But, of course, One-o-Ten had approached his home un-announced and caught Lambert off guard, just standing on his porch willingly breathing in the toxic air without so much as a scarf around his mouth. Everything about him, from his slippered feet to his uncovered face, screamed ease and relaxation. His cocky appearance alone would probably get his windows smashed, and his name and face plastered over every bulletin and screen across Canada.

"My brother was the first to die," his voice cracked. "I remember the night he died we got the call that Lily's swab had tested positive for the flu and my own was negative."

"Did you do anything different that prevented you from contracting the flu?"

Lambert was not use to talking to a Roborg. Never knew if the human side sympathized or if the robot side controlled all the emotions.

"I did nothing differently. In fact, I was hands-on with my mother and both of my siblings, because Dad still had to work, more so after than before the flu outbreak, and someone had to take care of them. That responsibility fell on me. I was only nine, but I was all they had while Dad was away. I cleaned vomit, administered meds, and sometimes I even slept in the same bed as my little sister, because she was so weak she couldn't turn and I didn't want her choking on her own sick."

"And now the Vancouver Island Marmot Flu is running rampant through your town, and you haven't contracted that, either. Everyone else has been plagued with tremors and seizures and you don't have so much as a cough. Do you think that's luck, Mr. O'Malley, or something else?"

"I watched my family die and now my neighbours are falling all around me, I wouldn't call that lucky. Would you?"

The Roborg turned to descend the four steps down from the porch, his human-like extremities fluid in their movements. Lambert thought he was leaving. It certainly was an abrupt end to the interview, and they hadn't even asked any of the questions he usually had thrown at him. He just assumed that with the way today's news broadcasts were handled that what he'd already said would be sliced and diced and just bits and spurts would make the final cut. He turned away as well, heading to the chair in the corner of the porch, glad to be done with the intrusion anyway.

The old rocking chair had seen better days, but Lambert had it so worn that the wood melded so that it conformed to his ass, a perpetual mug ring marred the wide arm of the chair, and the rocker tracks were etched in the thick veneer of the floorboards.

"Well, today is your lucky day," One-o-ten said, and out from behind the bushes Roborgs in white suits emerged.

"What is this?" Lambert turned, his glassy eyes, riddled with floaters, were large with surprise.

"People are dying Mr. O'Malley, and we believe you may be the cure."

The white-suited Roborg circled around to seize him. He was lifted into the air, his shirt tugged from the band of his pants. He felt someone grab the flesh of his belly, and someone else cup the ankle of his left foot. On the count of three he felt the subcutaneous injection at the same time as a second needle was injected into the dorsal venous arch of his foot. Within seconds his molecules jellied.

He'd never used teleporting as a means of travel before. He was old-fashioned, and a strong believer in 'if it's not broke don't fix it'. He'd always been curious about teleporting, but he stood steadfast in his promise not to adopt innovations where they were un-necessary. Although the thought of the experience excited him, he was terrified, too.

Even as he fought against the process, everything that made up his being seemed to pool around his ankles. Within seconds no one stood on the porch of the farm house.

It felt like cold water licking his bones. He tried to focus on his surroundings, but the water lapping at his extremities was trickling at such a slow pace that it was hard to focus on anything other than the tickle it was causing.

He began to be able to make out the laboratory around him. He could see stainless steel apparatus and utensils swimming into focus, and as the last of the trickle reached his head he realized that even the table he lay upon was stainless steel.

He moved to swing his legs off the table just as the click of his belt buckle sounded and he realized the teleportation process was tying up loose ends. The laces of his moccasins formed a sloppy bow in midair as he moved his feet toward the floor.

Realizing what was happening he held out his hand and watched as the scars he knew so well slowly formed on them. He reached for a tray in front of him; utensils clattered to the floor as he brought it up to his face. For a split second he saw what he would look like should he depend on machinery and artificial intelligence to live his life for him, while he sat on the sidelines no longer working hard for what he had.

He didn't like it. He liked the sense of independence and the satisfaction that came with having accomplished something. As the wrinkles, scars and callouses, and nicks and dings filled in on the canvas of his body he felt everything within him settle and he had a new appreciation for his faults. They were more like his me-dallions and trophies, and without them he was not truly himself.

"I know it's a little disconcerting Mr. O'Malley, but without a transport installation, we had to do this the hard way. After you get fitted with a port it will be a lot less intrusive and a more fluid transition on your next trip."

"I haven't consented to any of this," he said, dropping the tray to the floor and scrambling to his feet. His ankles flexed and his knees buckled. He tried to catch his footing but his feet couldn't find purchase, almost as if the floor was made of ice.

The tiled floor rose to meet him as he fell, but just before he crashed he felt hands wrap around his forearms and raise him back to a standing position.

"You're going to want to sit for a while, Mr. O'Malley. Between the photon wavelength and the photon and quantum entanglement that is needed to pass you through space, your body is in shock right now."

He felt himself being raised and then seated once again on the table.

"You just need a moment for everything to right itself and for your system to come back online, so to speak. Don't worry: the body automatically resets itself and everything falls into place. It's usually a very quick process, but with this being your first time, and taking your age into consideration, as well as the amount of trauma you've inflicted on your body throughout your life, we estimate it should take you upwards of an hour to readjust."

They lifted his legs back onto the table and easily pushed him backwards, a pillow wedged up under his head. He wanted to focus on the Roborgs around him. He wanted to argue with them and demand to be returned to his own home, where he'd never depended on society to help him survive in his life.

A patch of coolness pooled around his groin and quickly warmed, and Lambert sat upright again, reaching his weakened arms to cup himself. He was expecting his trousers to be damp, but they weren't, and he spread his legs to look down at the area.

"You haven't soiled yourself, Mr. O'Malley. Your body is acutely aware of everything, even your perspiration. Usually the skin oils are among the last things to regulate themselves again. Perhaps you will be back into commission sooner than we anticipated."

It felt like a million tiny needles were pricking him all over as follicles and pores opened up on the canvas of his body, and on each opening a small eruption of moisture chilled and then warmed him.

"I didn't consent to this." his words became muffled as a thermometer was thrust beneath his tongue and a strong hand forced his mouth closed around the tube.

"You keep saying that, Mr. O'Malley, as though we are not aware of it. I can tell you we are well within our rights as stated in the Government Code of Effective Standards for World Survival."

The white-suited Roborg nodded at One-o-Ten, and it began to read from a thin book. "In the interests of improving world harmony and survival, individuals found working against the greater good will be apprehended and forced to conform. If said individual refuses conformity, and poses a dire risk to survival, a Ward of State certificate can be obtained by following Ward of State protocol as stated on page one hundred fourteen of this Government Code of Effective Standards for World Survival. Also see page eighty-eight for proper protocol for whistleblower protection and provision. The main focus of this law is to maintain a fair and feasible—"

"Thanks, One-o-Ten. That about covers it"

Lambert could see the thermometer's red capillary spike silver as the liquid expanded all the way to one hundred six Fahrenheit and then plunged down below ninety-four within a few seconds. It was shooting red and silver, up and down, and he feared the little capsule of mercury might burst within his mouth. He thrust his tongue down and probed at the glass tube, sending it to the floor with the tray and the utensils he'd knocked over earlier.

"There is no such thing as a code of standards for world survival. You're making that up."

The Roborg laughed. It sounded human, but lacked real emotion, especially when the laugh was paired with paired with the flat facial expression. Although the Roborg had been programmed to smile with its mouth, its eyes never changed.

Lambert squinted, feeling his own eyes crinkle at the corners, and was relieved that the teleportation process had not forgotten his laugh lines. They were an important part of his features.

"Mr. O'Malley, one of the many down-sides of living in seclusion, as you have done for the last forty-odd years, is that you miss out on a lot of important things. It's 2062: the world has moved forward while you remain mired in the past. Consider this your comeuppance for your inattention to current law and the world situation."

"My comeuppance? Wouldn't that imply that I deserve this treatment? I haven't harmed anyone, have I? Just because I'm in a stricken community but not stricken myself does not give anyone the authority to strip me of my rights."

He could feel his strength growing even as his fight-or-flight response mode kicked into overdrive. "As for your implication that I am against survival, that couldn't be further from the truth. I have given and given to my community as best as I can without compromising my own survival. Is there a law that says I have to sacrifice myself for the greater good? What about individual human rights? Have we thrown those out the window too along with common sense?"

He could feel the spittle gather at the corners of his mouth, and see it flying as he spoke. "I have never been asked to give myself up for testing. I am all for helping out, had I been asked. You want a few vials of blood? Take it. You need a tissue sample? Take it. You need a shit sample?" he screamed, "take it, for Christ's sake."

He leaned forward until he was nose to nose with the white-suited Roborg. "But forcing me to use your means of transportation and to conform to your way of living is inhumane, indecent, and unethical. And if you intend to kill me, then that makes you all murderers no matter what some code of standards for world survival book tells you. A horse is still a fucking horse even if you say it's a dog."

"Are you quite finished, Mr. O'Malley?"

"Why? Am I free to leave?"

"Unfortunately. I can not allow you leave."

"Then no, I will never be finished. Not until you step aside and let me walk out of here. Otherwise I won't be held responsible for what happens to any of you."

"Is that a threat, Mr. O'Malley?"

"That's a warning, because, unlike all of you, I don't believe in sneaking around and pouncing on people without first warning them that I'm coming."

He felt his philtrum deepen even as he spoke, and the lid of his right eye droop as his body remembered his congenital ptosis. "Now we can do this the easy way or we can do this the hard way, but either way I'm walking out of here. If you need to test me, you can request my permission to do so in a civilized manner."

"Mr. O'Malley, I do believe we outnumber you six to one."

"If anyone were to take the time to really explain the situation to you it would blow your theory right out the window. However I can't explain it to you. I just need you to trust me on this. The last thing I want is to hurt any of you, but I will if that's what it comes to."

The stilted laugh from the Roborg echoed through the laboratory. "Mr. O'Malley, we have work to do and we don't have time to entertain your idle threats."

Four of the white-coated Roborgs moved forward. Lambert let them twist him around so he was lying flat again, and didn't struggle when they placed the tourniquet on his arm and inserted a needle to draw blood.

He felt them flick the vial and adjust the pressure of the tourniquet. A few more flicks, and then readjusting the needle within his vein. He was impressed that the Roborgs had been programmed to use curse words effectively and the order in which they strung them together would have made a sailor blush.

He felt his opposite arm being straightened and watched as they patted his protruding vein in the crevice of his elbow, and then a second tourniquet was wrapped around his upper arm and another needle inserted.

It was futile. No matter how much they twisted and probed, or flicked and patted, no blood was forthcoming. He had nothing to offer them.

He'd told them that, hadn't he? Without requested permission and his willingness to comply he would not be their test subject. It had been as simple as that. He could have told them that drawing blood from him was no easy task, and he could have explained what needed to be done to make his blood flow, but why would he when everything he'd ever said before had fallen on deaf ears?

It was no secret how Lambert felt about how the world depended on artificial intelligence, but few knew he had once loved AI so much that he often dreamed of their existence. He had spent lonely nights in the cold confines of an empty house creating the source code for the Roborg base program. As his father clung to life in the bed in the next room, Lambert compiled the binary code for the core program. He then created an API with which others could build on the system without ever seeing his own code.

After his work was complete he compiled it all in a sweet little package and sold it to a man who promised to cure his father.

The promise was a lie and less than two weeks later he laid his father to rest under the old oak tree with the rest of his family.

And he had one more secret he had never wanted to reveal, and now would be the first time in forty-two years that he uttered it aloud. He'd instilled a fail-safe command in the source code. A code he'd never told to anyone. It could stop all this craziness. It could end the corruption the world was now in. And although he knew that for humans the end of Roborgs could mean the end of a dependent society, a part of him still had faith in Roborgs. If only he, or someone, could find a way to show the world their true potential and still save humans from themselves. At the moment it felt impossible, but he was not ready to give up hope yet.

Lambert stared at the Roborgs around him. One of them situated the tourniquet lower on his arm, and another opted to try a different needle, determined that the current two were faulty.

"May I speak?" Lambert asked, and all six Roborgs stopped to study him. "When I created your source code it was not my intention for you to be used as human substitutes. Rather than be the human, it was my idea that you would better human life by working closely with people and helping them reach their full potential."

"Mr. O'Malley, it is obvious you are troubled, and that not all of your molecules have reset. We believe it is in your best interest to sleep for awhile, and let all your being settle before we subject you to further testing. Being certain that you are fully transported is vital to the accuracy of the testing."

"I never intended for the world to get so lazy. I never intended for humans to lose their roots, to turn from the land and just sit on the sidelines while life passed them by. It is my hope that this might change in the future. That the world will tire of nothingness and want to create again. That nature will call them and they will return to the comforts of company and a homemade lifestyles."

As the Roborg readied a sedative it said. "You'll go to sleep, and when you awaken all this crazy talk will be gone and you'll be as right as rain."

"Just know that it saddens me to do this, but I did give you the option to let me leave. You refused." he sat up on the table and gathered his knees to his chest. "You could have been great, but *make of none effect.*"

Make of none effect: his fail-safe command. It settled around him and worked its magic, just as he'd fashioned it to forty-two years earlier.

It was meant to be a fast process, but augmentations to the Roborgs over the decades slowed it down to some degree. He watched as the fluid motions of the Roborgs became jerky and then slowed to a complete stop.

He pulled the tourniquets from his arms and pushed the needles aside. He wasn't sure how to transport himself home, and after the experience he'd just had he didn't want to. Bodies were meant to stay intact, all their molecules and atoms were not meant to be jellied. Why was it that in a world where humans had made and expanded on super intelligent robots that could pass as human to an untrained eye, that the very same humans couldn't see how dangerous the whole teleportation process was on a human body that was already aging and slowing down a little more each day? Why couldn't they put together the common factor in the few of them not effected by the flu?

It was simple. They were the minority. The small group of people who did not fall victim to the easier way of life, but opted for traditional ways instead. It did not take a genius to see that.

Although Lambert wanted to run up and down the streets from province to province and state to state yelling, 'Make of none effect!', he did not. He wasn't ready for the state the world would be in if he did, and he knew that, should he tell them his theory of how they could fix what was broken, they would not believe him.

He left the facility resigned to living in a world of oblivion because, as sad as it was, the world was not ready for the truth.

It would be a long walk home, but he'd make it by supper, and he'd patch up his windows and be drinking a tea on the porch of his home in his favourite rocking chair by nightfall.

Woman, Seated

David Wiseman

Jonathan arrived early, one of a handful of press-ganged employees selected as a privilege to represent the firm at the art show opening. Their employer was sponsoring the event, but take-up of allotted tickets had been slow. Jonathan and his colleagues received the dozen or so remaining as a reward, a reward they were obliged to enjoy. Slight interest had been aroused when someone suggested that a show entitled *Corpus* might be a display of naked women.

The speculation was half correct. The gallery walls were covered with paintings, drawings and a few photographs of nudes, divided equally between the male and female form. A few androgynous examples bore the alluring qualities of both sexes, leaving some viewers confused and nervous, which was no doubt part of the artists' intentions.

Some pictures were mildly titillating, some were worth pausing over for their technique and observation but most concentrated on shape and form. What might once have been revealing or mildly erotic had long been devalued by commonplace nakedness and body-hugging fashions which left little to the imagination.

As he dutifully paused in front of each image, it struck Jonathan how differently the male and female subjects were depicted. The men seemed stuck in a different age, adopting the clichéd poses of The Thinker or Greek gods staring heroically into the middle distance, their muscular torsos flexed for action. Almost all seemed to have been working out in the gym, with toned bodies and competition-class definition. He wondered if it were only exhibitionist body-builder types who were prepared to stand naked in front of the artists. It was certainly something he couldn't imagine himself ever doing.

To Jonathan's eyes the women were different. They seemed to be more at ease sitting or, most often, reclining naked on a couch or cushions. He wondered if reclining was a word now exclusively used for an artist's model: none were described as lounging or lying or sprawled. All these reclining women were so much more ordinary, more everyday, than the men. He might see any of them on the train or the bus or at the supermarket check-out.

Such passing strangers, plus a handful of girls in the office, hardly out of their teens, blatant, pretty and empty-headed, were his only regular female contacts. A muttered "excuse me", an occasional "sorry", at most a "no, you were first" at the coffee machine, these were the extent of his conversations.

He and Megan, his most recent girlfriend, had parted sourly a few months previously, since when he'd found neither desire nor energy to embark on a new relationship, while his limited circle offered few opportunities. There were some amongst his male colleagues who wondered about his sexuality, wondered enough to have asked him on a date, although whether that was done for a bet or for real, he never knew.

As he lingered over the art, surprised to find himself enjoying it, Jonathan became aware that people had begun to coalesce in the centre of the gallery, where the volume was rising as the cocktails flowed. Self-consciously he moved away from a detail drawing of a defiantly posed youth. Even to his untrained eye the work was good, yet he saw no quality in the picture beyond the undoubted technical skill. Was that it? Was it just an exercise in observation and draftsmanship?

Unwilling to join the chatter, he looked for a less conspicuous position and a picture he hadn't already studied. He'd almost completed another circuit when he noticed an alcove a little away from the main area. At first, or even second, glance it wasn't apparent that there was a public space beyond the archway, but once there he found four more studies on display. Three were more of the same and he'd grown a little weary of ancient Greece.

The fourth was a drawing of a woman seen from her right side.

She was seated on a stool with her head turned to face the artist. It was a striking image, intense and personal in a way that was absent from anything else he'd seen that evening. The artist, using what seemed to be no more than a pencil, had conveyed the subject's shape and curves, her maturity—thirties was as close as he could guess—without specifics and yet with complete disclosure. But her face in that half-profile sideways look, her face was remarkable, unmistakable. Her eyes were riveting, looking directly at him, looking right into him, half in the surprise of recognition, half waiting for an answer.

Jonathan thought she was simply beautiful, not in the fashionable way of the catwalk willow nor of the unnatural implant, but completely beautiful, she personified all that could be beautiful. He knew she was full and round and wonderfully female, the artist had conveyed that perfectly even though she showed him nothing but limbs and shoulders, but he was drawn to the whole of her. What drew him was rooted in her eyes and her expression, the turn of her head and her cheek edged with straight dark hair cut to her jaw line.

He stood transfixed, engrossed in her, unable to take in enough of her. His mouth dried and he felt his heartbeat rise in his throat. He fancied that hers did the same as she looked at him. She'd spoken directly to him and waited for an answer but the words were fading and he struggled to find their meaning. He had a sense of it but longed for her to ask again.

The sign beneath the picture gave little away: *Woman, Seated - Alice Gorran. Pencil. POA.*

A female artist. Why had his first thought been of a man? There was no reason that a woman couldn't appreciate another woman, see the exquisite and, with sublime skill, share it with others.

With a conscious physical effort he turned away. The idea of buying the picture occurred to him, even though he'd never bought so much as a photo-frame in all his life. It seemed at once ridiculous and irresistible. What did he know of buying art, what would he do with *Woman, Seated*?

And yet the idea of having it, seeing her every day, drew him on.

The price would be beyond his means: "POA" always meant "too expensive to scare you by putting it on the ticket." But he could inquire, safe in the knowledge that he wouldn't be able to buy it.

He turned to face the main gallery, the buzz and the chatter suddenly switched back on. He'd been oblivious to it for as long as he'd stood with Alice Gorran's drawing. He scanned the room, wondering to whom he should apply to find the price. The artist? Were there any artists there? Should he peer at each badge in the hope of finding her?

For a few minutes he slowly patrolled the room, avoiding conversation with a smile or nod to his few remaining colleagues. Exploring further, he eventually found an office where a disinterested security guard waved vaguely towards the gallery and suggested he might find the Director there, or perhaps on the balcony where the smokers were congregated.

Back in the hubbub, Jonathan couldn't resist his picture. Yes, nothing had changed, she was as he'd left her, still intense, beautiful, waiting, still *Woman, Seated*. But the sign had an addition: POA was now terminated by a red dot. Did that mean what he thought it meant, that it was sold, sold in the ten minutes he'd been gone?

Looking about in disbelief he saw a man standing in front of another picture nearby and referring to a catalogue. He caught the slightest hint of red as a page turned. In another moment the man reached out and pressed another dot onto another sign. Jonathan approached him anxiously.

"Does that mean, er, has it," he pointed urgently back towards *Woman, Seated*, "has it been sold? Sold just now?"

"Red dot? Sold, yes, but I don't know when. I'm just going round with the list and the notes. Some sold tonight, some before, probably."

"Who would know?"

"The Director."

"Where is he, er, she...?"

The man looked around, then shrugged. "I don't see him. Could be anywhere, sorry."

Jonathan turned away in despair. No sooner had he set his heart on the prize than it was snatched away from him. Nothing increases longing more than denial. Whatever had been paid, he would offer more.

Even as he thought it, he knew it was pure foolishness. But he was consumed by the picture, by the woman, swept along by a desire he hardly understood.

Returning to the office, he found it locked. Back on the threshold of the exhibition space he was tempted to shout for silence and demand the Director and, if not the Director, then the artist. Then, two steps into the crowd, he saw a badge on a suit with the magic word engraved upon it. His quarry was talking earnestly about arts funding and the role of business sponsors.

"Excuse me, sorry to interrupt, I'm looking for the artist Alice Gorran, have you seen her?" he said, with as much authority as he could find. As an afterthought to justify his rudeness, he added, "It's urgent."

From the verge of being indignant, the Director became compliant, "Yes, of course. She was over there a moment ago, in the far corner, through the archway."

Back where he'd started. Jonathan muttered a thank-you and scuttled away before any details were required. It *was* urgent: urgent for him.

A diminutive woman in jeans and plain white shirt was alone in the side room, looking a little uncertain of herself. He wondered if she was hiding from the crowd or perhaps from someone in particular. Her wiry grey hair was tied back but threatened to escape at any moment.

He looked at her face and then at her hands, searching for some confirmation that she was Alice Gorran, the creator of *Woman, Seated,* but he found nothing. Now he had her, he struggled for words.

"Hello, er, are you, I mean did you...?" As he spoke he kept glancing at the drawing as if it would explain everything in his head without any need for question and answer.

"Yes, I'm Alice Gorran."

"Yes, sorry. I really like it," he heard himself say, as if it were the sum total of his feelings, lame and empty of the emotions churning through him. "Well, more than like it. It's beautiful, you've found her beauty, the lady, the subject, you've made her, umm, beautiful."

Beautiful. It was all he could think of and he kept repeating it.

"She is beautiful," said the artist.

"Yes, well, yes, maybe she is but what I mean is, you've…actually, I don't know what I mean."

"Thank you anyway," she smiled.

"I see it's sold. Was it tonight? I might've, you know, been interested."

"Oh, it could be available. Yes, it's sold but the owner might want to sell it."

"I don't understand, is the owner here, now?"

"Yes."

"Why would they want to sell it?"

"It's complicated. You should ask her yourself."

"She? Where is she? Who is she?"

"She's just there," she said, pointing a little beyond the archway.

He spun round and was astonished to see the woman in the picture. There was no mistaking her, the eyes, the look, the hair. As if reading his thoughts she turned her head slightly to echo her pose in the drawing.

She was seated, as in the picture, though not on a stool but in a wheeled chair. She wore a shimmering black dress with a high collar. A turquoise dragon-fly in gold and enamel clung to her chest.

"Sophie, this gentleman, he didn't tell me his name, he might want to buy your picture. Oh, and he thinks you're beautiful. Remember that when you're discussing the price."

"Jonathan, I'm Jonathan."

"Hello, Jonathan, I'm Sophie. Is one of you going to come and get me or leave me sitting over here on my own?"

"Me, me, me, it's all me with you, Sophie, you lazy trollop," Alice said straight-faced, in the way that only the closest friend can speak of another's disability.

Her chair had wheels in the style of a hospital chair, but was not a wheelchair that the occupant could propel with their hands.

Jonathan darted forward.

"Thank you, Jonathan. I could've waited all evening for Alice."

"Yes," he said uncertainly. Too many questions ricocheted around his head to make a sensible start to conversation.

He couldn't resist a sideways look at the picture, confirmation that Sophie and the *Woman, Seated* were one and the same. All he'd seen in her was true, her reality was as compelling as the picture had suggested, as irresistible as the expression Alice had captured so perfectly. He heard his heart bumping and felt sweat prickling on his scalp.

"Earth to Jonathan, hello, anyone there?" she said. What had he missed, what had she asked him?

"Sorry, I'm confused. It is," he paused and looked at the artist, "it is, as Alice said, quite beautiful. If you bought the picture why do you want to sell it?"

"It's a long story. Here's a short version. Alice and I have been friends for years and when she asked me to model, I agreed without a second thought. When Tony, my, um, boyfriend, found out, he was really upset."

"Ex, your ex-boyfriend," Alice chipped in.

"Yes, well, he was not happy, but he offered to buy the picture. Money being money and Alice being an artist, she agreed to sell it to him on condition it was exhibited here. He paid, then simmered about it for weeks. Finally he said he'd burn it as soon as this was over.

"We had a mighty row and split up soon afterwards. He said before he burnt it he was going to post it all over the place unless I wanted to buy it back. The price had gone up: his percentage, he said. I scraped around and got most of it, then borrowed the last hundred.

"Even then he didn't give it to me, he left it on Alice's doorstep. That's how it comes to be mine."

"But why was he so upset? I know you're, um, you know..." the words grew thick in his mouth as a vision of her body danced tantalizingly before him.

"Naked?"

"Yes, naked. But it's only your back, a leg, an arm. The rest," he felt the perspiration gather at his temple, "the rest of you is just suggested. It's wonderfully suggested."

"Don't look at me like that," Alice said to her model. "Tell him why. It doesn't matter, you might never see him again after to-night."

"All right. Look, Jonathan, I wasn't always like this, being pushed around like a tea-trolley. Tony and I have been together for years, off and on, years before this. I have what they call chronic fatigue syndrome, it's called a lot of other things too. It's been two years now."

"Chronic fatigue?" he asked.

"Yes. You know what it's like when you've just had the 'flu, when you're wiped out?"

He nodded.

"Well, it's like that all the time. A little better some days, worse on others. The chair means I can at least come to something like this, or the theatre or whatever, even if it'll still take me a day or two to recover. I can walk and talk and laugh and sing, but in small doses. Think flat battery that takes a day to charge and then only lasts five minutes."

Jonathan nodded again. He understood what she said to him, had a glimpse of the implications, but was thinking only of the sound of her voice, the candour of her story, the absence of self-pity, and what good company she'd be at that theatre or that whatever.

"Sorry, I still don't understand about the picture."

"Tony was all right to start with, but then he'd take me places just to show how caring he was, and talk about me as if I wasn't there. You know, speaking and answering for me, the old `does she take sugar?' thing. He got tired of all that and started looking for a way out, an excuse to dump me. The picture was just the thing. After he'd brooded on it, he announced that he found it disgusting."

"Disgusting?" Jonathan cried, "It's the very opposite."

"No, disgusting that someone who spends her life sleeping or being wheeled about should think it was all right to show off her body as if there was nothing wrong."

"You don't seem angry, I would be."

"Not any more, it takes too much energy. Alice does the angry for me, don't you?"

"I try," the artist shrugged.

For a few seconds they said nothing, like a stage tableau waiting for a prompt from the wings.

"Sophie, could you stand?" he said suddenly, afraid the moment would be lost forever if he didn't do something. "I'd like to know how tall you are."

Irrelevant and ridiculous, it was the first thing that came into his head.

"Yes," she smiled, "I can."

Jonathan bent down and slipped the foot-rests away from her feet, then offered his hands as she carefully stood up.

"We could dance if you like," she said as she took his arm.

"One day, maybe. But first, will you help me find the right place to hang your picture?"

The Meadow in the Middle

Gordon Wetmore

Part One: The Foxes Have a Problem

The meadow in the middle of the Milford Woods buzzed with excitement. All summer the rabbits and the foxes had been in furious competition. The rabbit population was the biggest in years and great gangs of the long ears had chomped almost all the greenest grasses and sweetest seeds.

The foxes were happy about that. More to eat, they thought. We'll get fat.

At first, hunting was good. They never got tired of breakfast, lunch and dinner of fresh rabbit. Snacks, too. But then something happened. The rabbits became harder and harder to catch. The foxes at first thought they'd just gotten out of shape from overeating. They went on diets and exercised hard. The rabbits still outran, out dodged and outsmarted them. What was going on?

You would think that the other small animals and birds, also part of a fox's balanced diet, would cheer on the rapid rabbits, but no. First, the bunnies didn't leave them enough to eat. Second, more and more of them were being gobbled up by the increasingly hungry foxes.

Only the skunks were not bothered. Foxes learned early not to attack the slow but stinky waddlers with the stripes and big tails. Rabbits avoided the skunks' favourite patches as well. Something about the smell of the plants there ruined their appetites.

One day, a young fox rested in a sunny spot just upwind of some grazing skunks. "It's a crazy world," he complained. "It's just not natural what's happening with those rabbits."

"It's not a big mystery, you know," said the oldest skunk, Smelly Mandel. "They've got a trainer."

"And you know this how?" sneered the fox. Foxes never considered anything slow-moving worth listening to.

"We notice things. You foxes are so busy running around that you don't see the big picture. Besides, the rabbits talk all the time and don't realize we listen. They're a lot like foxes that way."

The fox, whose name was Reginald but whose friends called him Fluffy (which he hated) because of his big tail, was about to bark at the skunk's rudeness, when it occurred to him that he might learn something valuable. "Tell me about the trainer," he said, and added "please" as an afterthought.

"Well," Smelly said, pausing to chew a dandelion leaf, "there are a lot of rabbits, so some are extra fast and some are extra smart. There's one named Lightning Lauren Lapin who's both extra fast and extra smart. She figured out how you guys hunt and taught the others how to avoid you."

Fluffy, head spinning from thinking for the first time in his life, sped back to the dens and told his mother what he'd learned. She called a meeting of the other adults. They were bewildered. Foxes had always hunted rabbits the same way. How could they change? What could they do?

One old fox, though, did think of something. "I have a grandson over in the next meadow. He tells me that they have a super hunter over there. Maybe he could help us."

"Send for him," they pleaded.

Early next morning, a strange fox came trotting up to the dens. He was very graceful. Muscles rippled under his shiny coat, his nose tapered to a fine black point and his bright black eyes seemed to take in everything. "I'm Rapid Ricky Reynard," he said. "I hear you've got a problem."

They all started yapping at him at once. It was quite noisy for a bit until he barked at them with a scary loud bark. They immediately quieted.

"Stop!" he commanded. "If you all yap at once, you'll never get anything straight!" Some younger ones began to yap about how he was right but the older ones quickly shushed them.

"Better," he said. "Now, just one of you tell me what's been going on."

All heads turned to look at the most senior fox, known as Creaky.

"It's like this," he said. "You know how when we spook a rabbit it runs in a big circle?"

Ricky puffed impatiently. "Of course."

"And how we run in a straight line to intercept it?" Ricky snorted, but the old fox wouldn't be hurried. "Always works. Well, almost always. Now, though, just as we're about to pounce, they do something crazy and get away."

"Nod if he's got it right," Ricky ordered. The foxes all nodded.

"Take me to where the rabbits graze. I want to see this for my-self."

A short time later, the foxes lined the top of a small rise. Below, in a large patch of clover next to a densely tangled hedge, dozens of bunnies nibbled, chewed and chomped on tender leaves. They seemed relaxed, even when the foxes were in plain view.

Rapid Ricky pointed with his nose at a large brown male at the edge of the patch. "Go for him," he ordered Fluffy.

With an enthusiastic yip, Fluffy dashed at the happy muncher. The rabbit took off in a flash of feet, speeding in the predicted circle to throw off his hunter. Fluffy immediately headed in a straight line to intersect the rabbit's path. Just as he had his teeth bared to seize its neck, the rabbit reversed so fast Fluffy somer-saulted trying to adjust.

By this time, all the rabbits had retreated to safety in their thorny refuge to watch the fun. The escaping rabbit dived into a hidey hole, pausing just long enough to wiggle his saucy tail at the fox.

Fluffy trotted back to the foxes, his tail down, while the rabbits thumped their hind legs in applause.

To the foxes' surprise, Ricky was smiling. "Just as I thought," he said. "Everybody, back to the dens."

Part Two: What's Bugging Lightning Lauren?

As the foxes left, the rabbits began leaping around and beating the ground with their hind legs. Thump-thump-bump! Thump-thump-bump! The rhythm spread until they all hopped, leapt and bounced in a crazy dance of victory.

All but one, that is. A lone female crouching on a grassy mound watched the foxes until they were out of sight. She was a light brown, almost blonde doe with sharp brown eyes.

"Come on, Lauren," a boy bunny said. He was a big buck named Billy, the one who had just made the fox look foolish. "Come and play. We won again. We don't have to be terrified by those dirty foxes anymore." He wiggled his nose at her. Billy was one of the cutest bucks and very popular with the does. They all loved when he wiggled his nose.

"No, thanks," she said. "I have some thinking to do."

"You're always thinking! You're no fun." But he could see that she wasn't hearing him at all, so he bounced back into the throng.

While the entire tribe cavorted around her, Lauren sat on the hummock and gazed at where the foxes had been before they left so quickly. Something was wrong.

She glanced over at the dandelion patch where the skunks had gathered to watch the show. She saw them look at the rabbits celebrating and then in the direction the foxes had taken, talk to each other, nod their heads. They definitely had noticed something.

She would talk to Smelly Mandel later. Right now, she had other business to take care of. And she was furious.

"All right, party's over!" she yelled. "Meeting in the hedge, NOW!"

"But—" Billy started to protest, but she cut him off.

"Hawk: check the sky."

They looked up. Sure enough, the curved wings of a goshawk circled high above.

"Foxes aren't our only worry," she said. "Get inside to the meeting pit. Go!"

They went.

Their thicket was a thorny jumble of gooseberry, blackberry and raspberry canes interwoven by wild rose vines. It was riddled with narrow, twisty tunnels that nothing larger than a rabbit could get through. Foxes were too big. Even Billy Buck had to move carefully.

In the centre, the rabbits had dug a wide pit and beaten the ground flat. They didn't like being by themselves for very long and in the winter it was a great place to keep warm. It was also a great place to hold meetings, only they didn't like meetings. Playing and snuggling, yes, but meetings, definitely not. Meetings meant they had to listen and often to think. Boring!

But when Lightning Lauren Lapin called a meeting, they listened. After all, her plan had saved a lot of their lives. It was her idea to do the double-back thing. It took her a really long time to explain the idea to them – they kept interrupting or talking to each other. Boy! Did she ever get mad at that! Then she made them practise until they got the timing right. Even more boring, but look how it had worked.

So why was her tail in a twist now? Hadn't Billy Buck followed her plan perfectly? Was she jealous because he looked so good making that stupid fox look so bad? Was that it?

It was an angry crowd of rabbits that Lauren faced when she mounted the speaker's mound. She didn't waste any time being nice, though. "Did any of you notice the new fox who ran the show this afternoon?"

New fox? No, they hadn't.

"He was bigger than the others, better fed, and he was smiling when Billy got away. Smiling!"

The pit suddenly grew quiet.

"And where were the lookouts who were supposed to warn us when a fox showed up? Wasn't that what you were supposed to be doing, Billy Buck?"

"Yes, but there hadn't been any foxes around for ages and I was hungry and—"

"You're supposed to watch until you're relieved. That fox almost caught you, and don't pretend he didn't. You were more lucky than good."

Billy wilted under her sharp glare.

"Also, foxes usually hunt alone. Didn't you find it strange that there was a bunch of them there at the same time? They're not pack hunters. But only one tried to catch just one of us, and then they all went away."

"What does it mean, Lauren?" somebody called out.

"I don't know, but we can't afford to get careless. When you're on lookout, look. Use your ears to pick up crawling sounds in the long grasses, sniff the air and scan the sky for hawks. Don't stop until your replacement shows up."

"But it's so boring!" complained a pretty young rabbit with very shapely ears and big blue eyes, which she actually rolled.

"Where's your mother, Chelsea?" Lauren replied, and heard gasps from the crowd of rabbits.

Tears welled in Chelsea's beautiful eyes. "Mommy was eaten. You know that."

"Yes, dear," Lauren said, "just before we started using lookouts and learned the double backs. That's why we need lookouts. And," she said more loudly, "that's why we're going to practise something new, switchbacking."

They complained but they did it, although in such a sullen manner that Lauren was more worried than ever.

Part Three: The Foxes in Training

Back at the dens, Rapid Ricky was feeling good. The other foxes had accepted his leadership without question. They were lean and hungry, desperate for a solution, and not very bright. He hadn't told them that he left his other group because the rabbits there were almost hunted out.

Here, though, the rabbit tribe was big, very big. He would train these bozos in his hunting techniques, take the best meat for himself, and when the rabbits grew scarce, he'd move on to a better meadow. Yes, he was very pleased.

The foxes lived in small dens that each family had dug into a low hillside. Unlike rabbits, who love togetherness, foxes like independence. Mothers and fathers lived with their cubs, but each family kept to its own place. Adults preferred to hunt on their own, except for a mother training her kits. They were not team players, but Rapid Ricky planned to change that.

On a flat spot below the dens, Rapid Ricky gathered the six males and three of the females. The three mothers nursing kits would listen from their dens.

"Here's what's been happening. You chase a rabbit, the rabbit doubles back, and you fall all over yourselves trying to keep up. It doesn't matter which of you goes after a rabbit, slow fox or fast fox, the rabbit escapes." He watched to see who would respond.

"Fluffy's the fastest of us. Maybe he's young and inexperienced, but nobody's got closer to catching a rabbit than him. He's not so hot on mice or birds, though. Too eager." As Ricky expected, the speaker was Creaky. His advice about den placement and hunting had helped the group for many seasons. He might be old and slow, but the others respected him.

"And that's as close as you'll ever get unless you change the way you catch rabbits altogether," Ricky snapped. He sounded like he was talking to ignorant children. "You're going to have to hunt... in pairs."

The foxes gasped and began yapping in confusion until Rapid Ricky barked the loudest bark they had ever heard.

Even so, old Creaky said, "That's pretty radical. I've seen a lot of foxes come and go, and none ever hunted in pairs."

"And you've never seen rabbits behave this way either, have you?" He asked the question so loudly, so fiercely that all the dumbfounded foxes could do was nod their heads. "Your kits need milk and all of you need meat. You're skin and bones. Those rabbits are doing something different, so you have to adjust. Do you get that?"

They nodded.

"Then get this. I know what to do. But you have to do exactly what I say. Exactly! Training begins now. And one thing more."

The foxes waited for him to say that one thing, knowing it had to be important.

"I'm going to be too busy planning and training you to hunt myself. So every team has to catch at least two rabbits and give one of them to me."

"Oh, now wait just a minute!" exclaimed Creaky. "That is not the fox way. Every fox has a right to keep any rab—"

Rapid Ricky was on him in a flash. Teeth bared and fur on end, he leapt on the old fox, fastened his teeth onto the loose skin on the back of his neck, lifted him high and slammed him onto the hard ground.

Even when Creaky rolled onto his back in the submissive position, Ricky did not step back, an unheard of aggression. With his teeth nearly touching the old fox's throat, he snarled, "Did everybody get the message? Yip if you did."

Everybody yipped.

"Everybody line up," he ordered. They did. Even the dazed old fox, shaking and dizzy, limped to the end of the line.

They practised until nearly noon, past nap time for foxes and rabbits both, who like early mornings and evenings best.

Part Four: Lightning Lauren Gets Some Smelly Advice

Lightning Lauren crouched in a tunnel opening and checked the meadow for predators. It was noon and the sun was hot. Except for buzzing flies, nothing much moved. Behind her, deep inside the thorny hedge, the rabbits dozed in the cool shadows. Lauren figured the foxes were resting as well.

Still, she took no chances, turning her head from side to side so that her ears would detect rustlings in the grasses. She sniffed the slight breezes and scanned the sky before hopping toward the dandelion patch. Like rabbits and foxes, skunks aren't usually active in the hot hours, but Smelly Mandel enjoyed "warming the old bones." This was a good time for a chat.

Lauren found him snoring near where the dandelions bordered the clover. She moved upwind of the odorous old omnivore. "Hi,

Smelly," she said. "Can we talk?"

The skunk lifted one eyelid and yawned, "Well, well, if it isn't Lightning Lauren Lapin. Been expecting you."

"I need to talk, Smelly. I'm worried." She told him about the strange behaviour of the foxes, their new leader and about the sour reaction of the rabbits.

"Well," he said, pausing to scratch behind his ear, "the foxes were pretty desperate, so I'm not surprised they'd be planning something. That new guy, though, I don't know anything about him. Not your regular red fox at all."

He paused to think for a moment. "I'm not even a little surprised that your rabbits were grumpy. They'd just had a big scare and then Billy Buck made a fool out of Fluffy. But just as they're starting to celebrate, you yell at them and make them feel stupid. I could hear you way up here and even I started to feel bad about myself. Then you made them work. They didn't even get to finish eating. You have some fences to mend, dearie."

It was a thoughtful Lightning Lauren that hopped back to the warren. At first she'd been angry with Smelly but the rightness of his comments gradually sank in. She had been so unsettled by the peculiar fox attack that she hadn't thought for a second how the others had felt.

Just before feeding time, she gathered the rabbits in the meeting hall again.

"Rabbits," she said, "I'm sorry I yelled at you. I was scared and upset. I made you practise new stuff before you had a chance to enjoy the idea that they ambushed us and still couldn't catch anyone."

To her surprise, Billy Buck spoke up. "I understand why you were mad. I was careless. But I wish you could have let us play a little more, and you were pretty mean to Chelsea."

"I was. It's true. I'm sorry, Chelsea."

"That makes me feel a lot better," Chelsea said. "Billy and I talked. I have to admit that if we'd had lookouts and your double-backing trick before, maybe my mother would still be alive. So even if it's really boring, Billy and I will be the lookouts this afternoon. We won't eat until we're replaced."

The rabbits thumped their applause. When that quieted down Lauren added, "And I'll be the third watcher. Those foxes are up to something. Chelsea, Billy, you guys are great!"

The applause was even louder this time.

"Okay, everybody," she shouted, "this morning we learned some new moves. Let's practise them now." As the cheers turned to groans, she added, "With a great big game of tag!"

She vaulted off the speaker's mound, turned a complete somersault in the air and landed lightly in front of a startled Billy Buck. Tapping him on the nose with her fore paw, she said, "You're it."

Suddenly bunnies were leaping and laughing everywhere, filling the tunnels and spilling out into the clover to eat and jump and chase each other.

At exactly the same time, the foxes filed out of their dens and padded toward the meadow with a new hunting plan in their minds and a scary new leader to keep them focused.

Part Five: Showdown

As the clover came into view, the foxes could hardly believe their eyes. The place churned with bouncing bunnies. No one seemed to be paying attention. This was going to be a feast!

"Don't get too excited," Rapid Ricky instructed. "Remember the plan. Anybody who gets careless and ruins the hunt will answer to me. Now set up like I told you and wait for my signal."

Immediately the foxes formed three groups. Crouching low to stay hidden by the bushes, one group headed for the far side of the clover near the dandelions. Another lined up with the middle and the third took its position on the near side. All looked back at Rapid Ricky, who stealthily climbed on top of a rock where they could see him and he could see everything.

But in his excitement, he overlooked the three bunnies hiding behind tufts of tall timothy grass, one with lovely ears on the near side, a burly one with a twitching nose in the middle, and, on the far side, the one with the sharpest eyes of all. The moment that

Rapid Ricky's ears showed above the top of the rock, all three spotted him. At once they simultaneously beat the ground with their hind feet: bang-bang-thump-bang, the signal for FOX!

Feeling the vibrations through the ground, the bunnies froze in their tracks, glanced up the slope to where the bushes hid the foxes, and then stampeded for cover.

"Go!" barked Rapid Ricky, and the foxes burst into action.

Three foxes, one from each side and one from the middle, charged into the panicky pack. The two from the sides quickly isolated two older, slower rabbits. When the chasers got close, the rabbits doubled back – only to be met by the chase foxes' partners waiting for them to make that move. Two quick chomps and two bunnies were dragged from the field.

Lauren was horrified. "They're hunting in pairs!" she thought. Never had she seen foxes behave like this. "Switchbacks!" she shouted. "Use switchbacks! Play tag!" Even as she shouted, three more pairs of foxes joined the hunt.

Somehow the rabbits heard her and changed tactics again. They dodged left, then right, and then doubled back, only to dodge in another unpredictable direction. A third older bunny got caught and one unlucky speedster dodged straight into a fox's mouth, but soon the clover patch was almost empty of rabbits. Almost, not quite.

Rapid Ricky was furious. Yes, they had caught four rabbits, but that was less than half a rabbit per fox and none left over for him. And, he thought, all because of her. He had spotted Lightning Lauren right away, the leader who had messed up his beautiful plan.

Then he noticed movement to his right. The team of Fluffy and old Creaky were pursuing a young doe. She had beautiful ears and a shiny coat. She will be very tasty, he thought. When those two caught her, he would claim her for himself. Let Fluffy and Creaky beg for scraps from the other teams.

Only those two were not having it easy. The doe was speedy and clever, and her dodging surprised the hunters time and again. But Fluffy was fast and fit, and Creaky was steady and calm. Tricky as she might be, Chelsea, for it was Chelsea the foxes were chasing, found her escape routes cut off, and she was getting tired. Then Fluffy closed in on her quickly, and when she doubled back, Creaky stood in her path, his wide jaws ready to bite.

What happened next shocked everybody. A big rabbit hurled himself at Creaky from the old fox's blind side. Billy Buck leapt high and slammed his hind feet into Creaky's jaw, knocking him over and leaving him stunned.

Foxes and rabbits alike gaped in amazement. A rabbit attacking a fox! Unheard of!

Chelsea sped by Fluffy heading for the briar patch. Too late, Fluffy gave chase and nearly got stuck when his nose slid into the mouth of the tunnel that Chelsea dived into.

Billy, though, was in big trouble. He had saved Chelsea but hurt his right leg with that kick. And now bearing down on him, eyes red with fury, was Rapid Ricky. Never had Billy been so frightened, and he couldn't run.

Suddenly Lightning Lauren was between them, so fast it was like she had magically appeared. "Stop!" she commanded Ricky. "I'm the one you want. You know it."

Startled, the big fox put on the brakes. With his black lips curled above his fangs, he studied the small creature sitting still in front of him. So this was the one who had spoiled everything. He forgot about Billy, forgot about the teamwork that he had drilled into the other foxes. He would make dinner out of this insolent bunny all by himself.

Snarling, he crouched low. Lightning Lauren sat unmoving, her eyes fixed on his. Abruptly he lunged. Almost before he had moved, she dashed off to his left. Expecting such a move, he zipped to cut her off, but she doubled back so quickly that she was sitting in her original spot by the time he had turned around.

This time he approached her slowly, his eyes focused on her shoulder muscles for a hint about which way she would turn. She held still. Then he charged straight at her. When she darted to her right, he kept on going straight and then whirled around to face her.

She was back in her original spot, sitting still, but now he was between her and the hedge.

Everybody in the meadow watched the life-and-death contest. Foxes watched from the low rise where the bushes gave way to the grasses. Rabbits lined the openings in the hedge. Even the skunks gave up their grazing to take in the spectacle. Smelly Mandel and three of his friends waddled to the edge of the dandelions to watch the drama unfold.

Fluffy, still beside the rabbits' lair, was too absorbed to notice Billy limp past him to snuggle down next to Chelsea.

It quickly became obvious that Lightning Lauren was too nimble for Rapid Ricky to catch with straight ahead lunges. But it was also obvious that the fox had blocked off all her routes to safety.

Worse, he was too fast for her to attempt a straight run out of the meadow. All she could do was keep dodging until either he got too tired or she did. However, her dashing left, dashing right and doubling back took more energy than Rapid Ricky was using. The advantage was all on Rapid Ricky's side.

The chase kept on from one side of the meadow to the other. By the time they were near the skunks in the dandelions, Lightning Lauren was slowing. Rapid Ricky placed himself between her and the dandelions, making sure he also cut off her path to the hedge. The end, he was certain, would come at any moment.

Rapid Ricky looked relaxed, confident. Lauren no longer appeared lightning fast. She made a half-hearted run toward the dandelions and Rapid Ricky easily got between her and safety. He was so close to the skunks that his tail nearly brushed them.

That's when she ran straight at his face.

Surprised, he hesitated for just a moment, and in that moment she leapt. High up she went, over his head, past his tail, to land among the startled skunks. Up went their tails just as Rapid Ricky, forgetting where he was, shot after her with a growl.

All four skunks fired off, straight into Rapid Ricky's open mouth.

A horrible cloud of gas enveloped the fox, who immediately collapsed in a ball. Choking, gasping, wheezing, he rolled about, trying to catch a breath. His eyes burned, his nose was on fire – he thought he was going to die. When he realized he wouldn't, he wished he could.

It was a long time before he could see and breathe properly. By that time, Lightning Lauren was safely back with the other bunnies. Exhausted by their experience, all the rabbits were taking a nice nap. The foxes had gone home, taking the caught rabbits with them. Even the skunks were long gone. They couldn't stand the smell either.

Epilogue

The meadow returned to normal for the rest of the summer, although things weren't quite the same. The rabbits became even better organized because Lightning Laura, Billy and Chelsea teamed up to keep them in shape. After the big battle, they were willing to practise even if they were tired or bored.

When Rapid Ricky finally crawled back to the dens, the other foxes drove him away with bared teeth and deep growls. They didn't want a leader who bullied them and took the food they caught. No one there heard from him again.

However, the foxes had learned things too. Teamwork and co-operation meant more to eat. Old Creaky took Fluffy under his wing and taught him some leadership skills, even started calling him Reggie. The other foxes began seeing him as grown up and a future leader.

The foxes continued to catch some rabbits using Rapid Ricky's techniques. Of course the rabbits didn't like it whenever one of them was lost, but at least it wasn't as bad as in the early summer. The foxes didn't starve and there was food left for the mice, chipmunks and birds.

But something still puzzled Fluffy/Reggie, so one day in late summer, he wandered over to the dandelions to see Smelly Mandel. "Smelly," he said, "would you help me figure something out?"

Smelly heard the respectful tone in the young fox's voice and was pleased. "Go ahead, Reginald," he said, speaking formally as he would to an adult.

"I still can't understand how what's-her-name got away from Rapid Ricky. He was bigger, stronger and faster, and he was really, really smart. She should have been lunch."

"Use her name," the skunk scolded. "Even if Lauren's your enemy, she deserves respect. The reason she escaped? Call it motivation, which is simple in one way but not if you really think about it. In the simple way, look at why she was running. Stinking Ricky was after her because he wanted revenge. She was running to save her life. When something is more important to you than to somebody else who's after it, you'll probably do better—if you don't panic. Lightning Lauren never panics. But that's not all.

"Ricky was greedy for power. He wanted to make you foxes do the work while he got the benefits. He was smart all right, but his thinking was narrow. Lauren, though, her goal is to keep as many rabbits as safe as possible. She has to consider all the dangers—hawks, snakes, you foxes especially—and get those scatter-brains willing to learn and work together. To do that, she had to get to know them, listen to them, pay attention to them. Did Rickey ever listen?"

Reggie shook his head.

"Of course not. Ricky commanded. Lauren led. In that final fight, because she was aware of so much, she knew all along where we skunks were and what we could do. Ricky never thought about us for a minute."

Reggie snorted, amazed. "You mean, she set Ricky up from the beginning?" The old skunk nodded. It made sense, Reggie thought.

The future leader of the foxes thanked Smelly and headed back to the dens thinking all the way.

Amo Amas Amat

David Wiseman

From her studio window she sees his car down in the valley. It slows and turns onto the track. It's made the turn a hundred times, maybe more.

"Jack's here," she says.

For a few seconds the car disappears as it rounds the hill and climbs to the house, bouncing across the ruts and bumps until it slithers to a stop by her kitchen doorway. The unexpected visitor is, like her, a Brit in a foreign land.

She welcomes him with their familiar loose embrace and touch of cheeks, the customary three times, left, right, left, as is the local custom. He holds her a little longer than usual.

"I saw you down the hill, raising a great cloud behind you. Billowing white dust, urgent yellow car, sea of lavender. You made quite the picture."

"Ah, Kate, you have an eye for such things."

She holds him away from her, her hands still on his arms.

"Are you okay? You look, I don't know, odd."

He does. Clammy, with pale skin leeching through his Provençal tan.

"Give me a proper hug, quickly," he says, pulling her to him, but she pushes against him, suddenly wary.

"Is it...Fabienne?" she says. It's all she can think to ask.

"Yes, in a way..." he begins, then sees her wide eyes. "No, no, she's away, gone to see her father."

"So what's happened? Why the dramatic entrance? Come to think of it, you look a bit dramatic yourself. I'm not sure it suits you."

He grips her arms tightly, looking straight into her eyes. He has light brown eyes; hers are bluey-grey. There is sweat on his brow; a single trickle runs from his temple, following his jawline.

"Kate," he says steadily, "it's the first day of the rest of our lives. Yours, and mine."

"Ye-es," she ventures. His intensity unnerves her. She looks for a gentle way to escape his hold. "You're being cryptic. A drink while you tell me?"

He releases her immediately, throwing his arms wide. "Yes, of course, sorry, a drink." He takes a deep breath and, head back, eyes closed, roars, "Now is the time!" for all Provence to hear.

She leads him into her kitchen and takes an open bottle and glasses from the shelf. She sits one side of the table, he drags a chair to the end so as to be half next to her, half facing.

"What are we celebrating, Jack? Come on, plain English for my pea brain, please."

"You said it yourself on Sunday, seize the day, the first day of—"

"Yes, the rest of our lives, you said that already. Did I say it too? Maybe I did, I'm good at telling other people they should act, follow their dreams and bugger the consequences."

She laughs but he does not, he is all seriousness.

"Yes, you do say that. You told me that. Thank you. It's what I needed."

He reaches a hand across the table, seeking hers, but she ignores it and takes a drink of wine instead.

"Jack? Tell me."

"Right. It's this. I've done it, I've left Fabi. I didn't know it would feel so wonderful, so liberating. I've never been so happy. I'm dizzy with it."

"You've left Fabienne? Just like that. Wait, does she know?"

"No, I took her to the station yesterday, then packed up my stuff this morning. Left her a letter. It's not a sudden thing, you know that more than anyone. We've waited long enough. What did you say, sitting on our hands moaning about missed opportunities instead of grabbing them? Something like that. Four years sitting on our hands, Kate, four years. Long enough."

She knows that is precisely the kind of thing she would say, probably did say, after a few glasses of wine in the company of friends, preaching resolve when her own was lacking. Now she's responsible for him seizing his moment. Or worse.

"Jack, Jack, you dear sweet man. You must tell me, say it straight, I'm scared of what you mean, half scared, half…something else."

"Yes, it is scary. Exciting scary. I love you, Kate. Simple isn't it? Just to say it out loud after all this time. I love you, I love you, I love you! I've loved you since the day we first met. Remember that day? You saw it too, I know, the way you looked, you saw it.

"Of course it was a crush to begin with. Fabi noticed, too; said I mooned over you. But you and I, we've grown together since then, love and friendship deeper by the day. I knew you didn't want an affair, didn't want me cheating on Fabi. I've known all along what I had to do. Finally it was you who gave me the courage. Who else would it be? Now I'm here, we're here, we start from today. My darling Kate."

She wants him to continue with his declaration of love so that she won't have to speak, but he stops abruptly and looks desperately at her, all boyish innocence despite his forty-four years. She could laugh if he wasn't so painfully earnest. Instead she pauses, searching for the words that will disappoint without crushing.

"Dear Jack, you're the kindest, gentlest man and we are good friends. I do love you in my way, although I could say the same to Fabienne."

He doesn't listen to her, he's too dizzy with love, but he smiles, happy to hear what he knows to be true. "Yes, you could, you're full of love. But you don't send Fabi home tingling from your touch, her cheek doesn't savour your goodnight kiss till morning."

"Are you sure?"

"I'm sure, Kate. Trust me, I know. You have such a way, you make everyone feel valued, unique, I know it's not just me. But I know your eyes, I know the look, the gentle squeeze of my arm, my hand. You don't give that to everyone. You make me feel very special, very loved."

"I don't mean to."

"Maybe that's part of the beauty. It's instinctive, unselfish."

"It's a curse."

"I'm not cursed," he protests, "I'm blessed."

"It's me. I'm cursed, Jack, cursed with people having crushes on me, fantasizing about me, loving me."

"People?" he says, as the first shadow of doubt touches his face.

"I get myself settled, a little circle of friends to share a few glasses, watch a sunset, enjoy a meal or the occasional treat together. People to be close to, friends to be comfortable with. Then someone finds me irresistible and friendships fracture and wither, relationships sour."

"Others?"

"Yes, there've been others. Old men, young men, and women, too."

"I don't believe you," he says, although he might.

"No, I don't suppose you do."

"Fantasies, yes, of course, I can see that, you're beautiful. A crush, too. Haven't I said so myself? But this is different."

"Oh Jack, yes, it's different, it's you, and it's once in your lifetime. You've summoned the courage, declared your love, and there is no other like it. You're bewitched by it. I know, I understand. You've risked everything. Thank you." She means what she says, she is grateful for his love, for his honesty, she doesn't say it to make him feel better.

"Thank you, but no thank you." A trace of bitterness leaks into his words.

"I have all I want, Jack. Good company often enough, a wonderful home here in Saint-Jean. I have my paints and beautiful light to use them by, enough money for the odd night away, a car that usually starts and a friend who'll fix it when it doesn't. All these things, and more: I please myself, I'm content in my own company, I answer to no one and no one answers to me."

"Sounds almost selfish." A hint of reproach mixes with the bitterness. "I'd give up anything for you."

"I couldn't carry the weight of your sacrifice, I couldn't bear the responsibility of your love. You dear sweet man, this isn't the way for either of us."

"No? What is the way for us now? Occasional lovers? It would be something, not much, but something. Is that really what you want after all?"

"No, Jack, you were right the first time." She reaches a hand to his to underline her sincerity. "I don't want an affair with you. Once, it might've been delightful fun, but we'd have done that by now if we were going to."

"You see! Listen to yourself, Kate. See how you touch, how you look at me. Tell me again this isn't love, tell me again I have it all wrong."

"Not all wrong, Jack, but wrong enough."

"Huh," he grunts, pulling his hand from hers, turning away from her.

"What do you think will happen now, I mean right now?" A firmness has entered her voice, a determination to guide him where he cannot go without her help. "No? Here's how it'll go. We'll finish our drinks, maybe talk about something else to calm ourselves while what's been said slides into the past, becomes something that was, not something that is."

"Pretend it never happened," he says. The bitterness level creeps higher.

"No, the opposite. We'll accept that it did happen, accept that today has not turned out how either of us expected when we woke this morning."

"You're a cool one."

"Cool? If you like, I prefer calm. Now, when do you expect Fabienne to return?"

"Tomorrow, maybe the day after. I can't go back, if that's what you're thinking."

"That's up to you, Jack. But with Fabienne away you have time and space to consider. You can retrieve your letter, then stay at the house or not, but you have a day to decide."

She's painted a picture he can imagine himself in, but he needs to be persuaded, to be convinced it could work, he needs objections overcome. He looks away, beyond her, beyond the kitchen window across the rolling purple fields, taking flight as a hawk, quartering the ground, searching for reasons to stay, reasons to go.

"How could I face her?" he says after a minute or so.

"You'll surprise yourself. You've been nursing one secret for years and managed all right."

"Not fair."

"Today isn't a new secret—yet. It could easily become one, but for now it's a part of the old one. You'll probably confess, sooner or later."

"Why would I?"

"Maybe you'll feel guilty and want to show your remorse by coming clean, except you won't tell everything, not the four years, not the words of the letter."

He already sees himself back at his house, unpacking his things, returning everything to its place, smoothing away the wrinkles in the fabric of time. The lie of the letter is one such wrinkle he can smooth immediately.

"There is no letter. I...I didn't write anything, I didn't know what to say. But I thought I should have, I thought you'd expect me to have done that."

"I did. And now you see how easily you confess to show your repentance."

"You're twisting everything."

"Or one day, when something slips out and you're challenged or when you're angry with me, feeling bitter or vengeful—"

"I will never be any of those things."

"One day you will, and when you are, you'll make a different confession."

"Different, how?"

"You'll tell friends you came here in a trance, under a spell I cast, enticing you, leading you on, just for the fun of rejecting you, just for the fun of taking you from Fabienne then throwing you away. And they'll believe it, because it's always easier to blame the single woman and they'll agree I'm a bitch."

"No. That won't happen. Fabi would know it wasn't like that. You and Fabi are good friends; close, almost sisters."

"Yes, we are. But friendships always end in treachery and betrayal."

"Now you're being dramatic, Kate."

"You don't know women like I do."

"I don't think I know women at all. There's a language barrier. Same words, different meanings. I never had a single doubt about us, Kate. How wrong could I be?"

"Don't say that. Think of it like this: you were nearly right. Maybe in a different life, a different version of this life..."

Abruptly he turns back to her, a flicker of hope rekindled. "There's still a chance? Don't tease me."

"No, you're right. Sorry, so unfair of me, unkind. Drink up, my dear friend. Time to go home and see how it feels. The sooner you go, the easier it'll be."

He stands awkwardly, uncertain how he should leave the stage, a tender embrace out of the question. He has his fingers on the door handle but stops to ask, "You really think I can salvage something from the wreck?"

"No wreck. Not yet. Grounded on a sand bank. You'll float off again when the tide turns."

"It's that easy?"

"Nothing's easy but you can try it."

"I still love you, Kate."

"I still love you, Jack."

As he slips into the car, she can just see clothes and boxes of books piled on the back seat. He reverses and turns. He does not look back or wave. In less than a minute he is gone. By the time she is back at the studio window the yellow car has raised a new plume of dust, reached the bottom of the track and is heading for home.

Fabienne stands behind her and puts her arms around Kate's waist.

"Why does he come?" she says softly. "Does he know, does he guess?"

"No, he knows nothing, *rien*. He came to tell me he loves me."

"He always loves you. Everyone loves you. *Tout le monde, et moi*

aussi. Je t'aime."
  "Dear Fabienne. One day, soon I think, you should tell him."

About the authors

Bob Bent was born in Amherst, Nova Scotia, lived most of his life in and around Lawrencetown, and now lives in Middleton and Cottage Cove. He has published stories in *The Nashwaak Review, All Rights Reserved*, and *Feathertale Review*; non-fiction in *The Barnstormer;* and a series of travel/running articles in *Run Nova Scotia Raconteur*. He published a collection of whimsical stories for children and grandmothers illustrated by Andrea Wood, *Have Yourself a Silly Little Christmas*, in 2013; and a collection of serious short stories, *The Last Time I Saw Alice*, in 2018.

Kathy Brooks had the good fortune to grow up as an 'air force brat' in the days when kids ran free all day, as long as they came home for supper. By the age of thirteen, Kathy had moved six times. She credits these days of adventure and exploration with developing her imagination and curiosity.

When not in the garden, Kathy can be found walking, cooking, reading, travelling, or squirrelled away at the library completing a biography, writing short stories or working on several novels at the same time. She prefers writing inspiring, up-lifting but gritty stories. "Go, Danny Boy, Go" won a prize in the White Rock Friends of the Library writing competition in British Columbia.

K. R. Byggdin was born and raised on the Prairies, but now lives and writes in K'jipuktuk (Halifax). K.R. has participated in the Writers' Federation of Nova Scotia's Alistair MacLeod Mentorship program and the Banff Centre's Emerging Writers Intensive program. Previous works have been shortlisted for the WFNS

Budge Wilson Short Fiction Prize and awarded the Sheldon Currie Fiction Prize by *The Antigonish Review*. Follow @krbyggdin on Instagram to keep up with K.R.'s writing journey.

Angel Flanagan lives along Bay Sainte Marie with her husband and two sons. She enjoys walking the beaches hunting for tiny sea glass treasures from the past. She is also a photographer who enjoys growing her own vegetables and even has a few chickens. Angel is inspired by the rugged Nova Scotia coastlines with their roaring winds and crashing waves. A fascination with changing landscape and abandoned places is explored throughout her work.

Flanagan's work has been published in The *Chronicle Herald*, *Le Courrier de la Nouvelle Ecosse*, *Xalt* Magazine, *Coastal Life* Magazine and *The Clare Shopper*. Moose House published her first novel, *Lost and Found*.

Rhoda C. Hill writes a broad array of fiction that spans several genres. Her writing has appeared in *The First Line*, and she was a finalist in Harlequin's Killer Voice contest in 2014. Moose House published her first novel, *Loving Number Seven*, and will be releasing the sequel sometime in 2023.

Rhoda thrives on the love of her family, rainstorms, books, and writing. She lives in Doucetteville, Nova Scotia with her husband, three children, and five furbabies. Rhoda can be reached on Facebook (rhodaswritingpage) and Twitter (@Creaeh).

Thibault Jacquot-Paratte, from the Annapolis Valley, travelled widely, studied in Europe, and writes songs, poetry, drama, and more. His first three books were published in 2016-17, and he has co-directed a film (2017). He has many publications in journals and anthologies, in both English and French. He works at Oui 98.5 FM in Halifax, and is currently a doctoral student in linguistics at the Sorbonne, as well as stage director with the Théâtre DesAssimilé in Halifax.

Connie Jodrey lives on North Mountain with her husband Tim, their lovable mastiff Lucy, three horses, two cats, and assorted barnyard birds. Recently retired from her dream job as Branch Manager of the Bridgetown Library, Connie has settled into her other dream job, making up stories.

When Connie isn't writing, you'll likely find her in her garden, watching curling on TV, kneading bread, or looking forward to a visit from her son Shea while sipping a glass of wine and cooking one of her homegrown chickens in the wood cook stove.

Grace Keating was born and raised in Antigonish, Nova Scotia, before she began her regular cross-country journeys switching her life between the east and west coasts. She has spent most of her working life in the world of costume and film, where she's absorbed enough stories to fill a whole bookshelf. Grace's short stories have won awards and been published across North America and in the UK. Lifelong interests include sewing, reading and storytelling. Grace has retired from themovie-making world and now lives in Annapolis Royal.

Kerri Leier is a teacher and theatre practitioner who grew up in Port Williams, Nova Scotia. She has an Honours BA in Theatre Studies and a B Ed from York University. She currently runs a community theatre company, Edalene, for which she writes, directs and occasionally performs. "The Little Red Sled" is a story about her grandfather, Phil Jordan, and her first published work. The little red sled is proudly displayed at Christmas time at her parents' house in Port Williams. Kerri resides in Hantsport with her two children (Xander and EvaJean) and her overly enthusiastic dog, Mokka.

Daniel Lillford is a professional actor and playwright who has been working in the entertainment industry for 40 years. He has had 35 productions (at last count) of his plays in Canada, The United States, Australia and Scotland. He spent his childhood in Jersey, Channel Islands; his formative years in Australia; and immigrated with his wife, Rachel, to Canada 22 years ago. They live in the Annapolis Valley with their three sons. Moose House is publishing his collection of short stories, *Ghost Breezes*, in 2023.

Gary Lovett became a stay-at-home dad after losing his sight, ending a coast to coast to coast career in mining. He began writing in earnest while attending Saint Mary's University in Halifax, where he received the Robert Hayes Memorial Scholarship for Creative Writing. He and his wife, Elizabeth, raised three children in Halifax. He continued writing poetry, lyrics and short stories to share with family and friends, winning a couple of radio contests along the way. Gary and Elizabeth divide their time between St Margarets Bay and an old farmstead in Annapolis County. This is his first published short story.

eloise comeau murray was born in Middleton, Nova Scotia and currently lives there with a wonderful life separating those two eighty-two year realities. She had many opportunities for education, travel and professional experiences. Her work was in educational institutions. Consulting included governmental, non-governmental and international organizations in many parts of the world. After making a transition from technical writing required by her profession, writing became a form of entertainment. Her preferred focus is on ordinary people, particularly middle age and older persons as they confront the issues of that life brings regardless of where they live.

Vernon Oickle was born and raised in Liverpool, Nova Scotia. He attended Lethbridge Community College. Upon his graduation in 1982 with an honours diploma in Journalism, he returned to Liverpool and began his career at the local newspaper, *The Advance*. An award-winning journalist and editor, Vernon is the author of 31 books, many of which collect and preserve the heritage and culture of Atlantic Canada. In 2012 Vernon received the Queen Elizabeth II Diamond Jubilee Medal, recognizing his contributions to his community, province and country, and in 2015 he received a Distinguished Alumni Award (Community Leader) from Lethbridge College.

Moose House is publishing Vernon's *Six Crows Gold*, the latest in his acclaimed 'Crows' series, in 2023.

P. E. R. Sprague is an air traffic controller in the Royal Canadian Air Force. While attending college in Saskatchewan, he worked as a tour guide at the Tunnels of Moose Jaw. His duty was to guide tourists through the tunnels beneath the streets and show them the lives of brewers and gangsters in 1920s Moose Jaw. He didn't develop an interest in writing until after college, when his wife introduced him to the wonders of literature. He became an avid reader and decided to try his hand at the craft.

Gordon Wetmore is grateful for having been born and raised in Annapolis Royal. That's where he began a teaching career of more than a half-century with stints in Nunavut, British Columbia and Quebec, where he now lives with Carol (Kemp), his wife of 48 years. The town also nourished his love of stories, history and people. Besides teaching, he has worked as a journalist and is youth and education editor with *Community Connections*, a bi-monthly magazine written and published by volunteers. Gord and Carol are active members of the community of Deux-Montagnes and have two sons and four grandchildren.

James (Jamie) Whidden grew up in Nova Scotia, Ontario, and Prince Edward Island. He attended Dalhousie University (BA) and McGill before completing his doctoral dissertation in History at the School of Oriental and African Studies, University of London. He has published two books, several articles and reviews. He did his field research in Egypt. After completing his doctorate, he taught in the UK and the USA before returning permanently to Canada where he has taught in several universities, including Acadia, Concordia, and Dalhousie. He now lives in rural Nova Scotia on a centuries-old farm.

Debra Whittall is a former broadcast journalist and speechwriter, living in Pleasantville, Nova Scotia. She belongs to several writers' groups, including the South Shore Scribes who meet regularly at the South Shore Libraries' Bridgewater location. Debbie regularly posts her short stories and memoirs to her blog: wordsbywhittall.blogspot.com. She is currently working on the second draft of her first novel and writing a memoir about leaving her small and close-knit community for the first time. "The Fall" is Debbie's first published story.

British-born **David Wiseman**'s writing, both short and long, is recognized and enjoyed on both sides of the Atlantic. His novels, of which *Casa Rosa* is the most recent, appear under DJ Wiseman. Lifelong enthusiasms include reading, maps, travel and photography. He currently lives in Annapolis Royal.